FALLOUT

D1262414

ALSO BY CARRIE STUART PARKS

Woman in Shadow
Relative Silence
Fragments of Fear
Formula of Deception

THE GWEN MARCEY NOVELS
A Cry from the Dust
The Bones Will Speak
When Death Draws Near
Portrait of Vengeance

FALLOUT

CARRIE STUART PARKS

THOMAS NELSON
Since 1798

*To my family, who understand the
importance of staying family*

Fallout

Copyright © 2022 Carrie Stuart Parks

All rights reserved. No portion of this book may be reproduced, stored in a retrieval system, or transmitted in any form or by any means—electronic, mechanical, photocopy, recording, scanning, or other—except for brief quotations in critical reviews or articles, without the prior written permission of the publisher.

Published in Nashville, Tennessee, by Thomas Nelson. Thomas Nelson is a registered trademark of HarperCollins Christian Publishing, Inc.

Thomas Nelson titles may be purchased in bulk for educational, business, fundraising, or sales promotional use. For information, please email SpecialMarkets@ThomasNelson.com.

Unless otherwise noted, Scripture quotations are taken from The Holy Bible, New International Version®, NIV®. Copyright © 1973, 1978, 1984, 2011 by Biblica, Inc.® Used by permission of Zondervan. All rights reserved worldwide. www.Zondervan.com. The "NIV" and "New International Version" are trademarks registered in the United States Patent and Trademark Office by Biblica, Inc.®

Scripture quotations marked KJV are taken from the King James Version. Public domain.

Scripture quotations marked NKJV are taken from the New King James Version®. Copyright © 1982 by Thomas Nelson. Used by permission. All rights reserved.

Publisher's Note: This novel is a work of fiction. Names, characters, places, and incidents are either products of the author's imagination or used fictitiously. All characters are fictional, and any similarity to people living or dead is purely coincidental.

Library of Congress Cataloging-in-Publication Data

Names: Parks, Carrie Stuart, author.
Title: Fallout / Carrie Stuart Parks.
Description: Nashville, Tennessee : Thomas Nelson, [2022] | Summary: "Bestselling and award-winning author Carrie Stuart Parks utilizes her expertise as a forensic artist in this gripping story that shows how the end doesn't always justify the means"-- Provided by publisher.
Identifiers: LCCN 2022007604 (print) | LCCN 2022007605 (ebook) | ISBN 9780785239857 (paperback) | ISBN 9780785239864 (epub) | ISBN 9780785239871
Classification: LCC PS3616.A75535 F35 2018 (print) | LCC PS3616.A75535 (ebook) | DDC 813/.6--dc23
LC record available at https://lccn.loc.gov/2022007604
LC ebook record available at https://lccn.loc.gov/2022007605

Printed in the United States of America

22 23 24 25 26 LSC 5 4 3 2 1

PROLOGUE

HANFORD, WASHINGTON
NOVEMBER 23, 1988

The November wind blew across the almost-barren plain, attempting to leach any warmth from the man's black wool coat. He pulled the woolen balaclava higher on his nose and wished he'd worn goggles. The wind raised icy tears that blurred his vision.

Snow clung to the scant protection offered by basalt outcroppings and meager shrubs.

The moon provided weedy light, enough to avoid the sagebrush and tumbleweeds, but not enough to reveal the ground squirrels' burrows. He'd fallen twice.

He paused for a moment to check his compass. He figured he'd covered about six of the eight miles. There was little chance he'd be detected. He'd approached the area by boat on the Columbia River, which flowed down the eastern side of the remote facility in South Central Washington State. Though the site was massive—570 square miles—the roads were heavily patrolled. After all, the Hanford Nuclear Reservation was the largest producer of postwar nuclear weapons.

Hanford's creation of the bomb dropped on Nagasaki, Japan, had provided the turning point in World War II. Afterward, the plant morphed into a Cold War arsenal against the Soviet Union until the last nuclear reactor finally shut down just a year ago.

He'd chosen the date carefully—Wednesday, the day before Thanksgiving. All the staff and workers would have left early in preparation for the holidays. Only a minimal number of employees would be working, and they'd not be inclined to venture into the frigid night.

Though he'd been on the Hanford Site since he'd left the river, his goal was the Hanford Tank Farms. The tanks held 53 million gallons of the highest-level radioactive waste found in the United States. He would be targeting the SY Tank Farm, three double-shelled waste storage units built between 1974 and 1976, located at the 200 West site. The tanks at this location were each capable of holding 1.16 million gallons of nuclear waste.

He shifted the backpack slightly. The bomb, made with C-4, was safe enough from his jostling cross-country run. It took a detonator to set off the explosion, which he'd rig once the materials were in place.

The tanks themselves were built of one-foot-thick reinforced steel and concrete and had been buried under eight feet of dirt, but the hydrogen from the slurry had built up in these particular tanks to dangerous levels. He didn't need to reach the tanks themselves, only disable the exhaust vent and the temperature thermocouple assembly. He knew no maintenance work was going on around the tanks that might create a spark or heat, so chance of discovery was extremely slim.

He paused for a moment to catch his breath. He'd paddled down the treacherous icy river, then jogged for miles, but his fury fueled his drive. In February of 1986, the Department of Energy had released nineteen thousand pages of documents describing the declassified history of the Hanford operations. Hints of a darker truth were written between the lines, and more evidence came out in the batch of documents released the following year. Everyone else would have missed it, but he'd been able to piece the sequence of events together.

They'd grown rich while he'd been discarded like so much trash.

Now was his time to get even.

He'd use the threat of the bomb to force the acknowledgment of their role and his own innocence. Anything less than the possibility of a Chernobyl-size disaster would lead to a governmental cover up.

A massive press conference. Facts and figures. Undeniable evidence.

In the meantime, he'd personally take care of those directly responsible.

He increased his pace. *Soon now.*

He knew this part of the facility well.

He found the location he'd identified before, knelt beside the various ports, detectors, and vents, and swiftly assembled the parts according to the bomb-maker's directions. All that was left was the trigger mechanism. He'd placed it in a secure box inside his backpack.

The box was gone.

He ran his hands over the backpack again. Then again. Then a third time. It was gone. *Did I forget to pack it? No.* It was here in this backpack when he'd left home.

He broke out in a clammy sweat and rocked back on his heels. *How could this have happened?* Where had it dropped out? Could it be back in the boat? Somewhere on the ground between here and the river's edge? Separated from him when he fell?

Calm down. He had a backup. Even if he didn't find the trigger, all it would take is a reasonable-sized explosion on the surface to start the process.

If it took the rest of his miserable life, he'd carry out his plan. They wouldn't get away with it. Not this time.

ONE

SEPTEMBER 2015

Bam! Bam! An engine roared, growing louder, closer.

I glanced up from the shading technique I was demonstrating for my elementary-school art class.

A black Suburban was barreling across the parking lot directly at my classroom.

"Run!" I screamed.

The children didn't hesitate, bolting for the door. I shoved the last boy outside toward the gym just as the Suburban smashed into the side of the building and plowed into the room. The portable classroom moved with a *screech*. Desks, chairs, books, glass, and chunks of the wall and ceiling exploded in a cacophony of sound and movement. Metal fragments, shattered glass, and hunks of wood pelted me. I found myself outside next to the gym doors, not knowing how I got there. I curled up and covered my head, praying nothing would crash down on me.

Hisssssssss. The stench of an overheated engine and hot rubber made me gag.

The crushed front of the Suburban had shoved the classroom into a covered storage shed before punching through the opposite wall. Fluids hissed and dripped from under the smashed hood, right beside me. The shed had collapsed onto the SUV.

I was shaking so hard I didn't think I could get my legs to work. *The children.*

Don't worry about the children. Someone will help them. Someone will help me. I just needed to stay put. *I'm safe here.*

But they wouldn't respond to someone calling to them. I taught them to be cautious.

If I move, the roof will come down on me. I'll be crushed. Stay put and be safe. Someone will come for me.

But my students are frightened. I need to help them. Heavenly Father, help me.

I placed my hands on the ground. White powder drifted down on my head. Carefully I crawled away from the SUV.

The beam shifted, sliding sideways.

My crawl became a scramble.

The beam shrieked as it slid across the metal desk holding it up.

I plunged, then rolled away.

The roof of the shed slammed against the ground, sending up more dust and powder.

Leaning against the school, I waited until I could catch my breath. The glass in the door to the gym beside me had shattered.

I couldn't see anything of the driver. I slipped through the frame, wincing at the stabs of pain from the hurtled projectiles.

Ahead of me was a second door leading to the front of the school. A quick glance into the gym showed it empty. I was pretty sure the children had raced through both sets of doors, scattered, and found safety. I'd trained my class of first-through-third graders on what to do in case of an emergency or active shooter. The school board had rolled their eyes at me, assuring me that this was covered in the student handbook and that school shootings wouldn't happen in a sleepy farming community like LaCrosse, Washington, population 330.

I'd finally convinced them. They allowed the drills and the self-defense class I offered on Tuesday evenings.

Fortunately, my art class was an after-school event, and the rest of the school was essentially empty. We met in a portable building because some of the classrooms were under repair for water damage.

I staggered outside. Mr. Parsons, the school maintenance man, rushed over to me.

"Samantha? Sam? Miss Williams? Are you all right? You're bleeding. What happened?"

"Help me find the children first."

"They're fine. They ran as you taught them." We looked around the manicured lawns in front of the school buildings.

"Olly olly oxen free!" I called out, voice shaking. I cleared my throat and tried again. "Olly olly oxen free!"

Slowly my class emerged from their hiding places. I counted them as they appeared. *Please, Lord . . . Five, six, seven, eight . . .*

nine. All present and accounted for. My stomach tightened on what could have happened, would have happened, if even one of them had paused to ask, *Why run?*

"Aren't you supposed to just say 'all clear'?" Mr. Parsons asked.

"I know the handbook says that, but anyone could access the emergency plans and use them against the children."

Several of the children had tear streaks running down their faces, but as soon as they caught sight of me, they started to giggle.

"Miss Williams, you're all white!"

"You have stuff all over you!"

"You should see yourself!"

I looked down. I was indeed covered in a white powder, probably from the recently installed smashed Sheetrock and insulation. "Oh my. It looks like I've turned into the magical snowman."

"Nooo!" The giggles grew louder. "It's not winter!"

I bent forward to be on eye level with most of them. "Maybe I've become Belle, the white Great Pyrenees from *Belle and Sebastien?*"

"That's a dog." The giggles became high-pitched laughter.

I grinned at them. "How about Casper, the friendly ghost?"

The kids were now laughing so hard they couldn't answer for a moment. Finally Bethany gasped out, "You're not dead."

Thank You, Lord. I straightened. "Well then, if I'm not a snowman, dog, or ghost, I must be Miss Williams, and you know what that means." As they eagerly lined up, I said, "'I am not afraid of storms . . .'"

"'For I am learning how to sail my ship,'" the children finished.

Leave it to children's books. As they approached me, each one gave me a sign as to what type of interaction they wanted. Hands out to the side, a hug. Hand held up in the air, a high five. Closed hand, a fist bump. Right hand sideways, a handshake.

They all wanted hugs.

So did I.

Bethany was the last in line. I tried not to hug her the longest. Teachers aren't supposed to have favorites.

The school buildings rested on a hill facing the town park. The wail of sirens and stream of cars and trucks announced the arrival of help and parents. I moved my small huddle of children around to the front toward the parking lot so their folks could find them. The parents, once reunited with their son or daughter, peppered me with questions.

"What happened?"

"Was anyone hurt?"

"Was that a drunk driver?"

"Are you okay?"

As I stumbled through various versions of "I don't know," a deputy from the Whitman County Sheriff's Department strolled over. He had to be at least six foot three inches tall, with silver hair, thick black eyebrows, and dark brown eyes that looked like they'd ferret out the facts of any case. He smelled of cigarettes. His name tag said R. Adams. "Ma'am. Looks like you were in the building when the accident happened."

"Yes. Is the driver—"

"Come with me." He had a slight New York accent. We walked to the gym, then around to the back side where the accident happened. I had to trot to keep up with him.

"Do you know if the driver is okay?"

His long stride covered a lot of ground. "We don't know yet."

The raised gravel parking area near the gym was filling with the LaCrosse ambulance, volunteer fire department, and sheriff's department vehicles. People were rushing around like ants in a disturbed mound. The Suburban was completely buried under the collapsed roof, and a large group of men and women were working to clear the debris.

Deputy Adams led me to the ambulance where an EMT waited. "Are you hurt?"

"I don't think—"

"You have a cut on your head." The EMT had me sit while he checked me over.

Deputy Adams kept an eye on the rescue efforts as he pulled out a small notebook. "You got all the children out safely?"

I winced as the EMT removed a sliver of glass from my hairline. "By the grace of God, yes. They're all on their way home."

He nodded and gave me a slight smile, softening his face. "Absolutely. How many people were in the SUV?"

"I don't know." I told him about what sounded like gunfire and the sound of an engine and getting the children clear of the room. I left out my cowering in the debris.

"Gunfire? Are you sure?"

"It could have been backfire."

He looked around, then motioned for an officer to come over. They spoke for a few moments before the man left.

I glanced over at the gathered first responders, parents, and neighbors. What if—

"When did you first see the SUV?" Deputy Adams asked.

I pointed. "He, or whoever was driving, must have come up either First or Hill Avenue, crossed this lot, then shot straight into the building."

A farmer drove up on a John Deere tractor and began lifting larger chunks of rubble with the bucket.

After the deputy took my name, address, and phone number, he handed me a business card. "I'll be contacting you soon for your statement. You might want to head home as soon as possible. We want to clear the area." He strolled away.

More people had arrived and pitched in to free the SUV and its occupants. A truck with a Miller Construction sign on the side parked next to us. Men in hard hats, work boots, and lime-green safety vests got out and set to work.

A pregnant woman in her thirties with long, dark hair pulled into a french braid drifted over and hovered nearby. When the EMT finished putting a bandage on my head and moved away, she approached me. "Hi. I'm Mary Thompson. I overheard you talking to that deputy. Do you mind if I ask you a few questions?"

"I guess. You're a reporter?"

"No. Copywriter for a medical company in Spokane." She rolled her eyes. "Booooooring. You're Samantha Williams?"

I nodded.

"Well, Samantha—"

"Call me Sam."

She grinned. "Sam then. You saved all those children. You're so brave. I would have been scared out of my mind."

Warmth burned up my neck and across my cheeks. "I . . . ah . . . so . . . um . . . what brought you to LaCrosse from Spokane?" I stood. "That's 86.9 miles from here."

"I was already here."

An officer started herding the onlookers away from the crash. "Move on, folks. Nothing for you to do here."

"Come on," Mary grabbed my elbow and pulled me into the shade under a tree.

My brain was buzzing from the adrenaline and all the activity. "I'm sorry. I'm a little—"

"I bet you are. I guess I should start at the beginning. I'm following the story about the body they found last week. And the one they just found." She waved her hand at the construction workers.

"Bodies?" I knew I was out of touch with the news. I didn't own a television, computer, or phone. "What bodies? Wait . . . I'm not sure I want to know." My legs started to buckle.

"Let me help you." Mary grabbed my arm and helped me sit on a patch of grass. She sat next to me. "Can I get you something or—"

"No, I'll be fine. Just a little woozy."

"Take your time."

Most of the onlookers had now moved around to the front of the school. With nothing to see, they started wandering back to their homes or cars.

She cleared her throat. "So do you want to talk about what just happened or—"

"No. You go ahead. You said there was a body . . . or was it two? Here at the school?"

"No, of course not. I followed someone to here and . . ." She paused at my expression. "I'm not weird or a stalker." She twisted her lips. "As you can see, I'm pregnant. The baby's father, my husband, Mike, disappeared two months ago. I reported it to the police but they're not doing anything. I mean, he could be dead!"

I blinked at her. "Why would you think that?"

"Mike had—I guess you'd call it a wild streak. He had . . . questionable friends. Some issues with drugs in the past, stuff like that." She absently rubbed her stomach. "I thought the baby would . . . redirect him." She looked at me. "He's a good man, just impulsive. And he'd never leave me. Not now. Not without telling me . . . something."

I took a deep breath. The shaking threatened to start again. "So you thought one of the bodies—"

"Could be Mike." She swiped a hand across her eyes. "That deputy." She pointed to Deputy Adams. "I was told he was the investigator on the case. I've been following him around trying to get him to talk to me, but he says it's an active case and won't talk about it. I followed him here to the school earlier—he has kids here that he was picking up—and was giving it one last go around."

"Did you find out anything?"

"No. Not yet." She reached into her purse and pulled out a

leather-bound notebook. "I keep track of everything." She flipped it open and fanned the pages, displaying a mass of tightly written notes. "I won't give up until I know for sure."

"'She made herself stronger by fighting with the wind.'" I muttered.

Mary stared at me. "What?"

"Oh. Sorry. A quote from *The Secret Garden*. You know, the book by Frances Hodgson . . . never mind."

Crash! A large piece of wall had fallen outward, releasing a cloud of throat-clogging dust that blanketed the scene for a moment. The dust settled, revealing the back end of the Suburban.

The workers surged to clear the rear door for access to the SUV. They soon had it open. An EMT who had been standing by crawled inside. "Two people!" he called out.

The first responders moved closer, talking to each other and to the folks inside the car. I couldn't hear their words, but shortly a man emerged cradling his right arm. Blood streaked his pale face. "I'm fine. Just a broken arm. Please, I'm fine." His deep voice carried clearly. He had even features, broad shoulders, and short-cropped, dark hair. The EMT ushered him to the ambulance near us, where he finally agreed to be looked at.

Mary nudged me and whispered, "Is it just me, or is that the hunkiest-looking guy in Eastern Washington?"

"Hunkiest? Um . . ."

"He could be the hero for a book." She looked down at her swollen stomach. "I'm not exactly heroine material at the moment. And you . . ."

"It's the buttered-toast phenomenon," I blurted out.

She frowned at me.

I sighed. "Just as buttered toast always lands butter side down, the best-looking guy I've ever seen shows up when I'm covered in white plaster and look like a zombie."

Mary grinned.

The medical worker who'd entered the Suburban crawled out again. The crowd grew silent. He signaled another EMT to come closer. "The driver is dead," he said quietly.

His voice carried clearly in the still crowd.

"Are you sure?" the second man asked.

The EMT nodded. "A metal beam came through the windshield. It was . . . not survivable."

My mouth dried. So close. I could have been dead as well.

I quickly glanced at the surviving passenger to observe his reaction. The other person in the car could be his wife, family, or a friend.

His jaw clenched and a vein pounded in his forehead. He stared sightlessly into the distance.

Deputy Adams moved over to the man. "They'll be taking you to Colfax soon to see to your injuries. Before you go, could you give me your name and the name of the driver?"

"Dutch, um, Dustin Van Seters. Dr. Van Seters. I'm an anthropologist working at Clan Firinn. The driver is . . . was Dr. Beatrice Greer, an art therapist also at Clan Firinn. We were heading over to Alderman Acres."

"Do you know what happened? What caused the accident?"

"Yeah. Dr. Greer . . . someone shot her."

TWO

Dr. Van Seters extended his arms to stay steady on his feet, then cleared his throat. The shock of the shooting and accident, along with the pain in his arm, made his stomach churn. He'd somehow known Beatrice hadn't survived. Between the gunshot and beam . . . He shook his head.

He'd answered the deputy's questions, then, left alone, stared into the distance, sorting his jumbled thoughts.

"Sir?"

He realized the EMT was addressing him. "Sorry. What were you saying?"

"I need you to lie down so we can get you to a doctor in Colfax."

He nodded. As he lay on the gurney, he caught a glimpse of a woman covered in white dust staring at him. She'd obviously been in the building when they'd plowed into it.

They'd almost killed her.

He met her gaze as he was lifted into the ambulance, then

quickly looked away. Somehow he'd find out who she was and apologize. He broke out into a cold sweat.

He reached for a small pebble he carried everywhere in his pocket—a reminder of his progress at Clan Firinn. Or rather, the lack of progress.

The EMT checked him over as they drove, finally leaning back. "You'll be fine once the doctor sees you and gets that arm fixed up. Why were you going to the school?"

"We weren't." Dutch checked his watch. "We were heading to where they found the most recent body. I should call to let everyone know we were in an accident. Do you have a cell phone I can borrow?"

"No. You're supposed to relax until the doctor can see you." His brow furrowed. "Didn't they find a body at that new place? The housing development?"

"Alderman Acres. Yes."

The EMT shook his head. "Then what were you doing driving near the school? The development is in a different direction and outside of town. And you were in a back parking lot. I don't know how someone could get lost in LaCrosse."

Dutch thought for a moment. "You can't." They were silent the rest of the drive. At the hospital, he found he was either being fussed over by a number of people taking X-rays or left alone in a boring emergency room. And no one would loan him a phone.

The doctor finally came in. "You're a lucky man, Dr. Van Seters. Fortunately, you won't need surgery. We'll be putting a cast on your arm, but we have to wait for the swelling to go down—roughly five to seven days. We'll splint it in the meantime and you'll need to keep it in a sling." After he took care of Dutch's arm, he said, "There's a deputy here to talk to you." He left and the deputy entered.

"Dr. Van Seters? I need to ask you a few questions before you leave." He took out a small notebook.

Dutch let out a sigh of exasperation. "I suppose."

"Could you tell me what happened? Why were you at the school?"

"Everyone seems to want to know the answer to that, including me. You'll need to ask the coroner why he wanted to meet there. We were headed to Alderman Acres from Clan Firinn."

"I'll follow up with him. What exactly did he say to you?"

"Not me. Beatrice took the call. She said it was from the coroner's office and that it was related to the body they found. She held up a piece of paper and said she'd drive us to this meeting, then to Alderman Acres."

"Then what happened?"

"Suddenly the window next to Beatrice exploded and she slumped over the steering wheel. Her foot must have pushed on the gas . . . I tried to get control, but . . . well, Beatrice was a large woman, and . . ." He felt clammy.

"I see. Did you or Dr. Greer have any enemies?"

"No. Not that I know of."

"What about the woman in the school? The teacher. Do you know her?"

"I don't even know her name."

The deputy paged through his notebook. "Samantha Williams. An art teacher. Lives in Pullman."

"No. Never met her." *But I need to.* Surviving an accident where there was a fatality could have a long-lasting impact on someone. He should know.

"What about Beatrice? Did she know the teacher?"

"Not that I know of. You sound like you think the shooting was deliberate."

"We're just looking at every angle." After a few more questions, the deputy left.

By the time he was released, his boss, Dr. Brùn, had arrived and was waiting to drive him back to Clan Firinn.

"Dr. Brùn! I'm surprised you're picking me up." Dutch smiled at the older man. "I figured you'd send Scotty."

The doctor was wearing his usual impeccable dark blue suit, snowy white shirt, and maroon tie. In his sixties, he had short gray hair, wire-rimmed glasses, and a small black ribbon on his lapel.

"I wanted to make sure you're going to be okay." Dr. Brùn gave him a piercing look. "And see to it that my number-one assistant doesn't get sidetracked."

Dutch again felt the stone in his pocket. "It's just a broken arm."

"I wasn't referring to your body. I meant your mental state."

Dutch continued walking toward the car. "I think I'll be okay. Yes." He stopped. "You're not thinking I should start over—"

Dr. Brùn paused next to him. "Good heavens, no! I've never seen someone work so hard and make so much progress in our program. You're one of our biggest success stories, going from . . . well, where you started to being on staff. I just want you to keep moving forward."

"Like I said, it's just a broken arm. And I really don't have time right now to think about it. I need to call—"

"I already did."

Both men continued walking.

Dutch cleared his throat. "About Beatrice—"

"Yes." The older man rubbed his face, then blinked. His speed increased slightly toward the parked SUV. "I guess both of us will be processing this for a while." He opened the door for Dutch, closed it, then got into the driver's seat. "Do you think the shooting was an accident? A hunter's bullet gone wild?"

"Hunting so close to town and the school? No. I don't think so." Dutch scratched at the sling, then his chin. "I couldn't get a direct answer from the deputy. I don't see how anyone knew where we'd be except the coroner, who asked to meet us."

"And was he there?"

Dutch shook his head.

"Strange all the way around."

Dutch borrowed Dr. Brùn's cell and dialed the coroner's office. He got an answering machine and left word for someone to call him, then disconnected. "I guess the answer will have to wait a bit unless you want to see if we can catch someone at the excavation."

"Considering you were just in a fatal car accident, it can wait."

———

As soon as the law-enforcement officers heard about a potential shooter, there was a palpable shift in energy and activity at the school. One man took charge, directing anyone not connected to the actual accident site to either do a sweep of the area or clear out.

Mary grabbed my arm and pulled me behind a dumpster. "Did you hear that? Someone shot the driver. And she was from Clan Firinn. I hadn't thought of that." She peered around the dumpster.

"And that's important because . . . ?"

"You *have* heard of Clan Firinn?"

"Sort of. A rehab place nearby, right? For drugs or alcohol abuse?"

"More than that. It's a primo program that's shrouded in mystery." She returned her notebook to her purse, scrolled through the phone, then handed me a short article.

Clan Firinn, located outside of Pullman, Washington, offers hope and rehabilitation to law enforcement and first responders suffering from various forms of PTSD and other disorders arising from their work. It is privately owned and funded. Clan Firinn does not accept general applicants but reviews referrals on an individual basis. While participating in the program, members experience therapeutic work, educational opportunities, physical training, a structured schedule, personalized feedback, nutritious meals, and spiritual guidance. Graduates are assisted with career counseling, job referrals, and relocation.

"I'm still fuzzy as to why that's important." I handed the phone back to her. "Are you saying the shooter is from Clan Firinn, or—"

"No, of course not. Drug rehab. Get it? Mike might be in some rehab or . . . or something." Her brow furrowed and she again rubbed her stomach.

I gently reached over and touched her on the shoulder. "Maybe. You could ask."

She glanced at me and nodded.

Deputy Adams discovered us. "You two. Move on. We need to clear the area."

I had to agree with him. Time to go. My head pounded, dust made my nose run, and various bruises were making themselves known. The children were safe. I'd go hide under that blanket at my apartment. I'd grab my purse . . .

My purse was somewhere in the debris next to a crushed woman. Compared to recovering the human remains, my purse would be a low priority to law enforcement. I didn't even have my car keys. And my car . . . I glanced around me. My car was gone.

"You have *got* to be kidding me." I looked around the parking lot for my Mini Cooper, bought used but well loved just a year ago. I soon found it.

I wanted to vomit.

The big Suburban must have clipped my tiny car in its out-of-control race to the school. My car had spun, flown over a retaining wall, and wrapped around a tree.

My mind blanked. Each part of my carefully crafted

world—the art class, children, books, the life I'd built in this dusty farming region of Eastern Washington—lay in ruined rubble or a tangle of metal.

"Is something the matter? Oh!" Mary had come up beside me. "Is . . . was that your car?"

I mutely nodded.

"Where do you live? Maybe I can give you a ride."

"Pullman."

"*Pullman?* That must be fifty miles from here over a boney winding road. Why so far from your work?"

"It's 45.6 miles." I didn't really have an answer. At least an answer I was willing to share with a stranger. "My keys, purse, everything is somewhere in that mess." I nodded toward the destroyed classroom.

"You do have that key." She pointed to the key on a necklace around my neck.

"That won't help." I tucked it into my blouse.

"Is there someone I can call?"

I haven't had anyone to call for a very long time. "No."

Mary tapped a finger on her lip. "I know for a fact that there aren't any hotels, motels, or car rentals here. I'm staying at the only bed and breakfast . . . wait, how about you stay with me until things get sorted out? The house has two bedrooms."

"Thank you. Maybe I can catch a ride home with someone else. I don't want to be a bother."

She waved her hand at the activities. "I doubt anyone's heading to Pullman tonight. And you wouldn't be a bother."

I couldn't think of another reason to turn down her offer,

though I was loath to be beholden to anyone. "If it's not too much trouble . . ."

"Not at all." She caught the deputy's attention. "Hi, Deputy Adams—"

"Didn't I just tell you to leave?"

"Yeah, well that's Sam's car over there." She pointed. "And her purse is somewhere in there with her ID." She nodded at the wreckage of the portable classroom. "If you need to be in touch with us, Sam and I will be staying the night at Rose Cottage Airbnb. We'd appreciate it if you'd let us know when you find her purse. And when you're ready to talk to me about those bodies. Here's my phone number." She handed him a business card.

It seemed so strange to have someone take charge. Normally I would have kept looking for a ride home. Normally I would have brushed off Mary's kindness as a charity. *Normally*. But there was nothing normal about today.

She aimed me toward the street, then to a dusty red Subaru, rear seat covered with boxes and bags. "Ignore the mess. I'm afraid to leave my good stuff at home."

I wanted to ask about that comment but thought it might be rude. *What if she's a hoarder?* Once inside with the air conditioner blasting, she turned toward the edge of town. "If it's okay with you, I'm going to drop you off and head back. If everyone is tied up at the school and searching for shooters, maybe I can get some answers at Alderman Acres."

My stomach gave a little lurch. "You're going to try and see the body?"

"If that's what it takes."

We pulled into the driveway of a craftsman-style bungalow with a wide front porch and parked near the rear of the house. "The back door is unlocked. The owner lives over there." "Over there" proved to be a modern rancher-style house visible through the plantings. "There are a washer and dryer, and the bedrooms each have plushy bathrobes—"

"When do you think you'll be back?" I blurted. *Pathetically desperate.* I tried to think of something funny. "I mean—"

"'S okay. You've had a rough day. I'll try to not be too late."

I stepped from the car. Mary gave a quick wave and backed down the driveway.

I walked with unsteady steps to the screened-in back porch, pausing to try for some semblance of normality. *The kids are safe. I'll try to find a phone to call in the report on my car to the insurance . . . tomorrow I'll be home. It's . . . Friday, right. Monday I'll be attending a lecture at the library on wilderness survival . . .* I ticked through my schedule, adding new items. I'd write everything down, just to be sure. To be thorough. *To be safe.*

"Stop it," I whispered and started humming to clear my mind.

"Hello?" A woman's voice came from my right.

I debated bolting through the door to avoid anyone else spotting me before I had a chance to clean up, but I wasn't fast enough.

"Hi. Can I help you?" She moved to where she could see me. "Oh! Oh my. Were you over at the school? Of course you were. I heard all about it. I'm Peggy. This is my Airbnb . . ." Her barrage of words hammered against me. "I left a note, but decided

25

to tell you in person—help yourself to eggs in the chicken coop and anything you can find in the garden, though it's pretty well tapped out—"

A small yellow dog flew past her and ran at me, yapping furiously.

My heart rate shot off the charts. I grabbed for the doorknob, missed, and turned to face the beast.

"This is Muffie. He won't hurt you. He's a Chihuahua-pug mix." Peggy snapped her fingers. "Come here, Muffie. Come to Mommy."

Muffie showed no inclination to go to Mommy. Instead, she stood on her hind legs, crossed her front legs, and walked around in front of me waving her paws.

"Oh, that's so cute!" Peggy grinned. "Muffie must really like you. She's dancing for you."

Cute-smute. The dog looked like she was judo-chopping the air. I gave Peggy a feeble smile, fumbled the door open, and slid through. Inside, I leaned against the door and took deep breaths. My fear of dogs was irrational, unfounded, and uncontrollable. Dogs, on the other hand, found me irresistible. They couldn't wait to deposit drool on my hands, fur on my slacks, or punch holes in my toes with their sharp nails.

The bed and breakfast was quaintly old-fashioned, with the typical heavy wood trim of the craftsman period. Computer printouts, a yellow legal pad, a stack of library books, and hand-written notes cluttered the kitchen table. A brick fireplace dominated the living room, with built-in bookshelves on either side.

I couldn't help myself. I checked out the books. *Diseases*

Among Swine and Other Domestic Animals. Palgrave's Golden Treasury. The Wizard of Oz. Alice in Wonderland.

Children's books. Thank You, Lord.

A short hall off the living room led to a bedroom on the left and right and a bathroom between the two. Mary's bedroom was easy to identify—tossed clothes and an open suitcase.

The smaller bedroom had a double bed, window seat, set of drawers, and desk. I caught sight of myself in the dresser mirror. No wonder the children had been so amused by my appearance. I looked like a mime, complete with tear lines running from my eyes. A cleared area near my hairline held a Band-Aid.

After undressing, I pulled on the fluffy white robe I found hanging in the closet and went in search of the promised washer and dryer. They proved to be in an alcove off the kitchen. I started my tiny load, then went to the bathroom for a shower.

The sun had set by the time I emerged. Mary had returned and was sitting in the living room with a glass of what looked like white wine. She looked exhausted. "Would you like a glass?"

"No thanks. Um . . . I know it's none of my business, but is that advisable while you're pregnant?"

"You're right." She took a deep breath. "It's white grape juice. I like to pretend. It's been a long day."

"Agreed." I pulled the towel off my wet hair and attempted to finger-comb it into shape.

"You'll find a hairbrush in my room. Go ahead and keep it. I have one in my purse. Just don't ask to borrow my toothbrush."

I grinned my thanks, found the brush, and worked the tangles out of my wet hair. She was still in the living room, now sipping water as I aimed for the laundry. After moving my clothes from the washer to the dryer, I joined her.

My stomach let out a prolonged rumble. "Oops. Sorry."

"Hey, I'm sorry. I should have brought something here for dinner. I didn't even think about it earlier. I'd guess you're starving like me. Of course, I'm always starving. You can't exactly order delivery out here, but I'd be glad to go back to the store—"

"Let me see what I can figure out." I stood. "Did you see . . . ?"

"The body? No. They had a guard. I ended up back at the school to see if they found your purse."

"Did they?"

"I couldn't get near. They'd posted officers around the school and park. I tried asking one of the guards, but they just looked at me and told me to move on. I watched from a distance. At one point there was a loud screech and I saw one guy run to the side of the school and vomit. I'm guessing it was . . . pretty messy."

I swallowed and headed for the kitchen, trying to keep any images from forming. *If I hadn't seen the SUV in time . . . if the children had hesitated . . .*

The refrigerator held half-and-half, a bag of coffee, a loaf of white bread, some butter, an almost-empty jar of jelly, a package of mixed cheese squares, and a plastic container of white grape juice. An open box of Ritz crackers sat on the counter next to a bottle of cabernet sauvignon. Toast for breakfast, and crackers and cheese for dinner. Looked like I'd need to earn my keep.

Several grocery bags rested on the top of the refrigerator. I grabbed one and started for the door.

"Where are you going?" Mary had moved to the kitchen table.

"To get something for dinner."

"Um, I don't mean to point out the obvious, but you can't drive without a car, and someone in the store might notice you're only wearing a robe—"

"I'm not driving or streaking. I'm foraging."

I stepped out the door and listened. I had unusually good hearing, which was useful for listening for the sound of a dog approaching. Fortunately, Muffie, the wolf in Chihuahua clothing, wasn't waiting for me. The garden was pretty well spent, but I found a couple of onions, a sprig of dill, and pinched off a handful of parsley. The row of potato plants had been recently dug up, but running my hands under the soil rewarded me with several potatoes.

The chickens were settling in for the night, but I found some eggs, which I gathered with only a couple of squawks and pecks of protest. I quietly sang the words to the theme song of "Chuck Chicken" to calm them down. I think a few of them bobbed their heads to the beat. Chickens I could handle. Dogs . . . not so much.

Mary hadn't moved since I left. "What are you, some kind of farm girl?"

"A regular Dorothy Gale." I emptied the paper sack onto the counter.

"*The Wizard of Oz*? I loved that movie."

"Don't forget the book. 'There's no place like home.' L. Frank Baum was a wizard, if you'll pardon the expression, with spinning iconic concepts—" I turned and looked at her in time to catch her eyes roll. "Never mind. Didn't you love children's books when you were younger? Especially those set on a farm? *Charlotte's Web*? Anything by Beatrix Potter?"

She shook her head. "I was never one for children's books. Probably because of my childhood. And farm books? Outside of coming to this dusty one-horse town, the closest I've come to farming was to drive a truck one day during wheat harvest for my uncle. He fired me at the end of the day, ending my farm experience." She stood and studied me from head to foot. "You read children's books. Teach art classes to children. What do you do for fun?"

"Those *are* fun. I read all kinds of books, attend lectures, and do jigsaw puzzles."

"Good grief! And I thought my job as a technical copywriter was uninteresting. I suppose the lectures are on such things as behavioral economics?"

"No, though that might be interesting. I just finished a series on verbal and written statement analysis and am taking one on edible plants and wilderness survival."

"Good grief!" she said again.

"Now that's an expression uniquely tied to the character Charlie Brown—"

"Sam, did anyone ever tell you you're a plethora of useless information?"

"You never know what could prove to be useful."

Mary refilled her water glass, then sat and caressed her stomach. "Wine is useful, at least when you're not preggers. Cell phones are useful. Credit cards are very useful. What brought you here? You're pretty. In fact, you're beautiful with that mess of auburn hair and those big blue eyes. You're smart. Young. Talented. Unmarried. A little on the boring side, but that's just me. You should have been scooped up long before this."

"What? And end my lucrative career as a spinster?" I muttered.

"What?"

"I just haven't met the right man."

"Not surprising. I'm sure the available male population is severely limited around these parts. But I bet men hit on you all the time."

"Not really. Once I open my mouth, they tend to lose interest."

"There's nothing wrong with your voice." She sipped some water.

"It's not my voice. It's what I say."

"So you have no filter."

I thought for a moment. "Sort of. I don't say anything rude or unkind. Most of the time I can't even think of what to say until hours later, when I come up with some devastatingly clever comeback. If I can answer, I tend to ramble, or say something dumb, or . . . quote people."

"Like Einstein or Emerson?"

"More like Dr. Seuss."

Mary sprayed out a mouthful of water.

I stopped in my preparation to hand her a paper towel. When she could speak again, she said, "You. Are. Kidding."

"I think of it as opening my mouth and the Sneetches fly out."

"Sneetches?"

"Birdlike creatures invented by Dr. Seuss. But I use it to describe whenever I'm nervous and say stupid things. You'd be surprised how fast a man backs away when you randomly say, '"Sometimes, I've believed as many as six impossible things before breakfast."' I turned to the counter, found a plastic bag, and filled it with a handful of crackers.

"So why *are* you here?"

"What brought me to LaCrosse was a job, though I also do freelance illustrations." I tried to make my answers casual. Using a rolling pin, I crushed the crackers and dumped them into a bowl. I didn't know if the silence behind me was from satisfaction with my answer or unwillingness to accept it. Only after I'd melted some butter, added it to the crackers, and pressed the makeshift crust into a pie plate did I risk a glance at her.

She was still watching me. "What are you making?"

"For dinner, a quiche. For breakfast, dilled scrambled eggs and fried potatoes with parsley if that's okay with you. We're a little heavy on the eggs, but at least they're fresh."

"Okay with me? Are you kidding? I was prepared for another cracker-and-cheese night! Did I bring home an angel?"

"Hardly." I preheated the oven, shredded the cheese, assembled the rest of the ingredients, then popped the quiche in and set the timer. Mary's curiosity about me was getting uncomfortable. "We have some time before it's ready. Tell me more about your search." I really didn't want to talk about missing husbands or dead people, especially at night, but I knew she'd take the bait. I sat across the table from her.

She shuffled the papers for a moment before placing a computer printout of the area in front of me. "I dismissed the report when it first came in. I mean, they were digging near a cemetery and they find a body? Duh. But I got a map to check it out." She pointed. "Here's the cemetery at the top of this hill. Down over here is where the excavation was going on. Not even close to the graves. Bingo, it's back on my radar. I called the deputy in charge of the case, Deputy Adams, and asked him about it. He wouldn't talk to me. Active investigation and all that. So I booked this place and sorta drove down and started following him around. That's how I knew about his kids and the school. Yesterday he finally confronted me and said all they found were bones."

"Bones?"

"That's pretty much it."

"But they're sure they were human, not some dead critter?"

"Not unless someone put a chiffon dress on their favorite cow."

"You're right. Cows look terrible in chiffon."

"Was that a Sneetch?"

"Yes. What did they do with the bones?"

"At first they didn't do anything. I mean, he said they basically stopped working and put up a tent until the experts could look at them. Then they sent the body to Seattle. End of that lead. Time to go home. But then early this afternoon, they found another body at the same place. Fortunately this house was available for another night."

"Thank you again for letting me stay here." How many times would Mary have hope to find her husband before she'd give up? I studied the map, then traced the road between the cemetery and the school. "And the guy in the SUV that crashed into the school was an anthropologist from Clan Firinn."

"Right. I overheard him talking to the deputy. He said he was going over to look at the latest find. Now, is it a coincidence that the body was found on land owned by Clan Firinn? I don't think so. There's some kind of connection. But what were they doing in that part of LaCrosse when Clan Firinn is"—she looked at the map—"here. And the bodies were found there." She pointed.

"Strange." I looked up. "They would have driven down Highway 26 to the LaCrosse Airport Road and should have turned here." I tapped the map. "The school is on the opposite side of town."

Mary leaned forward. "And there's nothing around the school but plowed fields."

"Maybe they wanted to speak to the deputy too?"

She shook her head. "They weren't there when I approached Adams about the second body. He didn't even let me get close to him. I waited for the busses and other vehicles to leave before I walked back to my car. That's when I heard what I thought was a backfire. Then the crash." She pulled her yellow legal pad in front of her. "So now we have another mystery. Why were they driving in the wrong part of town?"

"And why did someone shoot the driver?"

THREE

Mary wandered into the living room with her glass of water and yellow legal pad, leaving me to clear the rest of her notes off the table so I could set it for dinner. She thanked me and proceeded to clutter the coffee table.

The quiche turned out fine and the dinner conversation carefully avoided any mention of books, bodies, crashes, buried treasure, swine diseases, chiffon cows, or shootings, for which I was grateful. I wasn't used to sharing a meal with anyone, but Mary chatted up a storm. When she paused for breath, I asked her, "When are you due?"

"For what?"

"The grand opening. The blessed event. The visit from the stork."

"December 31. I'm hoping for a January first baby." She looked down at her rounded belly.

"Boy or girl?"

"Yes." She grinned. "I want to be surprised." Immediately

after dinner, she returned to her cluttered area in the living room. I washed up the dishes, then hung my now-dry clothes in the bedroom closet. Tomorrow I'd work out my new normal.

She soon brought me an offering of an oversize T-shirt to sleep in.

"Thank you again. 'No act of kindness, no matter how small, is ever wasted.'" Before she could ask, I added, "'The Lion and the Mouse.' *Aesop's Fables.*"

She grunted.

I started going around the house, checking that each window was locked. Mary trailed behind me. When I got to the front door, I stopped.

"What is it?"

"There's no deadbolt on this door."

"Is that a problem?"

"Anyone with a credit card or piece of flat plastic can open it."

Mary twisted her lips. "And you know this because . . . ?"

I grinned at her. "Part of that plethora of useless information. I read a lot."

"You're kinda OCD on security, aren't you? I mean, if we're not in the absolute middle of nowhere, we're certainly on the edge."

"You can never be too careful. Remember, someone shot that driver earlier today just a mile or two from here." The kitchen door proved to have the same locking issues. "I do know self-defense, but if furniture can do the job . . ." I jammed a chair under the doorknob, then picked up another to block the front door.

Mary stepped in my way. "Put the chair down and step back,"

she said in her best cop voice. "You can jam any furniture you want against your own door." She smiled to soften her words.

I replaced the chair. "I'm sorry. I'm on edge."

"I suppose you're allowed to be. You just barely survived getting crushed along with your entire class. You're entitled to a few quirks. And Sneetches. Besides, I'm armed."

I raised my eyebrow at her.

"Remember I said Mike had questionable friends."

"Is that why you travel with all your valuable possessions?"

"You got it. Laptop. A few pieces of silver. A camera in a drone. Anything that could be easily turned to ready cash."

I nodded and headed to my room. At least the door had a lock on it, albeit the same kind as the outside doors. I jammed the desk chair under the knob. *"You just barely survived getting crushed along with your entire class."* Mary's words swirled around in my brain. A car can be a pretty effective weapon. Was that weapon deliberately pointed at my class? One of my students? Me?

It couldn't be me. I was nobody. Just in the wrong place at the wrong time.

The sheets were crisp with a hint of lavender. I didn't think I could sleep, but the minute my head hit the pillow, I was out.

Creeeeeeaak!

I opened my eyes and listened.

The noise came again. A very subtle *creeeeeeaak!*

The house is probably settling. I sat up. The digital clock showed 3:20. A small night-light let me see the rough outline of the furniture. *Or maybe Mary had to go to the bathroom—*

Creeeeeeaak! Thump.

37

Louder now. Mary was definitely walking around the house. I wanted to lie back down and go to sleep, but a feather of unease tickled my neck.

A gentle squeak came from the door. I squinted to see in the dark room. The doorknob was turning.

"Mary?" I whispered.

Creeeeeeaak! Thump. Just outside my door.

"Mary?" I said louder.

Thump, thump, thump. Bang! The front door slammed shut.

I jumped out of bed, grabbed my pants, and pulled them on.

"Sam?" Mary called from the hall. "Are you okay?"

"Yes." I swiftly moved the chair and opened the door.

She had her phone to her ear with one hand, a holstered pistol in the other. ". . . yes, I'm sure. Someone just broke into our house." She gave the address. "No, whoever it was has gone. Yes, the doors were locked." She listened for a moment. "Yes." She looked at me. "They're sending someone. They want me to stay on the line."

"Are you sure he's gone?"

"Yes, but you might want to look around. Are you comfortable with handguns?"

"Yes."

"Then take this." She handed me a .38 snub-nosed revolver in a leather paddle holster.

I owned a Sig Sauer 9mm, but I kept it locked at home in my gun safe. "Do you think one of Mike's friends tried to get in?"

Mary looked at me for a few moments while she chewed her lower lip. "Look, Sam, I probably said too much about Mike and his friends. I don't want to drag you into this. Please don't mention that to the police."

"But they need to know."

She shook her head. "My experience has been when they find out who Mike used to run around with, they wash their hands. They don't want to look into his disappearance."

"But—"

"Really, Sam. Mike's friends have no quarrel with me." Mary moved to the front window to watch for the police.

I wanted to point out that she was the one carrying a gun, but she didn't look to be in any mood to discuss the subject. I inspected first the living room, then the kitchen, leaving lights on everywhere I went. If theft had been the motive for the break-in, they hadn't taken or moved anything that I could see. The kitchen looked the same, with dishes still in the drying rack, Mary's purse unopened on the end of the counter, and the chair still shoved under the doorknob. Before returning to the living room, I stepped into my room and put on a bra under my T-shirt. Life felt far more civil with a little undergirding. I left the pistol on the bed and returned to the living room where Mary was still at the window. "All clear."

"Good." She approached the front door and opened it before I could stop her. Any fingerprints were now smeared. She peered down the road, closed the door, then looked at the doorknob. "That was dumb. Why didn't you stop me?"

"I guess that simplifies the investigation."

Her lips thinned into a straight line. "Why don't you take over and let me get dressed." She handed me her phone.

Emergency lights flashed as the patrol car parked in front of the house. "They're here," I said into the cell before disconnecting.

"Is everything okay?" the officer asked as he stepped from the car. "You called about a prowler?"

"Yes. He's gone now. Nothing missing."

He nodded and flipped on his flashlight. "Sounds like kids. I'll take a look around outside." After disappearing for a few moments, he returned. "I don't see any sign of anyone, but I'll swing back by here a couple of times."

"Thank you, officer." I waited until he got in his cruiser, then stepped back inside the house. Mary, now dressed, met me as I walked toward the kitchen.

"Gone already?" she asked.

"He thinks it was kids. He looked around but didn't find anything." I reached the kitchen, retrieved a glass, and filled it with water. "I figured if someone was after something, they'd go for your purse on the counter, but it's undisturbed."

Mary's brows furrowed. She walked to her bedroom, returning a moment later with a leather purse. "It couldn't have been my purse. Mine was in my room."

The little hairs on my arms prickled. Slowly I turned and walked toward the purse. I hadn't really looked at it closely, just enough to see it was closed. Now as I approached, what had originally appeared to be an off-white purse was one covered in white powder. Like I'd been. The shape was familiar. "I think it's mine." Carefully, touching on the edges of the flap covering the opening, I peeked inside.

"Well?" Mary asked.

"Empty. My wallet's gone. Keys. Everything."

Mary rubbed her arms as if cold. "This is crazy. Someone broke into this house and returned an empty purse. Why? No one knew you were here, Sam." She turned to me.

I backed away and started pacing. The movement helped me think. "That deputy, um, Ryan Adams. He knows I'm here and where we're staying."

"You think—"

"No, no. I mean there were other people around who could have overheard."

"You're right," Mary said. "And anyone could have followed us here. We weren't paying attention."

"So the questions are, why would someone sneak into the school, find my purse in all that rubble, locate me, and break into this house in the middle of the night only to return an empty purse?"

"That's just creepy. Should we call that officer back and have him test for fingerprints or DNA or something like that?"

"That would be a waste of time. The only place where the powder is disturbed is where I touched the flap. Someone used a tool to open it, not their fingers." I picked up a kitchen chair. This time she didn't try to stop me from placing it under the knob in the living room.

I was too wound up to go back to bed. I didn't realize I'd started pacing again until Mary grabbed me by the arms. "Sam! Sit down. I have over seven trillion nerves and you're getting on every one of them."

"I'm sorry."

"Are you always this wound up?"

"Only when someone tries to run me down, kill my students, smash my car, and break in where I'm sleeping to return my empty purse. And knowing that someone now has my name, address, credit cards, and keys to my house—it tends to ping *my* seven trillion nerves."

We stared at each other for a moment before we both burst into laughter. I laughed so hard I cried. Then I just cried.

FOUR

Dutch looked out the window of his private living quarters on the third floor, where he'd been for the past three years. He'd moved to this room after going through the Clan Firinn rehab program, when both he and Dr. Brùn felt he needed more time. He took a job on staff teaching science while he finished up his forensic anthropology studies. He never tired of the view across the rolling farmlands, especially early in the day. It was a soothing sight this morning. He hadn't been able to sleep well with his aching arm and the restless thoughts on the accident. The list of work projects he'd jotted down this morning served as a reproach to his current lack of direction.

The best thing to do would be to jog. It would probably hurt like the dickens with his arm but would clear his mind. He pulled on some sweats and his jogging shoes, then stuck his iPod and earbuds into a pocket.

A few guests were roaming around the living area of the

lodge, waiting for their class or appointment to start. He waved at the few that nodded at him.

Outside he inserted his earbuds, cranked up the music, and started a slow jog to warm up. Gradually he increased his pace. His muscles hurt, his arm ached, and his breath came in jagged gasps.

He slowed, then stopped and looked around. *No wonder I'm tired.* He'd probably covered over nine miles.

He turned around and started walking back. Now the thoughts that he'd kept a bay crowded into his head. *Why did Beatrice get shot? Was it an accident?* He glanced around. Was a sniper still out there? He increased his pace. More thoughts elbowed into his brain. *Why her and not me? She didn't deserve to die.*

He got back to his room just as the phone on his desk rang.

"Dr. Van Seters."

"Hi, Dutch. This is Kay." Dr. Kay Solem was the state forensic anthropologist and a friend of his.

"You must have been reading my mind." Dutch pulled up a chair. "I was going to call you about the accident." He outlined the car crash into the school.

Kay was silent for a few moments after he finished. "That explains why I couldn't get ahold of you. I'm so sorry about the accident. Beatrice was a nice person." She paused and cleared her throat. "I know we arranged for you to come here to Seattle."

"Right. Reconstruct the face on the unidentified skull from LaCrosse."

"Last night I received a call from the Whitman County coroner on the latest set of remains found at Alderman Acres."

Dutch frowned. "So Rick has time to call you but not me? That's not like him. He was the one who sent us to the school. Said he wanted a meeting."

"You'll need to ask him. He wants me to take over the case. I'm on my way to LaCrosse now and should be there in another two hours or so. I thought I'd save some time and bring the skull with me so you could work on it there. But with your artist gone and you with your broken arm . . ."

"Well . . ." He really wanted to work on a case. Since finishing his degree, he'd had chances to work on only a few. *That teacher at the school is an artist.* Preparing the skull for a two-dimensional facial reconstruction wasn't all that difficult. He could easily direct her, and her artistic ability would do the rest. If Dr. Brùn approved, Dutch could ask her if she'd be interested in helping.

"Actually, that's great, Kay. I do have someone here, an artist, who might be able to draw the face for me. Let me ask her."

"Excellent. I'll meet you at Alderman Acres. You can work your magic while I process the current scene, then I'll pick up the skull at your lab and take it back to Seattle when I leave."

They disconnected. Dutch tried calling the coroner's office. When again he got the answering machine, he hung up without leaving a message.

He walked downstairs to meet Dr. Brùn for breakfast in the staff dining room. The older man had a cup of coffee, half a grapefruit, and a small plate of whole-wheat toast in front of him. Only the coffee had been touched.

"I saw you go out this morning." Dr. Brùn took a sip of coffee. "Did it help?"

Dutch sat across from him and poured his own mug. He took his time adding cream. "Did what help?"

"Running."

"I was jogging."

"Hmm." Dr. Brùn folded his napkin. "So what are your plans for today?"

Dutch pulled on his ear. "I got a call from Kay Solem. She's been called in on the latest body." He caught Dr. Brùn up on the discussion.

"Are you feeling well enough for me to drive you to the development today?"

"I can have Scotty drive me. You're busy—"

"Indulge me."

"In that case, I'm fine. I'll load up on aspirin."

"The deputy handling the school incident asked that we stop by the school before heading over. Although the SUV's been towed, he said he has some personal items recovered that we could pick up. He said he'd be there in about"—Dr. Brùn checked his watch—"about an hour." He picked up a piece of toast, then set it back down.

"I'm so sorry about your friend, Beatrice. If this wasn't an accident, who'd want to murder her? I liked her and didn't think she had an enemy in the world." Dr. Brùn stared out the window, then cleared his throat. "Of course, there is the possibility that she wasn't the target."

Dutch tried not to slosh his coffee. He hadn't thought about someone else being the target.

A female staff member approached. "Dr. Brùn? We've cleaned

out Beatrice's room and boxed her things. What did you want done with them?"

Dr. Brùn sighed and looked at his hands for a moment. "Beatrice had no family, so her clothes can go to the church's thrift store."

The woman turned to leave.

"Wait," Dr. Brùn said.

The staffer paused.

Dr. Brùn turned to Dutch. "About this artist that might help you with the reconstruction. The deputy told me her car was wrecked and her purse is missing. There's a chance she'll be needing a place to stay. How would you feel about her coming here? That would put her close by to help you."

Dutch tried to hide his grin. "Good idea."

Dr. Brùn looked at the woman. "See to it that Highland House is stocked and our guest has all she needs for the next few days. Just in case."

"Yes, sir. What size is she?"

Dr. Brùn looked at Dutch. "Did you see her?"

Dutch pictured the teacher he'd seen covered with plaster yesterday. "Beautiful." The word slipped out before he could clamp his mouth shut. Heat shot up his neck and onto his face.

Dr. Brùn raised his eyebrows.

"Small, slender, like you," Dutch finally mumbled to the staffer.

The woman nodded. "And which room?"

Dr. Brùn stared out the window a moment, then said, "She's an artist. Put her in Beatrice's room."

Once they were alone again, Dr. Brùn leaned back in his chair. "You seem interested in this artist, Dutch."

"Is that a bad thing?"

"Not at all. Not at all."

Dutch thought about Dr. Brùn's implied question. "I don't know why she caught my attention. Maybe it's because . . ."

"Because . . . ?"

"She reminded me a little bit of me when I first came here."

"And you were . . . ?"

"Lost."

———

Lack of sleep replaced my brain with cotton wool. Although I'd finally gone to bed around four thirty, I slept only an hour before rising and making a list of what I needed to do. By the time Mary fumbled her way into the kitchen, the list was done, the coffee was hot, and the sliced potatoes had been soaking in cold water for several hours.

She poured a cup of coffee, dumped in some half-and-half, and flopped into a chair. After consuming most of it, she straightened. "I suppose you have made your bed, rearranged the dishes, cleaned the oven, and organized your day. And you're cheerful in the morning. I think I hate you."

I slid the sliced potatoes into the melted butter in the frying pan. "Not bad. Two out of five. I didn't do the dishes or clean the oven, although it could use a cleaning. I stripped the bed, and the sheets are in the dryer. And I'm not cheerful. I'm . . . concerned."

"About what? I'm sorry. I'm not thinking. Not enough caffeine in my system. Your keys, credit card, all that. My cell is in my purse. Feel free to make the calls . . . um . . . but could you do that after breakfast? That smells heavenly and I'm eating for two." She went to her room, returning with her purse, then moved to the coffeepot.

I found her cell. "What's your password?"

She put down her cup. "Oh, sorry, that's my work phone. My personal cell is in a purple case." She took the unit from me, rummaged in her purse a bit more, then pulled out a cell and handed it to me.

I took the phone. "I confess, I don't even own one."

"I knew it. Admit it. You're a leftover from another era."

I grinned. "Flash frozen in 1937." After we'd eaten, Mary headed to her room to get ready and pack while I cleaned the kitchen. I was halfway through my calls when she returned.

"I got hold of the insurance company." I showed her my list. "They wanted to know where my car was towed or have a photo of it for the adjuster. I canceled my bank card, but it will be a few days before I receive a new one. My landlord was out, so I left word to check my apartment and call in a locksmith. Hope you don't mind I gave her your number to call me back."

Mary shook her head. "Did anything work out?"

"Just in reporting my stolen wallet."

Mary's phone rang. "Hello?" She listened for a moment. "Yes, I'll tell her." She disconnected. "That was your principal. He said he wants to address the staff around ten in the parking lot. Why don't you make the rest of your calls while we drive over to the school? We can also find out if anyone knows where they took your car."

"Sure."

Mary declined my offer to carry her suitcase and loaded it and her computer case in the car. She started the engine, pulled on a navy baseball cap and sunglasses, and cranked up the air-conditioning. While she drove, I continued making my calls. Requesting a replacement driver's license brought more bad news. I needed to pay for it with a check or credit card, and it would take several weeks to get the replacement. We arrived at the school before I could call the bank.

The crisp fall morning smelled of burning leaves, freshly turned earth, cut grass, and spilled gasoline. We had to park down the hill from the school and walk the remaining distance as the grounds were still cordoned off. The deputy watching over the scene stopped us at first. Only after showing him the staff ID card I'd been wearing would he let us through. I had to dust off my photo. He noted our names and the Airbnb address on a form attached to a clipboard. He said he had no clue as to where my car was but gave me a number to call.

As we cleared the gym and moved to the rear, we saw the SUV had been pulled from the classroom and taken away. The gaping hole in the side of the building looked even more shocking, especially with the crushed children's desks and chairs now exposed. More cadmium-yellow crime-scene tape fluttered around the perimeter of the building, and overall-clad technicians were picking through the debris. A number of official vehicles were haphazardly parked in the gravel lot.

Deputy Adams was speaking to a man in a hard hat from Miller Construction. The man was pointing to the collapsed roof.

As Mary and I approached, the two men turned toward us.

"Miss Williams," Deputy Adams said. "I heard about your break-in last night. How do you think someone could have found your purse in all that?" He waved at the debris. "Or get past our guard?"

I suspected there hadn't been enough guards to watch the entire perimeter of the school, park, and surrounding hundreds of acres of open fields. I grunted a noncommittal answer. "Would it be possible to go through the gym and look at the other side of the classroom?"

He gave me a skeptical glance, then said, "I'll find out if it's safe."

He turned to the construction worker. The man appeared to be about my age, with thick black eyebrows, deep-set blue eyes framed by black lashes, even features, and a cleft chin. His red-rimmed eyes and five o'clock shadow testified of a night working to remove the SUV.

"Leroy Miller, this is Samantha Williams." The deputy nodded at me. "Sam was in the school when the accident occurred. She wants to go into the other side of that." He waved. "Is that safe?"

Leroy checked me over as if examining a used bulldozer. "Depends. Why?"

That's none of your business. "Um, my desk could have been shoved clear of the shed and building, making it relatively easy to locate my purse."

"Women and their purses." Leroy grinned, making me want

to stomp on his instep. "They got a part of it taped off, but you can look."

With Leroy leading, I followed along with the deputy and Mary. Although the town of LaCrosse was an unassuming farm community dominated by grain elevators, the K–12 school was a meticulously maintained series of modern brick buildings. When the school had to close a section for repairs, they didn't want the temporary classroom to disrupt the beautiful campus. The thirty-six-foot mobile classroom, looking like something a semi would haul, had been tucked out of sight, with access both from the side and from the back through the gym. Now only the gym route was open.

The door opened to a tiny debris-filled area. The joist-roof structure of the open storage unit had completely collapsed. Peering below the edge of the roof, I shuddered when I saw just how flat the beam would have made me. My purse would have been easy to steal. I kept it underneath my desk, and it would have gone flying when the desk moved.

We walked back to the parking lot in front of the school, where small groups of local citizens, the school's principal, and several teachers mingled. The principal had already started speaking to several teachers and a few people I recognized as the school board. I joined the group. ". . . we will be assessing the safety of the building," the principal was saying, "so until we have a handle on the damage, school will be closed."

"Do you have a timeline?" someone asked.

"Not at this moment. We may be looking at bringing in more temporary classrooms."

I stepped away. I didn't want to think about my iffy future just yet.

"Miss Williams?" The principal waved me over. "Under the circumstances, we won't be offering an art class this year. We'll give you a good recommendation, of course."

A weight settled on my chest. "Thank you."

"Miss Williams? Miss Williams!"

I turned, smiling. The weight lifted.

Bethany Woods broke away from her parents and ran into my arms. Sunshine broke through the storm cloud on my heart. "Miss Williams, you're squishing me."

I loosened my arms. "I'm sorry, sweetheart. I'm just happy to see you."

Bethany's parents joined us. "Thank you for your quick action," Mr. Woods said. "You probably saved our daughter. Is everything okay?"

Over the lump in my throat, I managed to croak out, "So far. I'm just happy they got away safely."

"You let us know if you find out anything." Mrs. Woods held out her hand and Bethany grabbed it. The three of them strolled toward their car.

Mary came over. "One of your students?"

I nodded.

"Funny thing about small farming towns. Not a big gene pool. Everyone looks like they're cousins."

I narrowed my eyes and frowned at her.

She held up her hands. "Just saying." Her gaze went over my shoulder. "Well, hello. Who do we have here?"

I turned.

A white Cadillac Escalade was just parking. A man in his sixties wearing a dark-blue suit stepped out. Another man, with his right arm in a sling, got out of the passenger side.

I recognized the second man as the one who'd been in the SUV. Cleaned up, he looked even more handsome than he had yesterday.

Mary jabbed me in the back. "Wanna flip a coin for him?" she whispered. "Heads I win, tails you lose."

"What about Mike?"

She looked down and gave a half shrug.

Another Sneetch. I felt terrible about reminding her of her missing husband.

"Dr. Brùn." The deputy stepped forward with his hand held out. "Good to see you." The men shook hands. "How is everything at Clan Firinn?"

"Going smoothly . . . at least until yesterday." Dr. Brùn's forehead furrowed. "A terrible tragedy. Will you be investigating the accident as well?"

"No, just the bodies at Alderman Acres. Another detective and crime-scene team are working here. Which reminds me." He turned, walked to his squad car, pulled out something in a brown paper bag, and brought it to them. "They pulled this from the car. Some personal effects."

"Forgive my rudeness. Ryan." Dr. Brùn turned to the man with a broken arm. "I don't know if you had time yesterday to meet Dr. Dustin Van Seters. We call him Dutch." The men acknowledged each other. Dutch nudged Dr. Brùn and quietly said something. The older man turned and walked over to me. "I don't believe I've had the privilege of meeting you."

"Samantha Williams." My voice came out squeaky. Dr. Brùn, although barely taller than my own five feet six inches, projected power, money, and authority.

"Ah, the artist who saved her students." He gave me an approving nod.

My face grew warm. I was one step away from staring at my shoes and saying, "Ah, shucks, tweren't nothin'."

Dutch nodded at Leroy. "How's it going?"

"Good. Missed seeing you around lately. Drop by sometime for a beer and a can of SpaghettiOs."

"Tempting, Leroy, tempting."

Leroy and Mary introduced themselves, saving me from having to think of something clever to cover my awkwardness. Or from a Sneetch that might slip out.

Mary's phone rang. "Hello? No, if you're looking for Sam, she's right here." She handed me her cell. "Your landlord."

I moved a few steps away from everyone. "Hi—"

"I just got your message. Did you finally break down and buy a cell phone? Never mind. I don't really have time to talk. The insurance adjuster is here. I was ready to shoot you this morning. Now it makes sense in a strange way."

"What are you talking about?"

"Talk about shutting the barn door after the horse has bolted."

"I don't understand."

"I guess whoever took your keys let themselves into your

55

apartment and left all the water running. After they plugged the drains. Part of the ceiling in the apartment below yours collapsed. Water's everywhere, in the hall, running down the stairs. It's a mess."

FIVE

My landlord's statement about the flooding of my apartment left me speechless for a few moments. I finally squeaked out, "What!" I needed to sit. My legs felt like rubber.

Dr. Brùn, Leroy, Mary, and Ryan turned to look at me.

"Anyway, no rush to get your locks changed. Your apartment is off-limits until we can get someone in to see if we have more structural damage. I'll keep this number." He disconnected.

"What is it, Sam?" Mary asked. "You look like you just saw a ghost."

My little studio apartment, carved out of the attic of an older home, wasn't much, but it was my retreat, the place I felt secure and comfortable. Home, car, job, money, identity . . . I felt like I was floating, unanchored, and would soon be lost. My head buzzed and my vision narrowed.

"Miss Williams?" Dr. Brùn was holding my arm.

I gently removed my arm from his grasp. "Sorry. I . . . I'm fine. Just a water issue in my apartment."

"Like a backed-up toilet?" Mary asked.

"More like a personal tsunami." *Now what?* I had no car to drive anywhere yet, no apartment to go to, no way to get money from the bank or a replacement credit card to pay for a hotel. I didn't have any family or close friends. I couldn't touch the money I'd put aside. I reached for the key around my neck, then stopped. *No.* My classes were canceled. I bowed my head and prayed. *Lord, I could use a little help right now.* When I looked up, Dr. Brùn was watching me.

"Ready to get going?" he asked Dutch.

"Are you going over to where the latest body is?" Mary asked Dutch. She didn't seem the least intimidated by anyone.

"Yes." Dutch strolled toward the SUV.

Mary followed him. "Mind if I tag along?"

"I don't mind." Dutch looked over at Dr. Brùn. The older man gave a half shrug. "All right then. Just stay out of the secured scene." Dutch glanced at me. "How about you? I have something I'd like to discuss with you."

Staring at a collection of human bones was hardly my idea of a fun time, rather in the realm of a root canal. On the other hand, not being ready to pitch a tent under an overpass, I had no place else to go. And I was intrigued by what Dutch wanted to say to me. I nodded.

He held the back door open for Mary and me. I reluctantly got in. "Why don't we follow in your car?" I whispered to her.

"This way they're stuck with us," she whispered back. "They can't exactly tell us to go away if something juicy comes up. And we'll probably get a free lunch out of it. I'm starving."

"But—"

The men got into the front seat, started the car, and turned toward the cemetery. As we drove down Main Street, Mary leaned forward. "Dr. Van Seters—"

"Call me Dutch." He turned to look at her.

"Dutch, tell me more about the bodies." Mary took out her leather notepad and pen.

"Miller Construction, Leroy, was in charge of the initial excavation of the new housing development," Dutch said. "When he discovered the first set of bones a week ago, he called the sheriff's department and they, in turn, called the county coroner. Under state law, the accidental discovery of human remains on nontribal or nonfederal lands means that all work needs to cease until certain things are done."

"Like figure out if it was a homicide." Mary looked up from her writing.

"Right. First, determine if this is a forensic case," Dutch said. "The coroner, Rick, is a friend of mine and gave me a call. I met him at the excavation. Unfortunately, the coroner couldn't determine the cause of death, so he called the state forensic anthropologist, who took over the scene. The bones were transported to Seattle for analysis and possible identification. I was asked to go to Seattle and do a facial reconstruction."

"Is that where they put clay on the skull and make a face?" I asked.

"That's one way," Dutch said. "Or you can draw the face once the skull is prepared."

Mary glanced at me. "Good question." Then to Dutch: "Go on. Yesterday they discovered a new set of remains?"

"Correct," Dutch said. "Even though work had stopped, we still had someone patrolling the area. Once again the coroner took control of the scene and the anthropologist was notified. We were on our way to see the coroner yesterday afternoon when the accident occurred."

Mary jotted some things in her notebook. "And you, Dr. Brùn, are here because . . . ?"

"With his broken arm, Dutch needs a driver," Dr. Brùn said. "And I feel somewhat responsible. I'm head of Clan Firinn. I should have mentioned that during introductions. Clan Firinn is building these homes so my staff can live close to work without having to live *at* work. We always need to establish healthy boundaries."

I glanced at Dutch. He was staff and lived at Clan Firinn. Was it possible he had also been a guest at some point?

Mary nodded and wrote on her pad.

"Alderman Acres is a big deal in LaCrosse," Dr. Brùn said. "We plan on having a community center open to the public, and the neighborhood will bring in a boost to the town tax base. Finding the bodies there is . . . distressing."

"Beatrice was fascinated with my studies in forensic anthropology and occasionally volunteered to help," Dutch said. Both men had grown pale.

I wanted to pat Dutch on the arm and murmur comforting words but resisted.

"What were you about to say, Miss Williams?" Dutch asked.

"'Just think lovely, wonderful thoughts and they lift you up in the air.'" I blurted. My face burned. *Idiot.*

Mary's mouth dropped open.

A slow smile spread across Dutch's face. "If you say so."

"Actually . . . Peter Pan said that," I muttered.

"She's speaking in Sneetches," Mary added matter-of-factly. "Probably because we didn't get enough sleep last night."

"What happened last night?" Dr. Brùn asked Mary.

Mary updated him on the break-in while I studiously looked out the window.

We stopped. I'd expected the housing development to look . . . official somehow. Roads established, stakes outlining the new homes, maybe even pipes sticking out of the ground in anticipation of water and sewage. A concrete curb here and there. Instead, a sagging barbed-wire fence enclosed a dirt landscape, a bulldozer, a dusty 1987 red Ford Taurus, a rusty travel trailer, and a white pop-up tent with crime-scene tape fluttering around the outside. Next to the tent was a van with the word *Coroner* written on the side. A small white sign on the road quietly announced "Alderman Acres Coming Soon. A Miller Construction Site" followed by a web-page address and phone number.

A man emerged from the van wearing blue coveralls with *Coroner* stitched on his pocket.

Dutch walked over to greet him. "Hey, Rick. We've got to stop meeting like this."

"You've got to stop digging up bodies," Rick said.

A deputy had been leaning against the pickup. He straightened when we appeared, then sauntered over to the tent.

Leroy had followed us and parked next to the pickup, with the sheriff's SUV next, all in a neat line like a used-car lot.

We walked single file over to the pop-up tent.

I'd never seen a dead body. When I was six, my parents died and there hadn't been a funeral. I'd been shuttled off to live with my aunt on a farm outside of Washtucna, Washington. With no close neighbors and plenty of chores to do, I didn't have time to make friends. By the time I left the farm and moved to Spokane, I'd grown used to my solitary life.

My steps slowed as we approached. I was the last to arrive. The deputy kept us from getting too close to the body, but I could still clearly see everything.

The bones weren't white like the synthetic skeletons I'd seen in science class. These were brown like the surrounding dirt. The jaw wasn't near the rest of the head, and numerous teeth were missing in the skull. No sign of any chiffon on this one.

I expected to find the scene upsetting, perhaps even frightening. Instead, I was fascinated.

A second van arrived. This time a woman stepped out and stretched. "Long drive. Dutch, Rick, good to see you both." She removed a black case from the van and took out a camera. After a few shots of the overall site, she draped the camera around her neck and walked over to the tent, where Dutch introduced us. The woman proved to be the forensic anthropologist, Kay Solem. Dr. Solem smiled her greeting, then placed the case on the ground and pulled on some gloves. She photographed the bones from all angles, then took readings from a small GPS unit. After picking up a small brush, she moved next to the body. She swept away the dirt, looked closely at the skull, then moved down the skeleton to the pelvis. She finally looked up. "Who found the body?"

"I did." Leroy stepped forward.

After returning the brush to the case, she lifted out a field notebook, then looked back at Leroy. "You also found the first set of bones last week, right?"

"Yeah."

"Tell me about finding this body."

"I already told the deputy and the coroner what happened."

"Yes. But now I need you to tell me."

"After we found the last one, as you know, we had to stop work. I sent my crew home. Once we got the all-clear, I was going to use the dozer in this area. So while I was waiting, I walked around and checked things out."

"You stayed here?" Dr. Solem pointed her pen at the camper.

"Yeah."

"What time was this?" Dr. Solem asked.

"It was after lunch. About one fifteen to one thirty. Anyway, I spotted something shiny and walked over and found the apple." He nodded toward a golden apple lying next to the skull.

"You found it here." Dr. Solem pointed.

"Nah. It was over there." He indicated a spot about ten feet away. "I picked it up and started walking back to the camper when I saw them bones. It just chaffed my hide that there were more. I almost picked them up and threw them away."

"Good thing you didn't," Dr. Solem said. "Then what happened?"

"I called the sheriff. He told me to stop moving things and don't let anyone on the site."

Dr. Solem turned to Deputy Adams. "You got here when?"

"Fourteen-twenty hours. They were clearly human remains, so I immediately called Rick at the coroner's office. He got here at fifteen-fifteen hours. I was helping Rick to secure the scene when I got the call about the crash at the school."

The anthropologist picked up the apple, turned it around to examine all sides, then pulled out a plastic evidence bag and placed it inside.

Mary folded her arms across her chest. "How . . . how long do you think this person's been dead?"

Dr. Solem looked like she wasn't going to answer, but apparently changed her mind after looking at Mary's face. "A long time. Possibly years."

Mary closed her eyes.

An uneasy silence followed. I finally pointed to the apple. "What is that?"

"It's heavy, maybe like a brass paperweight," Leroy answered.

"Did they find a paperweight with the last body?" I asked.

"Yes," Leroy said.

"We're still investigating," Dr. Solem said at the same time, then glared at Leroy before placing the evidence in her case.

A shiver went up my spine. I'd seen a paperweight like this before. The memory was fuzzy, like a dream.

Dr. Solem wrote for a few moments before turning to Leroy. "Did you walk over this area before yesterday afternoon?"

"Yeah. I take a walk around the whole site every day. I'm supposed to keep an eye on the place."

She nodded. "Okay. I'll be here for a while documenting the site. Dutch, let me get you that skull so you can get started." The two of them moved over to her van.

"So." Mary moved closer to Leroy. "I have to ask. Were the bones here before yesterday afternoon?"

"Nope."

She looked at me. "This whole story just keeps getting better and better. Someone's plopping dead bodies here. Now I need to figure out why."

Dutch returned with a cardboard box and said to Mary and me, "Ready to leave?"

We nodded.

As we turned toward the line of vehicles, Dutch paused and looked at Rick. "I almost forgot. Why did you call me yesterday?"

Rick shook his head. "I didn't."

Dutch straightened. "What do you mean? You called Clan Firinn, or at least someone in your office did, and spoke with Beatrice. She said you asked us to meet you at the school around four. You said something about these remains. I left you a message on your recorder yesterday."

Rick's brows drew together. "No one from my office called you."

Dutch's face paled. "Are you sure?"

"Positive."

"Then . . . then someone wanted us to be by the school at that time," Dutch said.

Sweat dampened my hands and I wiped them on my slacks. If someone had lured Dutch to the school, had they been waiting with a rifle?

And had they planted the body to lure Beatrice or Dutch into target range?

SIX

Everyone was silent after Dutch's comment, the only sound the soft *whap, whap, whap* of the wings of a low-flying raven. The autumn breeze grew chilly and I pulled my light cardigan closer.

The noise of an approaching vehicle finally seemed to break the moment and everyone spoke at once.

"How can that—"

"What do you—"

"Did someone actually—"

"Please, please," Dr. Solem said. "I need to continue my investigation."

A shiny black SUV passed by on the road, slowing down slightly to rubberneck before resuming speed. Something bothered me about the vehicle, but no one else seemed to be concerned. Maybe I was becoming totally paranoid.

"So once you guys get these bones out of here," Leroy asked Dr. Solem, "I can get back to work?"

"Unfortunately, you're shut down again," Dr. Solem said. "I'll keep you informed of the progress."

Dr. Brùn, Dutch, Leroy, Mary, and I started moving toward the parked vehicles, leaving the coroner, the deputy, and Dr. Solem at the site.

"Ladies." Dr. Brùn stopped and turned to Mary and me. "Looks like we're done here for now. Back to the school for your car, Mary. Sam, where can I drop you?"

Where indeed? My mind blanked. How could I have gotten into a position where I had no place to go and no way to change that? Did Pullman have a homeless shelter where I could camp until I sorted out the various agencies and businesses where I'd placed my trust? I reached for the key around my neck, then shivered and dropped my hand. *I'd rather go to a homeless shelter.* "I, um, need to find a phone . . . my car . . ."

"Sam's in a little bit of a pickle," Mary said.

"I have an idea," Dr. Brùn said. "Until you get the details sorted out on your car and apartment, why not stay at Clan Firinn?"

"But—"

He smiled. "It's on the up-and-up. We have several guest houses on the property where some of the staff and visiting instructors stay."

"Well, I—I'll be fine. I really don't need help."

"Where are you going to go?"

"There's . . . um . . . I can find . . ."

"Highland House is empty now. You can use the phone to help you straighten out your affairs." Dr. Brùn gave Dutch a small nod.

"As I mentioned before, I want to talk to you about a project." Dutch smiled.

"Um . . . I . . . guess so." I glanced at Mary. With her along, I wouldn't be alone. "Do you have room for two? Or should I say two and a half?"

Mary winked at me.

"Mary's looking for her—"

"Researching."

I looked at her out of the corner of my eye. Her lips were pressed into a thin line.

"Researching . . . a . . . a possible book. I really need to stay in this area."

I nodded. "And the place we're staying isn't safe."

"That's right," Mary said. "I'm thinking along the lines of a true crime. Something like *In Cold Blood*. The next Clancy."

"Capote," I muttered.

"Capote."

We're both babbling Sneetches. "True crime is arguably the fastest-growing genre in the twenty-first century." I snapped my mouth shut.

An awkward silence followed before Dr. Brùn spoke. "Well, of course. It's a big place."

"Let's make this more fun," Dutch said. "Leroy, why don't you join us for dinner this evening. I'm sure it will be better than the can of SpaghettiOs you were planning on eating tonight, right?"

Leroy grinned at him, the smile transforming him into a surprisingly handsome man. "I'm all over that like a kid on a cupcake."

"Ryan, Rick, Dr. Solem," Dutch called over to the remaining three. "Dinner tonight at Clan Firinn?"

Both Dr. Solem and Rick shook their heads. "I need to get back to Seattle," Dr. Solem said.

"You betcha," Ryan said.

Dr. Brùn stepped away, made a phone call, then returned and smiled. "All set." He turned and strolled to his SUV.

The rest of us followed. I felt like a crumpled-up newspaper being tossed by the wind, and I hated going to a strange place. I just didn't know how to fix my situation. *Go with the flow for now.* By tomorrow I'd have contacted the bank, found my car, and started looking for a place to stay.

I slid into the front seat at Dr. Brùn's insistence. In short order we returned to the school where Mary had left her car. She got out and turned to me. "Want to ride with me over to Clan Firinn?"

Without thinking, I said, "I'm fine."

Her gaze slid over to Dutch, then back to me. "Suit yourself." She shut the door just a tiny bit too hard.

I thought about jumping out and joining her. She'd been more than kind to me, and I didn't want her to think badly of me. Before I could act, Dr. Brùn had put the SUV into gear and was rolling out of the school lot.

As Anna Sewell wrote in *Black Beauty,* "Do your best wherever it is."

We drove through the undulating Palouse farmlands laid out in bands of alternating beige and pale linen-colored fields, then turned on a narrow gravel road. I'd never driven up this way and probably would have passed right by the turnoff.

We stopped in front of a plain, galvanized livestock gate with a four-strand barbed-wire fence on either side. A cattle guard further discouraged cows from roaming off their graze land. Dr. Brùn put the car into Park, but before he could move I jumped out and swung the gate open. For a place rumored to be both mysterious and extravagant, the entrance suggested neither. It looked like a typical farm entrance. After Mary's Subaru passed through, I closed it and returned to our SUV. The road meandered through plowed fields until it took a sharp right turn and arrived at a second gate, this time wrought iron and cedar with a keypad. The matching fence surrounding the gate blocked the view of the facility, though I could see a high roofline. Dr. Brùn punched in the code and the gate slid open.

Two extremely large, grayish dogs raced up to us.

I shrank back in my seat. They were at least as tall as Great Danes. Muffie could have savaged my ankles, but these two looked like they'd consume me with room for dessert.

"Ah, Caley and Camden." Dr. Brùn kept the window down and petted the two great hounds. "Scottish Deerhounds. Very sweet dogs. Go play now."

The two gray monsters raced off as if in pursuit of an unlucky rabbit. Or person.

The hills of plowed fields formed a drab backdrop to this emerald-green oasis. Ahead of us was a sprawling three-story rough-stone-and-cedar lodge with a massive log entry. A Scottish crest with a lion rampant holding a fleur-de-lis was over the carved doors. Two other homes faced the lodge on either side, forming a large U shape. The landscaping was extensive and meticulously maintained. The gravel road ended at the gate and had been replaced by black pavement that circled the central commons. As we pulled up to the entrance, a middle-aged man emerged. Dr. Brùn parked, stepped out, and opened my door. "Miss Williams, welcome to Clan Firinn."

I carefully checked for the hounds of the Baskervilles. *All clear.* "Thank you."

Mary parked and joined us.

"Scotty, I'd like you to meet Mary and Samantha. Would you show them to Highland House?"

"This way, ladies." He swung his arm toward the house on the right.

Scotty? A rather fitting name for someone working here. All he needed was a kilt.

Highland House had the same crest over the entry with the name beneath. The unlocked front door led past a formal dining room to a well-appointed living room and kitchen dominated by a stone fireplace. "Through that door is two bedrooms." Scotty pointed. "Mary, you can choose whichever one you'd like. The front one has a small study and porch. Off that dining nook is another bedroom. Samantha, I think you'd like that room. There are several more bedrooms on the second floor, which you can reach through there. Dinner is at the lodge at six."

Mary immediately moved toward her designated room. I wandered to the dining nook, where I found the door Scotty had mentioned. The bedroom beyond was lit by recessed lights shining on the beige-and-cream decor. The limestone stone floor had fluffy cream-colored area rugs, and a fire burned in the raised stone fireplace. An office/sitting area was straight ahead with french doors opening onto a patio.

"I could live here!" The words were out of my mouth before I could stop them.

"It is a lovely room." Scotty had followed me in and smiled at my reaction.

To my left was a bathroom almost bigger than my apartment in Pullman. A walk-in closet opened off the bathroom. The closet was full of clothing.

"Oops." I turned to the man. "Looks like someone's taken this room already."

Scotty's jaw tightened slightly. "The room did belong to Beatrice, but her things are gone."

My stomach gave an uneasy lurch. "But she just was killed yesterday. And what do you mean by *gone*?"

"Forgive me, Miss Williams. I didn't mean to offend you. Beatrice had no family and had left instructions should anything happen to her."

The lurch became a blast of acid up my throat. "Happen to her? Why would she think something would happen to her?"

"I don't know. She just mentioned that once. She was a very . . . private person."

"What about these clothes?"

"They're yours to wear."

"Excuse me?"

"Many of our guests arrive here much like you, although for different reasons, with just the clothes on their backs. We're prepared to provide what they need physically until we can work on what they need mentally, emotionally, and spiritually." He turned to leave. "There's a three-ring binder with the Clan Firinn rules. You'll find the kitchen well stocked should you like a snack or a bit of lunch. The dining room at the lodge is at this end of the building. Just follow the signs." He left.

The feeling of being tossed about and rudderless morphed into a new emotion. Gut-clenching fear. What had I gotten myself into? Even though I'd dragged Mary along with me, this complex was remote, gated, and protected by two giant dogs. Everything I knew about Clan Firinn came from vague rumors and the internet article Mary had shown me. And what was with a binder full of rules? I thought I was a guest. I had blissfully jumped into the car of a stranger and allowed him to drive me here. *Dumb, dumb, dumb.*

Returning to the living room, I found Mary's suitcase. When I looked out the window, both her car and the SUV were gone.

"This place is fabulous!" Mary entered. "I don't have a room, I have a suite. Oh, good, they brought my suitcase."

"Your car is missing." I tried to keep my voice steady.

"I'm sure they parked it in a garage or something. I left the keys in it." She headed to the kitchen, where she opened the refrigerator and grabbed a Pepsi. "Want a soda?"

"Is there water?"

She reached in, grabbed a bottle, and handed it to me.

I opened it and took a long drink to moisten my dry mouth. "Did you know there's a binder of rules to follow?"

"Well what do you expect, Sherlock? This is a treatment center for people who have screwed up their lives."

"I didn't think about that. They put me in Beatrice's room and provided me with clothes."

"Awesome about the clothes." She popped open the can. "Well, maybe awesome. Depends on what they gave you. Hopefully not Beatrice's wardrobe."

She didn't seem the least bit concerned about anything except looking for her missing husband. Maybe *I* was overreacting. My trust in people was tenuous at best, and in the last twenty-four hours I'd almost been run over, had the contents of my purse stolen, my car destroyed, my apartment flooded, *and* someone had broken into the house where I was staying. That would be enough to make anyone squirrelly.

Dr. Brùn was being kind and generous in offering me a place to stay. That was all.

I slowly walked back to my room, where I found an old rotary phone. I tried dialing nine to get an outside line, but apparently all calls here went through a switchboard. The operator did connect me, and I was able to talk to my bank and put a stop to anyone writing a check. A few calls located my towed car. A few more calls to the school and my landlord updated them on my new contact number at Clan Firinn. At least someone outside knew where I was.

It was strange how much I'd come to rely on the sameness of my life. My own clothes, favorite books, the view out the window. Morning inspirational, coffee in the blue chipped mug, throw blanket on a chilly morning.

With everything different, new, unpredictable, and strange, I couldn't relax. I had to think about everything. What I said. How

I looked. Did I unconsciously talk to myself? What else did I do without thinking?

My face grew warm.

The wisdom of Sneetches would only go so far. The problem was, the only person I'd trusted in the past few years, Mrs. Gimble, was no longer in my life.

I ended up in the sitting area, which held a beige-and-cream plaid wingback chair, love seat, and matching coffee and end tables. A reclaimed-wood computer desk with an off-white chair faced a large window. I curled up in the wingback chair.

Something softly crackled underneath me. If my hearing wasn't so acute, I wouldn't have heard it.

Standing, I lifted the cushion and peered under. Spotless, like the rest of the room. I felt the cushion, but it seemed to be standard foam. I replaced the cushion and sat down again. The sound repeated itself.

This time I lifted the cushion and found the zipper in the back. Opening it, I found the foam had been split, forming a slot.

My muscles tensed in my stomach. Cautiously I reached in and pulled out three pieces of paper folded to fit a business-size envelope and bearing letters cut out of a newspaper. The first one said, "I know who you are. I'll be in touch soon." The second said, "Place $150,000 in a red case and leave it at the old elevator tomorrow." The third said, "Remember this?" Below the words was a scanned photo of a brass apple paperweight.

SEVEN

I felt chilled staring at the notes, as if someone had opened a door in the middle of winter. Beatrice was being blackmailed and now she was dead. And I was in her room. Had she left some other warning? Was this place—

Someone tapped on my door. Before I could stuff the notes back into the cushion, Mary entered. "What's that?" she pointed at the papers as she approached me.

"Um . . ."

She got close enough to read the top note. "That looks like a cheesy blackmail note. And the apple looks like the one found in the cemetery." She took the notes from me. "Holy moly, this *does* look like blackmail." Her gaze took in the unzipped and upended cushion next to me. "You found these? A little co-incidental, don't you think? Maybe placed so you'd find them?"

Her skepticism somehow reassured me. "No. I don't think even a thorough cleaning would have found them. You needed to actually sit in the chair, and even then you could have missed the slight crackling of paper." I showed her the cut foam.

She sat in the love seat. "Well, well, well. The plot thickens." She spread the three notes out on the coffee table. "Beatrice was being blackmailed and ends up dead. She received a mysterious phone call to meet someone, a call that the coroner said he didn't make. After that she was on her way to see a corpse with a matching apple paperweight."

The hairs on my neck prickled.

"Maybe she failed to leave"—she looked at a note—"the red case at the old elevator. Or someone other than the blackmailer picked it up?"

"Creepy all the way around. But the paperweight . . ." I picked up the note with the picture of the paperweight. The glue holding the scanned photo had been poorly applied, and I could rub off the excess where it had smeared beyond the edges. A sloppy blackmailer. "This paperweight looks a little different." The sense of familiarity returned, stronger this time and accompanied by a hollow feeling. I had seen a paperweight exactly like this before. A long time ago.

"You're the artist." She leaned forward and studied the notes for a moment before looking at me, eyes sparkling. "We can check it out."

I made a face at her. "Old elevator? Where? There are probably hundreds of old buildings with elevators in them in the state."

"Hey, for a hundred and fifty thousand bucks, we can at least investigate. We'll be like Sherlock and Watson."

"More like Nancy Drew without her friends." I zipped up the cushion and sat. I normally would have flatly turned down the whole idea, but that memory kept tickling the back of my mind. Could there be some weird connection between Beatrice, the bodies they'd found outside of town, and me?

The next thought chilled me. If I hadn't acted so quickly, I'd have been just as dead when her Suburban crashed into my classroom.

I couldn't deny that someone had stolen my purse from the school, deliberately broken into the house where I was staying, tried to open the door of my room, and left the empty purse for me to find. Not to mention the water left on in my apartment, making it unlivable. All those actions forced me to take the first offer of a place to stay—Clan Firinn.

I clenched my jaw. At this point, who could I trust? Not anyone at Clan Firinn. An awful lot of open questions floated around this place.

I looked at the woman in front of me. Mary, as far as I knew, had no connection to anyone in the area. She had no motive other than looking for a missing husband. And her advanced pregnancy put her at considerable risk.

"Let me think about it." I replaced the notes. "For now we need to keep this between us. Beatrice hid these notes from folks at Clan Firinn, and she didn't turn them over to the police."

"Agreed. For now. But don't think about it for long. I can't stand ignoring a few crumbs on what could be a lot of money. And speaking of crumbs, I'm starving. Can you rustle us a three-course lunch so we can get started without perishing from hunger?"

I raised my eyebrows.

"I'm eating for two."

"Don't you like to cook?"

"Ha! I'm on a first-name basis with a can opener."

"I see. I'm Chef Bobby Flay while you're more Chef Boyardee."

"Correct. But I'll make you a deal." She grinned at me. "While you're the chief cook and bottle washer, I'll search this room to see if Beatrice left any other clues."

"So you're going to start investigating even if I don't agree?"

"Hey, I said Sherlock and Watson. You're the one that mentioned Nancy Drew. Single detective."

"Have at it, Nancy." I headed to the kitchen. "And help yourself to the clothes in the closet. I understand they're an added bonus for staying here."

Once again Mary had taken possession of the kitchen table with her research, notes, and this time her purse and jacket. I'd bet her apartment in Spokane was equally cluttered. I tidied her things and moved them to a desk in the corner of the room. While I prepared lunch, my mind circled around how familiar the apple paperweight seemed. That *had* to be a coincidence. What could I have in common with Beatrice? I'd never met her or even heard of her. I didn't even know if Beatrice was the shooter's target. Dutch was in the car. What if the point of killing the driver was to send an out-of-control vehicle into the school? Into *my* classroom?

I stopped cooking for a moment. I *did* need to look into the events—if only to protect myself. The only question I had to decide was whether I'd look into it alone or ask Mary for help.

When I returned to call her for lunch, I stopped at the door to my room. The bed was stripped with the sheets and blankets on the floor. A small pile of dresses now covered the mattress. She'd tossed all the cushions from the chairs and sofa, and every drawer stood open. Mary was holding up one outfit and looking in a mirror.

"Did you find something in those outfits?"

"Um, I did find something, but not any clues." She twirled with the red dress she held. "I'm taking you up on your offer. I didn't pack for the Ritz, so can I borrow this? I think if I tied it higher like an empire cut, it's loose enough to fit."

The dress seemed to have a number of openings, side splits, and dips. "I'd never wear something so . . . breezy, so I guess so. Like I said, help yourself to whatever you want to wear."

"Thank you. By the way, the shoes are too big."

I shook my head. "What did you find . . . besides clothes and shoes?"

She dropped the garment on the bed. "A couple of things. Follow me." She walked to the wall opposite the door into the room and pushed. A panel opened into another room. "I wouldn't have found it, but I noticed a seam going up the wall."

We entered an airy, spacious, fully stocked art studio. "Pinch me," I muttered. "I think I'm dreaming."

Mary reached over and gave me a painful tweak.

"Ouch!" I rubbed my arm. "That was a figure of speech, not a request." The room was organized into art-medium areas, with an easel and taboret covered with acrylic paint tubes, a slanted drafting table with a corresponding tray of pencils and charcoal, an oversize metal drafting table, and a craft table. A generous set of flat files held different papers. "I see why Scotty aimed me to this room. This must have been Beatrice's studio. Just one problem."

"You can't live here indefinitely?" Mary was busy opening drawers.

"No. I mean, yes, sort of. I meant that all of her art is gone. I would have loved to see her work."

Mary stopped her snooping. "We shouldn't be surprised. Everything of hers is gone. Almost everything. I have one more thing to show you." At the far end of the room was a set of folding doors. She opened both sides. Inside the tiny space was a small table holding unlit candles, a lighter, a Bible, cushions, and a single chair. "This is totally weird."

"It's a prayer closet. Matthew 6:6. 'But thou, when thou prayest, enter into thy closet, and when thou hast shut thy door, pray to thy Father which is in secret; and thy Father which seeth in secret shall reward thee openly.'"

"So Beatrice was a religious nut." She glanced at me. "No offense."

"None taken." I picked up the Bible, engraved with B. G. in gold on the cover, and closed the doors. "What about—"

"Lunch?"

"Oh. Well, yes, it's ready."

Mary didn't waste time. She shot toward the kitchen. I followed and found her at the stove. "Oh, wow. What kind of soup?"

"Moroccan red-lentil quinoa soup with a honey chicken salad. I hope that's okay."

Mary didn't need to answer. She was already ladling soup

into the two bowls placed next to the stove. I'd set the table with the salads. We both sat. I placed the Bible next to me and said a quick prayer before trying the soup. I had to admit, it was good.

"I think this just replaced my favorite minestrone soup." She took another sip.

"I can make that next time."

We ate in silence for a bit before she leaned back in her chair and looked at me. "Where did you learn to cook like this? Did your mom teach you?"

"No."

I stirred my soup, hoping she'd change the subject.

"So who did?"

I put my spoon down. "My mother died when I was six. Actually, both my parents died in a car accident. I moved in with an aunt on a farm east of here. She was strict but taught me a lot of things."

"Like cooking?"

"Cooking, canning, gardening, sewing. Things you need to do on a working farm."

"So that's how you became so—" She hesitated.

"I'm sure you were about to say *capable*."

"Um . . . yeah." She ducked her head and whispered, "Boring."

"Did you want to borrow that dress?"

"Capable. I meant capable. But remember you had to bribe me to say it."

I was no longer hungry and stood to clean my plates. Mary must have gotten the hint. She brought her dishes over, then brought out her laptop and placed it on the table. After a moment she said, "The internet seems to be off." She pulled out her cell. "Yup. Cell service as well."

"Try calling the lodge."

"Didn't you hear me? Cell service is down."

I pointed a soapy finger at the desk. "Phone."

She stood, moved to the phone, and made the call. "Yes. I'm calling because I can't find the internet—" She listened a moment. "What do you mean there's no cell service or internet?" She slammed down the receiver and slumped at the kitchen table. "I'm ruined."

I figured this wasn't a good time to say anything. While I continued to wash dishes, I again pictured the paperweight on the blackmail note. I'd seen it—or one exactly like it—before I'd been sent to my aunt's farm. Somehow, someway, I was connected to Beatrice, but to look into it would require going back to my childhood. To step through a door I'd firmly closed. To cross a threshold where there was no turning back. I touched the key around my neck. "Mary, I . . . um . . . okay, on looking into Beatrice's blackmail notes—"

"What blackmail notes?" Dutch was standing at the entrance to the dining nook.

I mentally groaned. I wasn't cut out for this cloak-and-dagger stuff. Dutch would probably run straight to Dr. Brùn.

"We found some blackmail notes that Beatrice hid." Mary straightened.

"Where are the notes?" Dutch asked.

Mary pointed.

Dutch stalked across the dining area to my room, pausing at the door when he spotted Mary's search efforts.

"Coffee table," Mary said.

He crossed the room. Mary and I followed, stopping at the door. He picked them up and read them. "We need to take these to Dr. Brùn."

I knew it. "No!" My mouth and brain finally kicked into gear.

"Why?" he asked me.

"Beatrice could have given them to Dr. Brùn." I folded my arms. "Instead she chose to hide them. Maybe Dr. Brùn's involved. Maybe *he* sent them. Who knows? Beatrice is dead, shot, and it's looking less and less like it was an accident."

"Then we should turn these over to the police," Dutch said.

I sat on the love seat. "Yeeessss . . ."

"Do I hear a 'but' in that answer?" Dutch sat next to me.

I became hyperaware of his nearness, smelled his aftershave, felt the warmth radiating from his body. My mind went blank. I jumped to my feet and began pacing.

Mary grabbed my arm. "No wonder you're so skinny. You're a bundle of nervous energy. Now spill it. What's going on in that brain of yours?"

I was loath to share the vague memory of the paperweight until I had a chance to look into it myself. I'd just decided Mary might be an asset in helping me investigate. Now Dutch was getting involved. And Dutch worked for Dr. Brùn.

On the other hand, it wasn't really up to me. Dutch didn't need my permission to go to Dr. Brùn. There was only one way to handle this. *I'll have to lay out my ideas without revealing any personal connection.*

"Okay. Mary, before you manage to let the cat farther out of the bag, and you, Dutch, talk to your boss, we should probably at least do a little research." *If for no other reason than to make sure someone didn't try to kill me with that runaway car.*

EIGHT

Over the next half-hour, Dutch tried to place the newly discovered blackmail notes into what he already knew about Dr. Brùn, Beatrice, and Clan Firinn. He would have completely dismissed Sam's suggestion that Dr. Brùn was in any way involved in anything as sinister and evil—except for one nagging thought. Why didn't Beatrice show the notes to Dr. Brùn?

He couldn't, in his wildest dreams, imagine anything nefarious. He owed his life to this program. Yet . . .

After Sam explained their discoveries and thoughts, he saw the opening he was looking for. "I'm glad you brought that up, Sam. I'll be needing help working on the case, and I'd like you to be the one to help me."

"I don't see how."

"Dr. Solem has asked me to do a facial reconstruction, and I'm hoping you could do the art. We'd pay you, of course."

Sam slowly sank into the nearest chair. "I don't even know

what facial reconstruction is. Don't they use DNA for identification anymore?"

"They do, but DNA is a comparison between a known and an unknown—and it's our best way to confirm an ID. But we have to know where to start."

"What about the various DNA databases where people are researching their ancestors?" Sam asked.

"Public genealogy databases can only be used where participants opt-in for law-enforcement matches," Dutch said. "Facial reconstruction is a way to create an image to see if we can get a lead on a possible identification. Otherwise, we're looking at weeks, if not months, waiting for DNA results."

"That's fascinating." Mary's eyes sparkled. "This gets more interesting every minute. Can I watch?"

"Of course. How about it, Sam? Will you help me?"

"What do I have to do?"

Dutch held back his grin. "Can you draw a face?"

"Yes."

"Then we're in business. Are you ready to start?"

"I guess."

"Good. I'll give you a ring on the phone when I'm ready for you." Strolling back to his lab, he tried not to think about the blackmail notes or what they could mean. He had to concentrate on the bones Kay had left from the first body. He took the box containing the skull to his lab. Inside were the preliminary report and photographs. There were pathetically few bones—most of the vertebrae, pelvis, a femur, cranium, and mandible. The mix made him wonder if the choice of bones was deliberate to aid in identification. The pelvis would give them the sex of the body, the femur would give height, and the cranium and mandible would give ancestry, possible age range, and facial approximation.

Dr. Solem wrote that the remains were a Caucasian female approximately five feet six inches tall. The remaining teeth had no fillings or other dental work, which might have made identification easier. The femur showed signs of rounding from arthritis, and a microscopic exam of the bones for the size and number of osteons narrowed the age to between fifty-five and sixty-five.

She'd further noted there was no sign of an autopsy and no bone evidence to reveal cause of death. The body had been dead for at least twenty years.

On the bottom of her report she'd written, *These bones were placed in this location from another site, not accidentally dug up, and left where they'd be quickly discovered.*

She'd begun the process to extract DNA from aggregates of bone crystals. DNA would be definitive, but this was a cold case and wouldn't be prioritized. Results could take weeks.

As he picked up the phone to call Sam, he glanced out the window. A number of the guests were strolling around the grounds, sitting in lawn chairs, or talking in small groups. Classes were over for the day and everyone was relaxing before dinner.

Mary stood in front of a newly arrived guest, animatedly speaking. The pale man had crossed his arms and was trying to back away.

Dutch leaped to his feet. "No, no, no, no!" He raced outside.

Both the man and Mary saw him coming. While Mary's

attention was focused on Dutch, the man took the opportunity to race away.

One of the counselors had also seen the exchange and was running toward them. When he spotted Dutch, he gave a thumb's up and changed direction, now charging after the guest.

"Mary," Dutch called. "Can I help you? Do you need something?"

Mary shook her head. "I was just asking if he knew someone or . . . had seen someone here . . . um . . ."

He reached her side. "Mary, you can't be talking to our guests."

"Why not? I'm a guest too."

"You're different. They have to be protected until they've gone through the program and can return to society as a whole, functioning person."

"It was just a simple question."

Dutch ran his hand through his hair. The Clan Firinn program was intensive, comprehensive, and far more than he could explain quickly enough to quench her interest. What he needed was a distraction. "Could you get Sam for me? I was just about to start the reconstruction on the skull. You said you wanted to watch."

"Sure."

"My lab is over there." He pointed. "Turn left inside the door."

Mary turned and walked toward Highland House. Dutch watched long enough to be sure she wasn't going to talk to someone else. After she disappeared inside, he ran back to his lab and dialed Dr. Brùn. Whatever was going on with those blackmail notes, he'd have to concentrate on the immediate problem.

"Yes, Dutch?"

Dutch shook his head. Dr. Brùn was his mentor, friend, and rudder. He *couldn't* be involved with Beatrice's situation. "We may have a problem. Mary has taken an interest in talking with our guests."

"I see. Were you able to tell her how fragile our people are during recovery?"

"I'm not sure she's listening."

Dr. Brùn was silent for a moment. "Of course, the easy answer would be to simply ask her to leave."

"We could." Dutch said slowly. "But that might make her wonder if we have something to hide. And Sam seems to want her here."

"True."

"Didn't they say Mary is writing a book? What if . . ." Dutch tapped a pencil on his desk. "What if we kept Mary's focus on research for her book? Kept her off the grounds as much as possible?"

"That's good. How would we do this?"

"I'm not sure yet. I'll look for opportunities."

"I like that," Dr. Brùn said. "But we need to make sure that Sam is safe."

Dutch was silent for a moment, digesting what Dr. Brùn just said. "Agreed. The purse theft, break-in, apartment flood— they're all very personal and directed actions."

"My thoughts exactly. Where is everybody now?"

"Mary is supposed to bring Sam to my lab to help me with the reconstruction. I can keep both women busy while we work out the next step."

"Good." Dutch could almost hear Dr. Brùn's mind ticking. "We'll talk later."

Dutch disconnected. *Now all I have to do is keep Sam safe and Mary busy.* Not to mention figure out Beatrice's blackmail notes, possible murder, and why someone was leaving dead bodies at Alderman Acres.

NINE

After Dutch and Mary left my bedroom, I looked at the black-mail notes. Probably the best hiding place for them, at least until I worked out what to do about them, was where I'd found them. I picked up the cushion and placed the papers back inside.

I'd started cleaning the cyclone aftermath that Mary had left in my bedroom when she popped her head into the doorway. "Dutch wants you to join him in the lab." She wiggled her brows at me.

I turned away for a moment and finished tucking in a sheet while my cheeks burned. I didn't like her implying he wanted me there for anything more than to do a job. "Okay. Do you know where to go?"

"Follow me." With Mary in the lead, we trouped outside, across the lawn, and around the rear side of the lodge to a set of stairs leading down. The door opened to a hallway. On the left was an oak door with a small brass sign saying Dustin Van Seters, PhD. We entered Dutch's lab.

High windows around two sides provided plenty of natural

light. Built-in cabinets, a stainless-steel sink, and a variety of instruments, including microscopes, filled the remaining space. A glassed-in display showcased a collection of antique medical instruments—glass syringes, vintage magnifying glass, stethoscope, scissors, pillboxes, and barbaric-looking surgical tools. The center of the room had two tables, one of which was covered with white paper. Several skulls lay on the table.

I moved closer. Some of the skulls were intact; many were in pieces. Once again I found myself riveted by the scene. "Are we working on one of these?"

"No. Over here." He reached into a box and placed a skull on the empty table. "Ready?"

"Yes."

"You'll find exam gloves over on the shelf." He pointed. "You'll also find some clay, cotton balls, and white glue. Although I have a computer program that can do facial reconstruction, I prefer the hands-on method."

While I retrieved the items, Mary found a rolling office chair, pulled it over to the table, and sat.

"We normally would insert and glue any teeth that have been found separate from the skull," Dutch said. "The holes in the maxilla and mandible indicate teeth were present peri- or postmortem. The rounded part shows where teeth have been missing for some time. There are enough teeth to align the jaw, but we'll use the clay to give some structure. We'll be gluing the mandible to the maxilla and closing the jaw."

I picked up the skull. It looked small and not quite real. Except for the teeth. They were worn and somewhat yellowed.

"We can't just glue bone on bone, because skulls have connecting tissue." Dutch pointed to a small depression in the maxilla. "You'll need to glue a small piece of cotton there in the mandibular fossa, then glue the mandible to it."

I followed his directions as he pointed out each step. He then handed me a clipboard and form for measurements. Using a digital caliper ruler, I measured and recorded in millimeters the nasal aperture, nasal spine, gum line, and other parts of the skull. I used the clay to fill in missing teeth, and a wedge of clay extending from the nasal spine to represent the tip of the nose. Two small pieces of tape marked where the outside of the nostrils would be.

While I was doing all that, Dutch handed Mary a chart, marking pen, craft knife, small miter box, box of strip erasers, and metric ruler. "You are going to cut the tissue-depth markers."

"What's that?" she asked.

"Precisely cut lengths of eraser that will be glued at specific locations on the skull to represent the thickness of the muscles, tissue, and skin." He poked his cheek. "This area, for example, is quite thick, but here"—he touched the corner of his eye socket—"Has very little between bone and flesh."

After I finished measuring, Dutch brought me a heavy-duty tripod with a strange-looking bolt attached at the top. "The toggle bolt will go through the foramen magnum, that hole in the occipital bone. Between the toggle bolt, which will flair open inside the skull, and the large washer on the outside held up by a hex nut, the skull will be anchored in place so we can apply the tissue depth markers and photograph it."

"That is so cool!" Mary took out her phone to photograph the work.

"Sorry, Mary, no photographs. This is an active case."

Mary reluctantly put her cell in her pocket.

Dutch brought me a diagram of a skull showing where the cut tissue-depth markers were to be glued, then pointed to the locations to be sure I understood.

I didn't notice the passage of time before I stepped away from the completed reconstruction. "This. Is. Amazing. Whoever thought of putting a face back on the bones like this?"

"His."

I glanced at Dutch. "His what?"

Dutch smiled. "Wilhelm His, a German anatomist, in 1895. He reconstructed the face of Johann Sebastian Bach. Many decades passed before the concept was used for forensic cases."

I'd always avoided anything related to death or dying, but this was different. I could use my artistic talents to help others. A door opened up to new possibilities. "What does it take to be a forensic artist?"

"You already have the artistic ability." Dutch stood and moved to the counter, where he picked up a camera. "So it would be a matter of picking up some specialty classes. When we finish, I'll look up some training for you." He handed me the camera. "Place this on the smaller tripod over there."

Once done, he arranged the skull and the tripod. "Okay, the skull is in the Frankfort horizontal position." He snapped a number of digitals. "You'll be drawing a face over the skull, basically connecting the dots of tissue depth markers. I can put this onto a digital tablet or print it out for pencil sketching."

"Let me guess," Mary said. "Pencil. Right?"

I nodded. She was right. I was boring. And predictable.

Dutch printed out the digital images and handed them to me. "Beatrice has a light table and drawing supplies in her studio. Once you've finished this, just bring it over and we'll run it through some facial-recognition software."

"Wait a minute." Mary stood. "Isn't facial-recognition software only available to law enforcement?"

Dutch moved to the door of his lab and opened it. "Let's just say I have some connections."

"I think I'll just wander around the grounds while Sam is drawing—"

"Ah . . . Mary . . . why don't you stay and help me?"

"Well . . ." She unconsciously fluffed her hair. "If you insist."

Poor Mike. The words came unbidden to my mind. Maybe his not returning to her wasn't about foul play. Not that it was any of my business.

After checking for dogs, I scurried between the lodge and house. Clan Firinn was remarkably quiet. I had no idea of how many residents and staff worked here. The uneasy tickle between my shoulder blades returned and remained until I'd firmly shut the door to Highland House.

As Dutch mentioned, I quickly found the lightbox in the art room. The tray on the drafting table held an assortment of pencils, erasers, and blending tools. After taping down the photo of the skull and placing drawing paper over the top, I began the drawing.

"I knew I'd find you here." Mary held a glass of grape juice. She noted my gaze and lofted the goblet. "As the saying goes, it's not good to keep things bottled up. I'm counting the minutes until I can drink the fermented cousin."

"Even if you could, I thought this place was a dry community."

"I could always come prepared for drought. Actually, I licked so many envelopes shut I deserve a reward." She walked over and looked at my drawing. "That's amazing!"

"Thanks. I'm almost done." I lifted out some white lines to give the image a salt-and-pepper hairstyle. "I'm just guessing on hair."

"Good guess. It looks realistic. I wish I had a pinch of artistic talent."

"Drawing is a learnable skill. Otherwise I'd be out of a job." I picked up the drawing and tucked it into a small portfolio I'd found. "Come to think of it, I *am* out of a job."

"Maybe they'll hire you to work here."

I paused, then shook my head. "Step into the shoes of a woman who was being blackmailed, then murdered? I don't think so."

"When you say it like that . . ."

I started moving toward the door. "What did you and Dutch work on after I left?" I tried to sound casual.

She wrinkled up her nose. "Unbelievably boring. He had me remove the tissue-depth markers and clean the skull, then box everything up."

"Oh." I tried not to grin.

"It gets better. He asked me if I wanted to see their 'library.'" She made quotes in the air. "I said sure. We walked across the hall and looked in. Guess what they had?"

"Um, books?"

"Books. Magazines. An antique card file. A microfiche machine. I got excited when I saw a computer, but it's not connected to the internet."

"Positively medieval."

She narrowed her eyes at me, then sniffed. "Why do I bother telling you these shocking revelations? You probably love that kind of thing." She waved at the sketch. "Do you want me to take the drawing over to Dutch?"

In a pig's eye. "That's very sweet of you to offer, Mary. I need to stretch my legs a bit, so I can walk it over."

"I'll go with you."

Of course you will. I tried to shove down the thoughts that kept flashing into my head. I wasn't jealous. I wasn't. She was a married person. And pregnant. And searching for her possibly dead husband. And my motto was to steer clear of men.

Dutch was bent over his desk writing when we entered his lab. He looked up. "Almost perfect timing. Dr. Solem picked up the skull, but I can send your drawing over. I can't wait to see your work."

Warmth shot up my neck. I bent over the now-cleared table and pulled out the drawing.

Dutch took it but didn't speak for several moments.

The warmth became a burn that shot up my cheeks. *He hates it.* I turned to leave.

"This is great. Perfect. Better even than Beatrice's work, though I shouldn't speak ill of the dead. Let's see if we can get a hit." He stood and moved to a counter holding a computer and scanner. After placing the drawing on the scanner, he typed in a few commands, then pushed Enter. "The program will take a bit." He glanced at a wall clock. "Why don't both of you get freshened up for dinner. Hopefully, we'll have some results by then."

I looked down at my clothes. "Define *freshen up*. What's the dress code around here?"

Dutch smiled. "We encourage our guests to change into business casual–type clothes. We want them to see mealtime as a chance to get connected, participate in interesting conversation, and enjoy excellent food. Some of them haven't engaged with anything outside of a bottle of liquor, a hypodermic needle, or a destructive relationship in years."

"How do you know someone is cured?" Mary asked.

"We don't really say someone is cured, because trauma or stress can reoccur. We teach our guests to develop coping strategies. When we feel the individual is close to a return to society, their counselor gives them three stones and a Bible verse. They're not told what to do with any of it."

"Let me guess," I said. "They're to use the Bible verse as a beacon to move ahead, and get rid of the stones as they overcome the burdens they represent."

"Very good guess." He opened the door for us.

I kept my head down and clamped my mouth shut to keep the Sneetches at bay. *If Dutch were both a guest and on staff, did he still carry any of his pebbles?*

The sun was low in the sky and the temperature had dropped as we returned to Highland House. The tang of dried grass and plowed earth perfumed the air. "I'm going to wear that dress I borrowed," Mary said. "But I'm going to need to borrow a shawl too."

"Help yourself. Like I said, they're not my clothes." Back at the closet I found a self-belted, floral dress and matching tan pumps. An oatmeal-colored wrap, which I found on a shelf, would keep the cool evening at bay. I joined a splashy-attired Mary in the living room.

"Holy moly," she said when she saw me.

"What? This looks bad? I can change."

Instead of answering, she pulled out the label at the collar of the dress, then ran her hands over the wrap. "That's an Oscar de la Renta dress, what looks like Roger Vivier pumps, and a Sofia Cashmere baby alpaca cape."

"The only part I understood was baby alpaca cape."

"You're wearing about four thousand dollars' worth of clothes."

My hands became cold and I gaped at her. "You're kidding. I can't wear these—"

"Too late." She grabbed my arm and yanked me out the door. "You don't have time to change before dinner."

"But what if I get spaghetti sauce or dribble cottage cheese—"

"Ha!" She raced across the lawn toward the lodge, moving lightly for one so pregnant. "People rich enough to provide designer clothes to houseguests don't serve spaghetti or cottage cheese to their dinner guests. They fix . . . um . . ."

"Coq au vin and Gâteau St. Honoré?"

"What you just said." We'd reached the back of the lodge. Stairs led down to Dutch's lab, while the ground-level door led to a foyer.

Scotty stood by an open door. "Ah, ladies, right this way."

As we followed him, I asked, "What do you do here, Scotty?"

He paused. "My actual title is head of security. What I do is anything that needs to be done." He ushered us to a small dining room with an oval table in the center covered with a white linen tablecloth, crystal, and what looked like Spode fine china. I couldn't think of any way to casually look on the back of a plate for the manufacturer's stamp. I had a hunch that women wearing four-thousand-dollar outfits probably didn't look for stamps.

Deputy Ryan Adams and Leroy Miller, both now dressed in slacks and sports jackets, were talking to Dr. Brùn. They stopped and turned toward us as we entered.

"Samantha, Mary, you both look lovely." Dr. Brùn looked even more distinguished in a dark navy pinstriped suit and shirt so white it gleamed. He smoothly pulled out a chair. "Samantha, why don't you sit here? Mary." He waved his hand and Deputy Adams did the same with another chair. "Please sit there." We were on opposite ends of the table.

I felt like Alice falling down the rabbit hole, transported to a surreal situation. Just yesterday I was homeless, jobless, and without identification. Now I was dressed in the most expensive outfit I'd ever worn, sitting at an elegant dinner table, and staying in an exquisitely appointed bedroom. *Just keep in mind that exquisitely appointed bedroom belonged to a woman who was blackmailed and probably murdered.*

Dutch entered and sat across from me. He'd changed into a tweed jacket and open-collared checked shirt. I caught a whiff of spicy aftershave.

I didn't know where to look and not stare at Dutch. My hands suddenly felt like they'd grown into baseball mitts, capable of knocking over the crystal water goblet. There seemed to be an inordinate number of forks and spoons. And what if they served radishes? They always made me burp.

Scotty entered, breaking up my frantic thoughts. "Miss Samantha, what would you like to drink?"

"Wa . . . water."

"And you, Miss Mary?"

"I'm heartily tired of grape juice. What I'd really like—" She glanced at me.

"Soft drinks, iced tea, water?" Scotty didn't smile.

"Pepsi."

Leroy opted for Mountain Dew, which set my teeth itching thinking about the sugar. The rest had water. Scotty returned shortly with the drinks and a soup tureen on a tray. After serving the drinks, he placed the tureen on a sideboard, then stood next to it, head bowed. The scent of male aftershave was replaced by the odor of coconut and curry.

Dr. Brùn bowed his head and we all followed suit. After a short prayer, he looked up and signaled Scotty to begin serving.

I copied Dr. Brùn's selection of cutlery. I was pretty sure I knew how to use most of the flatware, but when you lived alone, a single spoon or fork would usually suffice.

"I got a hit on the facial reconstruction," Dutch said quietly.

All eyes pivoted to him.

"Of course"—Dutch removed the silver ring from his napkin and placed the cloth in his lap—"reconstruction isn't an absolute and we'll need additional confirmation, but at least we have a valid direction to look."

"Don't keep us in suspense," Mary breathed. "Who was it?"

"If what I think is true, her name was Edwinna Zaring West, born in 1940 in Othello. She passed away in 1987."

Someone gasped.

"Murdered?" Mary asked.

"No proof of foul play." Dutch said. "But this is where the whole thing gets even more interesting."

I smoothed my napkin. "More interesting than her bones ending up in a construction site over twenty-five years later?"

"Indeed." Dutch tasted his soup, then added salt. "She died and was buried in Suttonville. A small town south of here."

I frowned at him, then glanced at Dr. Brùn. The man was staring at Dutch, the spoon in his hand motionless halfway to his mouth.

Ryan shifted in his seat, then cleared his throat. "That's a name I haven't heard in a long time." His face was pale.

"What's so special about Suttonville?" I asked.

Ryan leaned forward. "It was pretty much a ghost town, but in 1987, Suttonville's water supply became contaminated. Poisoned. The remaining population, all twenty-eight souls, died."

TEN

Everyone spoke at once.

"Died? But how—"

"I've never heard—"

"Are you sure—"

"Why would—"

Dutch held up his hand. "Easy, easy. One at a time."

"How can you be sure it's Edwinna?" Mary asked. "DNA?"

"There's an easier way of checking, and much faster." Dutch caught Dr. Brùn's attention. The older man gave a slight nod. "It's Dr. Solem's case and I'll call her first, but we can just drive over to the Suttonville cemetery and see if Edwinna's grave was disturbed."

"What about that apple paperweight found with the body?" Leroy asked.

"I don't know. Let's keep an eye open for any possible explanation," Dutch said.

"Sounds reasonable," Ryan said. "If her grave was disturbed as a prank, someone is in for a shock. It's a Class C felony to desecrate a corpse. Up to five years in jail and/or a fine of up to ten thousand dollars."

"Do *you* think this was a prank?" I asked.

Ryan shrugged. "I have no idea what the motivation was, but I can drive over to Suttonville tomorrow and take a look at the cemetery."

"This whole thing just gets more interesting every minute." Mary looked at Ryan. "Can I go with you? Pretty please?"

"Well—" Ryan glanced at Dr. Brùn. "I can pick up a waiver for a ride-along, I guess."

"Excellent," Dr. Brùn smiled. "You can stay here, Samantha, and—"

"Actually, I'd like to go along," Sam said.

"Oh." Dr. Brùn glanced at Dutch again.

"Well, then, since it sounds like an outing," Dutch said, "I'll go also. If I can convince Leroy to drive, you won't even need a ride-along waiver, Ryan."

"If Suttonville is a ghost town," Sam said, "will we be able to go into it?"

"Yes," Ryan said. "We'll just be visiting the cemetery."

Dutch relaxed. This little jaunt would keep Mary away from the guests, and Sam would be safe with three men to protect her. He also wanted to get some distance from Clan Firinn. He wanted to think about the implications of Dr. Brùn's possible involvement in the recent events. Or did he? Clan Firinn was

Dutch's world, his life, his security, the only thing that had kept him sane over the past few years.

Did he really *want* to know the truth, no matter how devastating that truth could be?

———

I needed to find out more about Beatrice but wasn't sure how to start without internet access. When the conversation turned to books, I saw my chance. "Tomorrow when we drive to Suttonville, do you think we can stop by a library somewhere?"

"We have a library here," Dr. Brùn said.

"I was thinking along the lines of one with internet. I need to do some research."

Ryan furrowed his brows. "We'll be somewhat close to Pasco."

"Thank you." I looked around the table. "I hope you don't mind. I won't take long."

"If you just need to look something up on the internet," Mary said, "once we get into range you could use my cell phone."

I really didn't want anyone to know what I wanted to look up. "Thank you, Mary. I . . . um . . . was thinking about local history and . . ." I clamped my jaw shut in case a Sneetch was lurking, waiting to jump out.

She shrugged. "Just let me know."

Dr. Brùn stared at me for a moment. If he asked me what I was researching, I'd probably start babbling. Making up lies on the spot was a skill I hadn't mastered. Before we could head down that slippery slope, I turned to Mary. "You said you're a copywriter. Tell me about that."

"Not much to tell." She took a sip of water. "I grew up in Spokane. I needed a job and sort of fell into copywriting."

"Is that what led you to think about writing a book?" Dutch asked.

"Yes. The book." Mary didn't look at me. "I'm tracking unidentified bodies looking for a possible . . . um serial killer in the area."

"Robert Lee Yates operated out of Spokane and killed at least thirteen people before he was caught," I said. *Amazing how a simple lie gets so complicated so fast.*

"Right," Mary said.

"Family?" Dr. Brùn asked.

"I'm married. Mike is a long-haul truck driver."

"I bet you're both looking forward to the happy event," Dr. Brùn said. "Do you have extended family in the area to help you?"

"Mother died when I was born. Father raised me until he offed himself with drugs and booze."

"I'm sorry about that," Dr. Brùn said quietly. "What did your father do before he died?"

"He was in the military, air force. But all he ever flew were drones to monitor the Fairchild Base perimeter. Passed over for promotion, probably because of the booze. He died a bitter, angry man." She reached for her glass of water and took a gulp. "Like I said, not much to tell."

My heart went out to her. That certainly explained her at-times sharp edges. I'd at least had loving parents for the first few years of my life. "Mary, I—"

"Let's talk about something else." A vein throbbed in her neck and her gaze went around the table before sharpening on Dutch. "How about you? What do you do for excitement around here?"

Before Dutch could answer, the door opened and Scotty appeared pushing a cart with covered plates. By the time he cleared the soup dishes and served the main course, Dr. Brùn had changed the subject. To my relief, the rest of the meal passed quietly.

After dinner, Ryan arranged to arrive at ten to drive to Suttonville.

Dutch offered to walk Mary and me to Highland House. Both of us took him up on the offer. Before exiting I stopped at the door to be sure the dogs were gone. They were.

We each took a proffered arm, and I tucked my hand under his sling. The fabric of his jacket was nubby and he radiated warmth. The night was clear and cold, with a million stars spread across the indigo sky. Back in my small apartment in Pullman, I would sit on my minuscule porch and enjoy an evening like this.

Once at the house, Mary headed for the kitchen, grabbed something from the refrigerator, then headed for her room.

Dutch and I were alone. I didn't quite know how to start a conversation. How did I manage to get so awkward around people, around men? I finally blurted, "Could you tell me—"

"Are you worried—" he said at the same time.

"You first," he said.

I waved toward the living room. "Please have a seat. I'd like to ask you about Beatrice." I took a chair, not wanting to end up on the sofa with him. I needed to stay focused. "How well did you know her?"

He sat. "I worked with her on forensic cases over the past few years. She had a drafting background and we both lived here at Clan Firinn, but we didn't socialize much. She seemed to be quite close to Dr. Brùn, which isn't surprising. They were about the same age."

"If she was so close to Dr. Brùn, it seems strange that she didn't show him the blackmail notes."

He leaned forward. "That same thought stuck me. Not to mention that she'd be the last person in the world I'd expect to be blackmailed. She seemed to be deeply religious—"

I jumped up. "That reminds me." Beatrice's Bible still lay on the table where I'd left it. I picked it up, brought it into the living room, and handed it to Dutch. "I didn't know if you were aware she had a prayer closet. I found her Bible in it."

He took it. "She bookmarked something." After opening it, he read, "'For my iniquities have gone over my head; Like a heavy burden they are too heavy for me.' Psalm 38, verse 4. She underlined it."

I cleared my throat. "Sounds like Beatrice *did* have something to hide."

"Is that why you wanted to stop at a library tomorrow?"

"One of the reasons. I don't suppose you heard if they found any indication of who made that phone call pretending to be the coroner?"

He shook his head. "Just a feeling that whoever did call was probably the same person who shot her."

I looked out the large window in front of me. The lights at the lodge were all on, as was the porch light here at Highland House, but the trees cast inky shadows. "Those two dogs?"

"Caley and Camden?"

"Are they good watchdogs?"

Dutch followed my gaze out the window. "They are, but this time of night they're not running loose. Don't worry about it, Sam. You're safe here."

I hope so. I wanted to ask him if he had any idea who might have taken and returned my purse, then filled my apartment with water. But if the purpose of all that was to force me to stay here, he could be in on it up to his eye teeth. "Well," I stood, "tomorrow will be a busy day."

Dutch slowly stood. "Sam . . . I . . . I guess I'll see you in the morning."

After escorting him to the door, I leaned against it. *What was Dutch about to say?*

———

The next morning, Dutch met Dr. Brùn for breakfast. He and Scotty were deep in conversation when Dutch entered.

". . . so let me know about his progress," Dr. Brùn said. "Was there anything else?"

"No, my friend, but you'll let me know if *you* need anything." Scotty stood, patted Dr. Brùn on the arm, nodded at Dutch, and left.

"What do you think Sam wants to look up at the library today?" Dr. Brùn carefully spread preserves on his toast.

Dutch picked up his coffee and took a sip. *I might as well be honest.* "She has a lot of unanswered questions about why someone would play games with her purse and apartment. She's without work, a place to stay, a car . . . technically her life is on hold. Maybe she's trying to find an underlying reason."

"Mmmm." Dr. Brùn finished spreading the preserves, then took a bite of the toast.

"I'm rather wondering the same thing. Is what happened to Beatrice at all connected to Sam?" Dutch waited.

Dr. Brùn finished chewing his toast before answering. "Are you asking me if I can guess?"

"You knew Beatrice for a long time."

"Indeed." Dr. Brùn took another bite.

Dutch toyed with the eggs on his plate.

Dr. Brùn sighed. "Dutch, you know we never discuss why someone is here. They've destroyed their life, career, and often those around them, as you well know. Beatrice is gone now, God rest her soul, so it's not going to harm her personally to share a little background, but please be discreet." He waited for Dutch to answer.

"Of course."

"Beatrice was the reason I started Clan Firinn."

"Oh." The sound was more of a gust of exhaled air. He blinked at Dr. Brùn, then gulped his coffee.

"I knew her . . . before. I knew certain events that were out of her control sent her into a tailspin. I thought I could help her. And I did. That's what gave me the idea to create this place." His gaze drifted to the window, then back to Dutch. "There were dozens more out there that needed this kind of help. When she conquered her demons, she worked with me to help others. She even started a well-funded educational foundation."

"Were the two of you . . ." Dutch didn't quite know how to ask.

"Were we involved? No." Dr. Brùn reached for another slice of toast, picked it up, then replaced it. "I decided early on to devote my life to Clan Firinn. This"—he waved his hand around him—"became my family."

"These 'events.'" Dutch made quotation marks in the air. "Could they have created any enemies, someone who might wish to harm her?"

Dr. Brùn carefully wiped his hands on his napkin, then placed it on the table. "What happened was a long time ago. If there were any . . . well." He stood. "I don't even want to imagine holding on to something so long and hard that it's festered into . . ." He started walking from the room. "God help us all," he muttered.

ELEVEN

After Dutch left, I'd been unable to rest until the room was back in order. I did my exploration of the area in the process. Nothing new showed up. I didn't think I'd sleep, but lack of sleep from the night before caught up with me.

The next morning, I slipped out of bed, dressed in jeans and a sweater, then drifted to the kitchen where I found Mary had started the coffee maker. She'd been cleaning her pistol. Newspapers covered the counter. A box of bullets, a gun-cleaning kit, and the revolver were where she'd left them. Used cleaning patches and a slightly oily silicone gun cloth showed she'd finished. The room smelled of solvent and oil.

I strolled toward her bedroom to ask her to move her things so I could set the table for breakfast. As I grew closer, I could hear her speaking on the phone.

"I'm sorry about the deadline, but you said I could have this time off. Yes, but . . ."

I walked back to the kitchen table. My aunt had been a stickler for order, and nine years of her discipline had stuck with me.

Mary came in. "I didn't think I'd be on the phone so long. I'm sorry about the mess."

"I'll help you clean up."

"Thanks." She sealed the solvent and oil while I collected the used cleaning patches and threw them away. After collecting the rod, cloths, and solutions, she started for her room.

I held up the bullets. "Loaded or unloaded?"

"Doesn't do much good unloaded."

I loaded the revolver and clicked on the safety, then placed it in the holster and moved them to the desk.

Mary returned. "What's for breakfast? I'm starving."

"That seems to be your constant state."

She patted her belly. "This little guy is growing fast."

"I thought you said you didn't know the sex?"

"I don't. Boy or girl, *it* is hungry."

I opened the refrigerator. "Well then, I can make you a Denver omelet, french toast, eggs Benedict—"

"Eggs Benedict."

I pulled out the ingredients. "You know, the origin of this dish is disputed. Some people believe a drunken Wall Street broker—"

"You *are* a glut of useless information! Wait. Don't tell me. 'You never know what could prove to be useful.'"

"You're starting to know me too well." I grinned at her. "I may yet convince you to read a great children's book and join me in jigsaw puzzles."

"Never."

After breakfast, while Mary lingered over her coffee, I cleaned

CARRIE STUART PARKS

up. I'd just finished when Dutch came in. He wore stonewashed jeans, a gray sweater over a black, red, and white plaid shirt, and a leather jacket. "Ready to go?"

"Yowza!" Mary murmured. "You should put him on your list as a keeper. He looks good enough to—"

"Shh." I looked at Dutch. He *was* easy on the eyes. "I'll be right there." I ran to my room and grabbed a jacket and over-size tote bag. In the kitchen, I packed several bottled waters, Pepsi, and Mountain Dew from the refrigerator, added a note-pad and pen, then joined everyone outside. The white Cadillac Escalade, with Leroy behind the wheel, waited in front of the lodge.

"Ryan called and said he'd meet us outside of Suttonville." Dutch opened the passenger-side door for me. "He sent directions."

I got in. "I confess. I'd never heard of Suttonville before last night. How far is it from here?"

Dutch jumped into the back seat. "About forty miles as the crow flies, but several hours for us."

"I don't mind." Mary put on her sunglasses and smiled at Dutch.

"Me neither." Leroy shifted the car into gear and drove forward, then gave me a sideways glance. "What's goin' on with you, Sam?"

I shifted in my seat. "What do you mean?"

"You know. Where'd you come from? Where have you been all my life?"

Mary smirked at me. "I'm waiting."

"'From there to here, from here to there, funny things are everywhere!'"

Leroy's head snapped in my direction so fast I thought he'd pull a muscle. "Are you okay?"

I looked at Mary. "Sneetches."

"Sorry. I'm missing something here. What are you two talking about?" Leroy flushed.

"I'm sorry, Leroy. Sam and I had an . . . interesting conversation. She said whenever she's nervous or in an uncomfortable situation, she blurts out Dr. Seuss or something equally . . . strange."

He looked at me.

I shrugged.

Dutch said, "Something like this? '"The time has come," the Walrus said, "To talk of many things: Of shoes—and ships—and sealing-wax—Of cabbages—and kings."'"

"Very good, Dutch!" I turned to Mary. "See? It isn't just me."

"Do you put together jigsaw puzzles?" Mary asked Dutch.

"No."

"See?" Mary looked at me. "It *is* just you."

I looked out the window.

"I'm sorry," Mary said. "I was just being funny. Um . . . tell us about living in Pullman."

"What can I say? My apartment is . . . *was* very comfortable, and the price was right." I shifted and tried to think about something to change the subject.

"How about before you moved to Pullman? Or did you grow up there?" Dutch asked.

"Um . . . well . . . when my aunt died, I moved to Spokane. I was fortunate enough to find a house-sitting job for a woman who traveled a lot with an accounting firm. She'd come home every week or two to do laundry, pick up her mail, and have a few days off. Pretty boring stuff."

"Wait a minute," Mary said. "Speaking of kids' books. You're kinda like that character you mentioned before from *The Wizard of Oz*. Dorothy Gale."

"Why do you say that?" Dutch asked.

"The boring life. No offense. You know," Mary leaned forward. "Dorothy, like you, lived with her aunt on a farm. One day a tornado, in the form of an out-of-control SUV, crashes into your 'house.' You're swept away to the Land of Oz, also known as Clan Firinn—"

"So is Dr. Brùn the Wizard?" Dutch asked.

"Right," Mary said. "Now here you are setting out on an adventure with the Scarecrow (Dutch) and Tin Man (Leroy)—"

"This is ridiculous." Leroy looked at her through the rear-view mirror. "Why are we even talking about kids' books?"

"Chill, Leroy, and just admit I'm the good witch," Mary said. "What's-her-name, with the big pink dress and crown."

"Glenda," I said automatically.

"Yeah, right, and Ryan is the Cowardly Lion."

"Not a very good analogy," Dutch said.

"Actually," I said slowly, "I think it's rather clever, at least to a certain point. The Scarecrow, who wanted a brain, was smart all along. He just needed a degree, right, *Dr.* Van Seters? And the Cowardly Lion was brave but just needed a medal, or a badge, like *Deputy* Adams. I don't know you well enough, Leroy, to know about your heart . . ."

Leroy's knuckles whitened as he clenched the steering wheel. He gave a humorless chuckle. "Nothin' wrong with my heart. Like I said, a stupid subject." He took a swig of his Mountain Dew.

After a few minutes of awkward silence, Dutch asked, "How about you, Mary? How long have you wanted to be an author?"

Mary launched into a lengthy discourse about her writing while Dutch peppered her with questions. I was amazed at her creativity. Leroy seemed focused on driving and gradually his grip loosened.

We eventually turned off Highway 395 and headed east on a two-lane, paved road. Leroy handed me a piece of paper. "You'll need to be my navigator from here on."

"Okay. Stay on this road for six miles. After six miles, look for a road on your left."

No one spoke. Leroy kept one eye on the odometer, finally slowing down. "Should be around here."

"Is that it?" Dutch pointed at what looked more like a field access than an actual road.

"I don't think so," Mary said. "Drive up a bit farther."

Leroy drove another mile before turning around. "There's nothing here. It has to be that one we saw earlier." He found the dusty track again and turned on it. Grasses brushed the underside of the SUV as we drove up a small hill, crested it, and started down the other side. Ahead we could see a Whitman County squad car. We pulled in next to it, and Leroy turned off the engine. We were parked on a sharp cliff overlooking a coulee, a valley carved from glacial floods from ancient Lake Missoula. We got out and joined Ryan, who'd been leaning against his car and smoking.

"Down there." Ryan gestured with his cigarette.

We moved to the edge of the precipice. Through a rusty chain-link fence below, we could see a series of old decaying houses. Dead trees and yellow, wispy grasses marked where lawns once were. A sagging chain-link gate blocked the road down with a No Trespassing sign.

"We walk from here." Ryan looked at Mary. "You okay with that?"

"I'm pregnant, not crippled." She glared at him, then reached into the car, pulled out her baseball cap, and put it on.

He gave a tug on the gate, and it shifted enough for us to slip through.

We all trooped down the switchback road. The walls of the coulee rose above us, layers of basalt scrubbed clean from the centuries-old flood.

At the valley floor, the breeze blew stronger, sending the dried grasses into a hushed *shhhhhh* whisper. Somewhere a door squeaked in its hinges, while a magpie harshly chirruped his displeasure at our presence. The boarded-up houses, with peeling paint and sagging front porches, looked like a set for a post-apocalyptic movie.

Goose pimples tripped down my spine.

"I kinda expect zombies to come out from one of the houses." Mary brushed her hair away from her face.

I cleared my throat. "Or maybe winged monkeys. Certainly this qualifies as the haunted forest."

Ryan looked over at us. "What are you talking about?"

"Nothing. Nothing." I swallowed my grin. On impulse, I trotted up to the nearest house and tried the front door. It was unlocked.

Inside everything was gray, covered with a thick layer of dust but perfectly intact—as if the occupants had merely stepped out for a moment and forgotten to return. A book lay facedown on the coffee table, knitting needles protruded from a basket near the far wall, and a pair of overshoes sat on a throw rug by the door.

The goose pimples returned.

"Come on, Sam," Ryan called.

I closed the door and joined the other four.

"The cemetery is just ahead." Ryan strolled swiftly down the tumbleweed-strewn street.

I caught up with him. "I take it you've been here before?"

"Yes."

I kept pace with him, but he didn't elaborate on his answer. We passed by a burned-out house, only its charred chimney still standing.

"Doctor's office," Ryan said. "Cemetery behind it."

Handy location if you're a lousy doctor. I bit my tongue.

A rusted wrought-iron fence surrounded a patch of earth where gray headstones poked out in tired rows. Toward the rear of the graveyard stood a small, simple mausoleum. None of the ground looked disturbed. Ryan paused at the open gate. "Spread out. See if you find any signs of digging."

I walked left, reading the names on the gravestones while looking for any disturbance. I hadn't gone far when I came across a series of five small headstones lying flush with the ground. A cherub statue stood at one end with the date of 1986. I caught Mary's attention and waved her over. "Does this look like what I think it is?"

Mary's lips tightened for a moment. "A baby cemetery." She pulled out her cell and took several photos.

"That's what I thought." I moved on, but something nagged at me. The last three graves had a single headstone with the last name of *Adams*. John Edgar, 1948, Martha Eve, 1950, Peter John, 1977. All had the same final year, 1987. The year the town was poisoned. A very dead bouquet of flowers tied by a bleached ribbon lay on the headstone.

"Over here," Ryan called from the mausoleum.

I trotted over. The door was open. Inside were two caskets placed on either side of the door, leaving a small area between them. Carved into the wall above was the name *West*. Both caskets stood open.

"A lot easier to force a door and break open a coffin than dig one up," Dutch said.

I leaned against the side of the building. My stomach clenched. I felt like I held a jigsaw piece in my hand and had just spotted where it needed to go. "Ryan," I said slowly. "Last night—"

"Yes." He narrowed his eyes and stared at me.

The feeling grew stronger, as did my twisting stomach. "Um . . . you knew all about the town. Did you guess the body came from Suttonville as soon as you heard the name?"

"Why would I think that?" Ryan folded his arms. A vein pounded in his forehead.

"Because you know this cemetery, the names of people interred here, Ryan *Adams*. You've been here often—to visit your family's graves. They're buried over there." I pointed. "All of them poisoned in 1987."

TWELVE

Dutch felt his mouth drop. He made an effort to shut it, then asked Ryan, "Is that true?"

Ryan gave a noncommittal shrug.

Dutch waited a moment to see if Ryan would offer any other comments, then entered the mausoleum. The air was full of dust motes floating in the light streaming through the door and the stained-glass window in the rear. The open coffins had been damaged by whatever someone had used to open them. The bodies inside were a jumble of bones and ragged fabric, but he could easily see the skulls were missing as well as other bones—bones that he was sure were sitting in Dr. Solem's lab in Seattle.

He turned and nodded to the four standing outside. "Looks like we found the graves. I'd bet the farm that the most recent set of bones are from here as well." He didn't want to address Sam's comments just yet. Instead, he exited the mausoleum and crossed over in the direction Sam had pointed. He found the graves, along with a dried pile of flowers tied by a limp ribbon.

He thought back to the conversation the night before. Someone had gasped when he mentioned 1987. Had that been Ryan?

He slowly returned to Mary, Ryan, Sam, and Leroy. How did Ryan, the doomed town, the excavation at LaCrosse, the apple paperweight, and the break-in at Mary and Sam's place fit together? Or did they?

When he drew close enough to speak without raising his voice, he asked Ryan, "It was no coincidence that you ended up working on this case, was it?"

Ryan took out a cigarette and lighter, then slowly lit it. He didn't speak until he'd taken a deep puff and let out the smoke. "No. No coincidence." He shifted his weight.

"You got any idea what's going on?" Leroy asked.

"No." Ryan started walking back toward the road. "But I intend to find out."

I followed as everyone trooped from the graveyard. I still wanted to ask Ryan about the small headstones. I soon caught up. "Ryan?"

He slowed but didn't stop.

"What are all the baby graves from 1986?" I asked.

This time he did stop. "The town doctor delivered babies from all over the area."

"That's really not an answer," Mary said. "Why so many deaths in the same year?"

Ryan looked down. "I don't know. My folks moved to Suttonville from Brewster, New York when I was in high school. All this happened after I'd left for college."

"So yet another mystery," Mary licked her lips and leaned toward him. "When did the doctor's office burn down?"

"Nineteen eighty-seven," Ryan said.

We started moving again. We'd just reached the point where the road started to climb when a flash from the cliff above caught my attention. I squinted to see. Parked next to Ryan's squad car and our white Escalade was a third vehicle, a black SUV. I could see someone standing on the far side. The flash came again. Binoculars. "Hey guys, we've got company." I jerked my head toward the cliff.

Leroy, Ryan, and Dutch spun toward the crest of the hill, then sprinted up the road.

The person with the binoculars jumped into the SUV. Before the men could reach the top of the coulee, the rig was gone.

"Why would someone spy on us?" Mary asked. "Come to think of it, how did anyone even know we were here?"

How indeed? Instead of heading up the road, I turned and strolled back to the cluster of houses.

"Hey, where are you going?" Mary caught up with me.

"That could have been a passing motorist, but that's highly unlikely because the road is almost impossible to find. Or someone is following us, again unlikely, or . . ." I checked each abandoned house, then the trees. I missed it the first time. "There." I pointed. "A game camera."

"That's creepy. Someone's watching this place." She rubbed her arms. "But then again, it makes sense. The fence across the road says No Trespassing."

"True. But the guy with the binoculars—"

"It was a guy?"

I thought for a moment. "Yes. In a dark suit. Anyway, he wasn't trying to stop us. If he were law enforcement here because of trespassing, he'd be driving an official vehicle, and he wouldn't be wearing a suit. And he'd cite us, make sure we got out. It's like he was . . ." *The excavation site.* The memory of another event pushed into my brain. "Mary, this isn't the first time a black SUV checked on us. I'm pretty sure, no, I *am* sure that same vehicle drove past us yesterday at LaCrosse when we were looking at the bones."

Mary's brow furrowed. "How can you be sure? Black SUVs are pretty common. Maybe you're stuck on that particular type of car because that's what drove into the school."

A slight shiver went through me. *Maybe I am obsessed.* I closed my eyes. Because of the return of my purse and deliberate sabotage of my apartment, I knew someone was aware of my location. What was the probability that my stalker and the driver of the black SUV were the same? I couldn't be sure.

"Do you have some kind of map or satellite app on your phone?" I asked Mary.

"Sure." She fiddled with the cell, then handed it to me.

I found a map showing the roads around LaCrosse. I switched from map to satellite view. "Look." I turned the display so she could see. "There's the cemetery, excavation, and road. Yesterday I saw a black SUV heading north."

"And this is important because . . ." She looked at me and raised her eyebrows.

"Look again. That road goes nowhere. It takes you to a couple of farms."

"Maybe they live on one of those farms."

"I thought you were the one with the imagination." I turned and trudged back toward the parked cars. She caught up with me but didn't speak until we'd reached the top.

"Hey, I'm sorry," she said.

"It's okay. I am being paranoid." Even as I said it, I didn't believe it.

───

Dutch was winded by the time he reached the top of the cliff. The SUV had already driven off. Tire tracks marked where the vehicle had parked, but the hard earth didn't record any footprints.

"Can we make tire imprints?" Leroy asked Ryan.

"Why? The driver broke no laws." Ryan stomped out his cigarette, then moved to his squad car and unlocked the door. "You going to call Dr. Solem about the graves?"

Dutch nodded.

"Okay then. I'll drop in on the Franklin County Sheriff's Office and let them know." He got in, but before he could start his engine, on a hunch Dutch strolled over to his window and made a sign to roll it down.

"Yes?"

"This may sound strange, but do you know of any old elevators around here?"

"Not off the top of my head. Is it important?"

"It could be."

"Okay. I'll call you if I find out anything." He started his engine and drove off.

Leroy looked at Dutch. "What was that all about?"

"It may be nothing." Dutch looked around for the women. He thought they would be behind him when they raced to the top of the coulee. He moved over to the edge. Below, Sam walked toward the town with Mary following. They both stopped and Sam turned in a slow circle.

Leroy joined him. "What's going on? Where are the girls?"

"Still at the town. Sam seems to be looking for something."

Sam finally pointed. Dutch's gaze followed her finger.

Of course. "I think she's pointing to a game camera."

"If someone set up a camera, then they should have a record of who could have moved those bodies."

"That's true. I'll call Ryan and let him know." Dutch pulled out his cell. "No service here. I'll try later." He leaned against the SUV. "Looks like we've solved the mystery of the unknown remains. I suspect Dr. Solem will want to confirm everything, but it's probably a case for the Department of Archaeology and Historic Preservation over in Olympia. They handle nonforensic remains. Looks like you can go back to work on the development pretty quickly."

"Yep," Leroy said softly. He moved away, staring at the

ground. His jaw clenched and unclenched and he rubbed the back of his neck.

"Something wrong?"

"Nah. Just . . . thinking."

The wind kicked up, sending a dust devil twirling between the sagebrush. A red-tailed hawk floated on the updraft, watching the ground for a tasty mouse.

Soon the two women joined them, slightly out of breath from the climb.

The sound of a diesel engine and a cloud of dust preceded the arrival of an older blue Ford truck. It parked on the road and a man in a battered cowboy hat, red plaid jacket, and jeans stepped out. His face was a network of wrinkles, and a small white mustache lined his upper lip. "Can I help you folks?"

Dutch stepped forward. "We were just leaving."

"I see." He looked at the women, then Leroy, before addressing Dutch. "Did you find what you were looking for?"

"I believe so. And you are . . . ?"

"Hank. Hank Jenicek. I own this." He waved his hand at the surrounding farmland. "I kinda keep an eye on anyone paying too much attention to Suttonville, especially this time of year."

Dutch's forehead wrinkled. "Why this time of year?"

"We're coming up on September 29. The anniversary of the town's . . . I guess you'd call it death. People used to come by pretty regular, lay flowers on the graves, even some protesters, but not much anymore. People forget."

Samantha walked over to Hank. "Are you the one who put in the game camera?"

"Game camera?" Hank asked.

"Someone installed a camera on one of the trees down there," Sam said.

"No," Hank said. "But that's not such a bad idea. What's your interest in the town?"

"I'm sorry. I should have answered you." Dutch stuck out his hand to shake Hank's. "I'm Dr. Dustin Van Seters." They shook hands. "We believe someone removed some bodies from the Suttonville graveyard and we're following up on it."

"Some bodies? Which bodies?"

"The West family."

"Edwinna and Ned?" The old man shook his head. "He and his wife were good people."

"You knew them?" Sam asked.

"Yep. Shameful to disturb the dead." He turned toward his truck.

"One more thing, Mr. Jenicek." Sam brushed her hair from her face. "There are a number of baby graves all from the same year, 1986. Do you know anything about that?"

"I heard rumors, that's all." He gave a half-wave, got into his pickup, and drove off.

"Every so often I wouldn't mind hearing a few rumors," Sam muttered.

Leroy unlocked the car door. "Lunch?"

Dutch nodded. "Head to Pasco." As soon as they reached the highway, he was able to get cell service and updated Ryan on the game camera. After he disconnected, they drove in silence.

When they reached the edge of town, Leroy found a small restaurant in a strip mall and parked.

Mary had been bent over her phone since they'd left Suttonville. Once inside and seated, she finally looked up.

"What are you looking for on your cell?" Sam asked her.

"I think it's more what am I not finding." She waited until the waiter took their orders and moved away. "There's surprisingly little known about what happened in Suttonville. Rumors flew that the doctor poisoned the water, then committed suicide. They think he started with the children and babies."

"That's so sad," Sam said. "He had to be a monster to do that. No one was even allowed to bring him to justice."

"There'd be no closure for the families. And speaking of which"—Mary took a sip of Pepsi and showed Sam her phone—"the most interesting thing of all is who discovered all the bodies. None other than Deputy Ryan Adams."

No one spoke for a few moments while Sam read.

"I wonder why Ryan didn't mention his connection to Suttonville last night at dinner," Dutch said.

"He probably didn't want to think about it." Sam looked at each of them. "He found his parents' and brother's bodies. That had to be a terrible shock."

"It was worse than that," Mary said, taking her phone back. "On September 29, 1987, there was a terrific windstorm. A lot of damage and power outages. No one was able to connect to Suttonville, but because of the storm, no one thought this was unusual until the power grid was restored four days later. By the time Ryan went over to check on his family, they'd been dead for several days."

THIRTEEN

The revelation about the fate of Suttonville nauseated me. I shivered, though the day was warm. The waiter brought our orders and everyone began eating. I played with my food. "Do you suppose that Ryan could have been the one to move the bones so we'd find them?"

"Are you thinking that Ryan was trying to bring attention to what happened to the town?" Dutch asked.

"It sure didn't make much of a splash at the time." Mary touched her cell. "But it's been something like twenty-eight years. Why wait so long?"

"Well, September 29 is coming up real soon. Maybe somethin' changed." Leroy spoke around a mouthful of food. He finished chewing. "Remember, it weren't just the one body. Maybe that didn't get the attention someone wanted. So he, or she, planted the second set of bones with a second brass paperweight."

"True." Dutch thought for a moment. "Ryan didn't seem surprised when I told him you found a game camera, Sam. Maybe he set it up."

"To keep an eye on the town?" Mary nodded. "Makes sense. What about the link of the paperweight to . . ." She quickly glanced at me, then Dutch.

I knew what she was about to say. She was about to mention the blackmail notes.

"The paperweight to . . . ?" Leroy said.

Mary fiddled with her phone, then stuck it in her pocket. "To anything."

Leroy narrowed his eyes at her, but she ignored him and turned to me. "Have you heard anything from your insurance company?"

The conversation turned from bones, bodies, paperweights, and Ryan to insurance claims. Leroy listened without saying anything, his gaze going from person to person. I could tell he wasn't satisfied with Mary's answer, but already too many people knew about the blackmail notes.

Dutch picked up the check, which I was grateful for. I hadn't thought about being penniless when I ordered.

We soon found the library. Leroy wanted to get some coffee to go and gas the SUV. He dropped us and drove off.

I found a vacant computer and typed in *Beatrice Greer*. The search returned eighty-eight women by that name, with the only residents in Washington State having an average age of ninety-eight. I tried alternate spellings of her last name and had no results. Next I typed in *accident, LaCrosse, school*. A brief article appeared with no mention of the dead woman, only "name withheld pending notification of next of kin."

I leaned against the back of my chair. Beatrice Greer didn't seem to exist. So who was the blackmailed woman from Clan Firinn who was probably murdered?

Blackmailed and murdered? A blackmailer would hardly be shooting at the victim . . . unless the victim didn't pay up. What if the shooting was meant to force Beatrice to cough up the money, but it went horribly wrong?

What if several people had Beatrice on their radars? A blackmailer who wanted her money, and a killer who wanted her dead?

I wrote some notes on the pad of paper I'd brought with me, then turned to the brass paperweight. I found numerous pictures of apple-shaped paperweights—glass, brass, antique, copper, metal—but none were an exact match.

The words *apple* and *Washington State* in the computer's search engine were even more frustrating. Apples were Washington's state fruit, and they represented 65 percent of the apples grown in the United States. I did discover there were seventy-five hundred varieties of apples. I printed that chart.

Surprisingly little news covered the tragedy at Suttonville. I stood and moved to the resource desk, where a young woman was working. "Excuse me, but is there someplace I can read more about Suttonville?"

She wrinkled up her nose. "Um . . . I think . . . you tried the computer?"

"Yes."

"Let me ask." She looked around the room, spotted an older man reading at a table near the window, and approached him.

After a whispered conference, the man slowly stood, coughed

a few times, then came over to me and said in a hoarse voice, "You were asking about Suttonville?" He had wispy hair, a thin mustache, and wore a too-large jacket over a white shirt. He reminded me a little of Don Knotts.

"Yes."

He coughed again, straightened, and tilted his head backward. "I was there."

"And you got out alive?"

"Well, no, not in the town, but nearby." He rubbed his neck and coughed again.

I took a half step backward.

He noticed. "I'm not contagious. Thyroid cancer." He coughed again. "After that happened, a lot of strange things cropped up."

"How so?"

"The fence, for one thing. They put the fence up almost immediately." Another cough. "I drove over there probably three days after they found . . . what they found. They were still working there. They'd blocked the road and had someone watching it, but I know the area." He motioned me closer and lowered his voice. "They were down there walking around in white suits, like space suits." Cough.

"Biohazard suits. Not surprising. After not being found for four days."

"True. True." He glanced around to be sure no one was paying attention. "Nobody had any kind of official markings." He smelled of mothballs and garlic.

"Official markings?" I tried to breathe through my mouth.

"You know. Like police, or sheriff, or coroner. Unmarked. Catch my drift?"

I was certainly catching some of his olfactory drift. "I see. Could I have your name and number should I have any more questions?"

He reached into his pocket and took out a grimy business card, straightened the edges, and handed it to me. It read *Norman Bottoms, Accountant,* followed by a phone number. "I'm retired."

"Thank you very much, Norman. If you think of anything else, call me." I gave him the number at Clan Firinn.

Mary caught my attention and pointed at her watch. I gratefully moved toward the exit. I didn't know if I'd learned anything of use. I just needed to watch, listen, and pray for inspiration.

Dutch was already outside, sitting on a bench in the shade working on his cell.

Mary followed me out. "Did you find what you were looking for?"

"Unfortunately no."

"I . . . um . . . I did a little research on you."

"Me?" My voice came out high pitched. "What did you need to know about me that you couldn't have asked?"

"You said your parents died when you were six in a car accident. I couldn't find any record of that—" She stopped, reached into her pocket, and pulled out her cell. "Hello?"

I continued forward to give her privacy.

"He's right here. Would you . . . Okay . . . Uh-huh. Hello? Hello? I'm losing you. Okay, you're back. Right . . ."

Leroy pulled into the lot, his cell to his ear, and put the SUV into Park while he spoke on the phone.

I moved to the SUV.

"Dutch." Mary trotted over and held out her cell. "Ryan wants to talk to you."

Dutch took the phone. "Van Seters. Uh-huh. I hadn't thought of that. Where?" He made a motion to indicate he wanted to write something. "Hold on a minute."

I handed him my notebook and pen.

"Okay. Yeah, got it." He looked at his watch. "About an hour and a half."

Mary drifted closer.

"Meet you there? Sure, I guess." Dutch disconnected.

"What did Ryan want?" I asked.

"I had asked Ryan if he was aware of any old elevators," Dutch said. "He called back to ask if we meant grain elevators."

"Grain elevators," I said slowly. "Of course."

"There's one about an hour and a half from here." Dutch handed me my notebook. "Directions are in there. I figure it's worth checking out. It's roughly on the way back to Clan Firinn."

"Wait a minute." Mary's lips had formed a thin line. "You didn't just say you'd *meet* him there, did you?"

"He wanted to meet us there, so yes—"

"You idiot!" Mary practically hissed. "We may have had a chance to recover one hundred fifty thousand dollars and you just invited a *cop* to join us?"

"Mary, even if we *do* find the blackmail money, and that's highly unlikely, it's not ours to keep—"

"Haven't you ever heard of finders keepers?" Mary's face had turned red and her eyes glittered with unshed tears. "Do you have any idea how that money . . . never mind." She jumped into the car.

We all joined her. She stared out the window, jaw working. I wanted to tell her I understood what it was like to be poor, to have doors slammed in your face, but I couldn't. I could never find the right words. I wasn't being very much of a friend.

"Where to?" Leroy asked.

"A slight side trip." Dutch gave directions.

Leroy put the car into gear and pulled into the road. "What's there?"

I leaned slightly forward to look at Dutch.

"Probably nothing." Dutch glanced back at Mary.

We drove for a number of miles in silence. I thought about the blackmail notes and about Mary looking into the deaths of my parents. Why didn't she just ask me?

Dutch's phone rang. "Van Seters." He listened for a few moments. "We're on our way and should be there by evening." He listened again. "Will do." After dropping the phone into his pocket, he leaned forward. "That was Dr. Brùn. He wanted to let you know, Sam, that some boxes arrived for you. They're in Highland House. He's invited everyone for dinner, including you, Leroy."

"Sounds good," Leroy said.

The two men talked the rest of the drive while I watched the passing Palouse countryside.

The grain elevator wasn't hard to find. Made of wood, the over seven-story structure was sagging along one side. If it had ever been painted, the color was long gone, and the boards had weathered to various shades of brown and gray.

"This is it." Dutch pointed to a wide spot in the road.

"You're kidding me." Leroy shook his head and pulled off.

Dutch had already jumped from the car. Ryan soon parked next to us.

Mary got out. "So." She gave Dutch a hard look as if defying him to question her authority.

"Go ahead, Mary." Dutch gave her an encouraging smile.

The dump shed extended from the side next to the road and was open at either end. The grain trucks would have pulled off the road, had their load weighed and emptied, then pulled out through the other side. Mary pointed in that direction. "Ryan and Sam, why don't you go through there? You should find a door or some way to get inside."

Before she could assign him a task, Leroy shook his head. "I'm staying here."

Mary shrugged. "Whatever. I'll go left around the outside and Dutch, you go right. Look for a way to get into the building."

"It looks like it's going to collapse at any minute," I said.

"It's looked like that for years," Ryan said. "I doubt it will fall down today." He looked at Mary. "What are we looking for?"

"Anything that looks like it doesn't fit," Mary said.

"That's helpful," Ryan muttered as he walked.

I slowly followed, pausing and peeking through the broken boards before entering the dump shed. Ryan was already out of sight. No sign of a case, red or any other color.

The wind whistled through the holes and gaps between the

boards, as if a small band of off-key pipers were warming up. It smelled of rodents and dried grasses.

A door on the far side should have opened to the storage area of the building. The door was stuck, but the rotting wood beside it easily gave way with a shriek before dropping off the rusted nail holding it to the building.

"Samantha?" Ryan called.

"Yeah. Here." I peered into the cavernous space of the main part of the building where the massive storage bins would have been. Sunlight poked through the siding, creating spotlights around the room. The breeze sent the grain dust twirling in the light. I stepped inside.

"Can you be more specific on 'anything that looks like it doesn't fit'?" Ryan pulled out a cigarette, then swiftly clicked open his lighter.

"Ryan, *no*—"

The flame ignited the grain dust. The massive fireball blew outward.

I flew through the opening, landing on my back.

I couldn't catch my breath.

Black smoke roiled overhead.

A jolt of adrenaline shot through me. I rolled to my stomach, curled up, and buried my face in the dirt.

Searing heat hit my back.

I grabbed the earth and clawed forward.

One hand grabbed me up, then pulled me from the inferno.

The fire roared behind me like a locomotive.

Once outside, my rescuer, Dutch, continued to haul me

forward with one arm around my waist. We fled, tripped, fell over chunks of dirt, scrabbled up, and raced away from the devouring flames. Finally we paused in the middle of the field and turned.

The grain elevator was a massive, towering blaze. With Ryan inside.

FOURTEEN

Dutch's heart slammed against his chest and he sucked in air as if he'd been underwater. Mary and Leroy soon joined him and Sam in the field.

"Are you okay?" Sam asked him. "You're white as a sheet."

"I will be." Dutch wiped sweat off his brow. He tried to keep the memory bottled up, but it bubbled to the surface. He was back in Boise, working his shift as a firefighter. The alarm came in. A fire at an apartment complex. When they reached the building, the structure was already engulfed in flames. Just like the grain elevator in front of him.

He shook his head, trying to sort the two images.

They merged. Again he was facing the apartment, and someone said there were people still trapped. A child.

He saw an opportunity and ran toward the end of the building, then inside. The flames rolled up the walls. He ran. Without knowing how he got there, he was in a baby's bedroom. The baby was still in the crib.

His rapid breathing rasped loudly in his mask. He snatched up the baby.

Not a baby. Just bedding over a stuffed animal.

No time. The smoke cleared enough for him to shoot through a doorway, down a short hall, then outside. The ceiling collapsed after him, sending a wave of smoke, firebrands, and flames upward and outward.

Stop it. He wasn't in Boise. He was in Washington. And someone was talking to him.

"Dutch." Sam was shaking his arm. "Dutch, what's wrong?"

The vision retreated, leaving the leaping flames of the grain elevator.

"What happened?" Leroy asked. "One minute I'm walking around the edge of the building, the next I'm on the ground and Dutch is running inside."

"Ryan." Sam's lips were pale. "Ryan lit a cigarette. I guess he didn't know how flammable grain dust is."

"Ryan is in there?" Mary turned toward the inferno.

No one answered.

"Leroy . . ." Dutch's voice came out high and scratchy. He tried again. "Leroy, you'll need to move the SUV farther up the road."

There was no way anyone would miss the fire for miles around, but he'd need to call it in just the same. Before he could pull out his cell, the distant wail of a fire engine and shriek of police cars told him they knew.

A car swung around the corner, slowed at the fire, then sped away. A black SUV.

"If that isn't proof we're being followed . . ." Sam quietly said.

A sheriff's cruiser pulled in next to Ryan's patrol car, followed by a fire truck. After checking out Ryan's vehicle, the officer started walking toward them. Dutch met him halfway and explained what happened. Mary and Sam followed.

The officer took notes while the firefighters worked to keep the blaze from spreading to the nearby fields. When the wind shifted and sent the smoke over them, the officer gave Dutch his card and arranged to meet the next day.

Dutch turned to the two women. "We'll be in the way at this point. Let's get back to Clan Firinn."

As they made their way across the field to their SUV, Sam said to Dutch, "You probably saved my life back there. Thank you."

Dutch kept his gaze on their vehicles, unable to look at either the fire or Sam. "You're welcome," he finally managed to croak.

When they reached the SUV, they all got in. Dutch reached for the stone in his pocket. *Have I done it? By saving Sam, have I finally released the burden I carry?* When Leroy turned toward home, Dutch rolled down the window and threw the rock away.

———

Dutch was seated behind Leroy. I turned to watch him as we started toward Clan Firinn. He'd saved my life, but he seemed a million miles away. His jaw clenched and unclenched. Finally he pulled out a small stone, looked at it, rolled down the window and threw it out. Could that be one of the stones he mentioned earlier?

Mary was directly behind me. I couldn't see how she was taking all this. Did Ryan's horrible death remind her of her husband's possible end? Was she upset that we hadn't found any money? I felt beyond cruel to even think she'd be so shallow. "Mary, are you okay?" I finally asked.

"Not okay. That was . . . horrible."

My face burned. It was a good thing no one could read my thoughts. Sneetches thoughts.

When we reached the first gate, I jumped out and opened it. The second wrought-iron and cedar gate had been left open. Leroy parked in front of the main lodge.

"Thank you, Leroy," I said as Mary and I headed for Highland House. As soon as we were inside, I grabbed a bottled water and bolted for my room.

The door was open to the studio, and the two huge dogs lay sprawled on the floor.

My heart raced, pounding in my ears. I stopped dead. I couldn't speak, couldn't call for help.

The dogs raised their heads and looked at me.

Mary didn't know the dogs were in here. *I need to shut the door so they can't get to her.* I willed my legs to move, to turn and run, but they'd become rooted to the floor. The sealed bottle of water dropped from my hand.

"What are you doing, Sam?" Mary came up behind me, picked up the water and handed it back to me, then calmly walked over to the dogs. "Hello there, boys." She scratched them on the head, then glanced at me. "Good heavens, Sam, you're white as the proverbial ghost. Don't tell me you're afraid of dogs?"

Mutely I nodded.

"Come on." She snapped her fingers at the dogs. They stood and followed her to the studio. The outside door opened, then closed, and she returned. "You'd better sit before you fall down."

Again I nodded and stumbled to the nearest chair.

"Why are you so afraid of dogs?"

"I don't know. Or maybe I don't want to remember." I opened the water and took a drink.

"You're rather a complex person, Samantha Williams."

"So I'm maybe not so boring?" My voice was still squeaky, but at least I could speak.

"I'll give you a test. Have you ever folded all your socks in your sock drawer?"

"Doesn't everybody? But I arrange them by color."

"Still boring." She started for the door. "I'm going to lie down before dinner. I'm not even sure if I can eat. Catch ya later."

"Okay."

She quietly shut the door behind her. I sat and stared at the wall for a few moments. Who'd have thought a simple day trip would end up with someone dying?

Maybe Suttonville was cursed? Anyone drawing near to the place would suffer? Look at that poor Norman Bottoms, the man with thyroid cancer. He was there . . .

"Stop it," I whispered. "'You're mad, bonkers, completely off

your head. But I'll tell you a secret. All the best people are.'
Thank you, Lewis Carroll."

I needed to refocus my attention. The promised boxes from
my Pullman apartment rested at one end of the room. The
pathetically small containers held all my earthly possessions.
Not surprising, as I'd never collected knickknacks and usually
gave away anything I wasn't using. When I opened the first box,
the stench of mold and mildew from my damp clothing filled the
room. I lifted the entire box, transported it to the laundry room,
and started a load.

The second box held my gun safe, which would now need a
locksmith as the key was on the missing keyring. Also inside
were two jigsaw puzzles, a children's Bible, and a small collection of children's books. The books were all I had when I was
sent to live with my aunt. The damp had seeped into the pages,
causing them to ripple, and the cover was separating from the
inner paper. I carefully smoothed the front page of my favorite
Dr. Seuss book, the one my parents had inscribed:

Our dearest daughter,
    Should you ever need any guidance in your life, note the
gifts given to you this Easter, 1997.
                    All our love,
                    Mommy and Daddy

The cardboard in the jigsaw puzzles had pulled away from
the images printed on the front of each piece. I left the books on
the window ledge to air out and dry.

I'm officially homeless. Nothing remained of my life in Pullman.

"What's it gonna be, Sam?" I whispered. "Whimper and feel sorry for yourself? Afraid of everything?" I crossed the room, then returned to the empty box. "You know what you are?" My voice grew louder. "A scaredy-cat." I kicked the box across the room. It slammed into a chair. "A lily-livered scaredy-cat." I chased after the container and kicked it again, this time sending it into the wall. "A dithering jellyfish!" Another kick sent the box into the coffee table. "A whiney, simpering coward!" *Wham!* The final kick sent the now-torn box into Mary's legs.

"Ouch! What. Are. You. Doing?"

My face burned. *Lord, anytime now, You can open up the earth and swallow me.* "I'm acting completely illogical with this childish outburst." I clapped my hands over my mouth.

Mary stared at me. "You do realize how odd that sounded? Did someone say that to you a lot as a child?"

Now it was my turn to stare. *Did* someone often say that to me as a child? I didn't remember. Just as I didn't remember why I was so afraid of dogs. "I'm sorry."

"No reason to be sorry, but are you quite finished?"

"I still had namby-pamby, pantywaist, and milksop wussy poltroon," I muttered.

Her mouth dropped for a moment. "Are you prone to these . . . childish outbursts often?"

I thought for a moment. "I don't know."

She yawned. "Can you finish up quietly? I'm going to bed." She turned and closed the door behind her.

I picked up the shredded cardboard and placed it next to the garbage container. "Namby-pamby, pantywaist, milksop wussy poltroon." Picking up the jigsaw puzzles, I moved them into the studio and threw them into the garbage. *Jigsaw puzzle.* I stared at the colorful boxes for a moment. *I have a personal jigsaw to assemble.*

I soon found a sketchbook, scissors, and Sharpie marker, then pulled the chair out and sat at the drafting table. After cutting up a few pieces of paper, I wrote a word on each sheet—*1st body, 2nd body, blackmail notes, accident, shooting, break-in, water damage, purse, paperweight, Suttonville, Beatrice, Alderman Acres*. Pausing after writing *fake coroner call,* I thought a moment, then added *time.* Collecting the paper and some pushpins, I moved over to a corkboard on one wall above a small bookshelf. I was about to assemble the words, but paused. Anyone walking in would be able to see my notes.

I soon found foam-core board in a wide drawer under the counter near the sink. I exchanged the pushpins for tape, then returned to the drafting table. "This all started when someone put a body where it would be found immediately," I whispered, then taped *1st body* and *2nd body* to the board. "Why put bones taken from a grave in Suttonville in the excavation at Alderman Acres? Does it make a difference where they found the bodies? Or where they placed them?" I taped up *Suttonville.* "Of course, it could be that because of the fence around the town and the mausoleum, those bodies were easy to retrieve, but I suspect there's a connection. And speaking of connections . . ." I grabbed more paper and wrote *Ryan Adams*, then put his name between *Suttonville* and *Alderman Acres*. "The second set of remains had a paperweight. Nobody said one was found with the first body. It could be that someone chose the object simply because it was shiny and would draw attention to the bones before the bulldozer smashed everything to dust, but the apple also appeared in the blackmail notes to Beatrice." After adding *paperweight* to the board along with *blackmail note*s, I placed Beatrice's name in the middle. Next to *paperweight* I attached the printout from the library on apple varieties. I taped *accident, shooting, fake coroner call,* and *time* near Beatrice's name.

I attached the remaining notes having to do with the break-in, my apartment, and my purse in a second grouping.

Beatrice seemed to be connected to most of the incidents, and my brief research into her life left more questions than answers. I couldn't see any relationship between the events of my life and Beatrice other than the accident itself and a vague memory of the paperweight.

I placed the foam-board chart into a flat file and covered it with paper.

Returning to the bedroom, I found my children's books drying into crinkled fans. Maybe if I closed the books and placed a weight on them, they'd flatten. When I lifted the first book, the one with the inscription, I saw the end paper had pulled off the cardboard cover, exposing the edge of something. I took the book into the studio, found a pair of tweezers, and pulled out a strip of black-and-white film negatives. Taking the negatives to the lightbox, I turned it on. I recognized the images immediately. Our last holiday together, Easter 1997, when I was five.

A hollow feeling filled my chest. I remembered when my dad had taken the photos. My folks were marginal Christians, but that year they went all out with a new dress for me, a basket filled with goodies, and we'd attended church. I was so proud of that fluffy pink Easter dress as I sat on the piano bench in our home with my Easter basket on the seat beside me. Dad had arranged the basket, adjusted me slightly, and snapped a photo. He did that a number of times until I became restless.

Why did my parents place negatives into my book? It was almost . . .

A creeping ripple of unease tripped down my spine. *Go ahead. Think it.* For some reason they were hiding them.

Only the first negative was in good shape. The other four had a sepia stain over one side, obliterating most of the images.

The contents of the Easter basket—the Bible and children's books—must have prompted him to write the inscription pointing me to the Good Book for guidance. Could they have somehow known their own lives would be cut short?

I found a magnifying glass and looked more closely. Perhaps there was a golden apple paperweight on the shelves visible behind the piano?

No such luck.

Could they have known this would be our last time together?

Time.

Once again I looked at the inscription at the front of the book.

Our dearest daughter,

Should you ever need any guidance in your life, note the gifts given to you this Easter, 1997.

All our love,

Mommy and Daddy

In 1997 I was five. I knew my parents died after that Easter. But I didn't end up at my aunt's until I was six.

What happened to that year of my life?

My stomach churned. Leaving the negatives on the lightbox, I entered the kitchen and poured a glass of water, leaning against the counter as I drank it.

How did this fit in with anything going on now? Or did it?

Mary wandered from her room, hair and clothes rumpled from her nap. "Good. You're over your temper tantrum." She gave a jaw-cracking yawn. "Wow. I'm still sleepy. I'm going to skip dinner."

I'd forgotten about dinner. I wasn't the least bit hungry. I picked up the phone and got the switchboard. "Could you tell Dr. Brùn that neither Mary nor I will be present for dinner?"

The buzzer on the washing machine announced my clothes were ready for the dryer. I shook my head to clear it of the swirl-ing doubts and disturbing thoughts. Mary followed me to the washer and watched as I transferred my laundry. She picked up a couple of my blouses and looked at them. "Gray? Black? Are you a nun or something? Don't you wear anything colorful?"

I took them from her. "These are obsidian and smoke. That's colorful." I tossed them in the dryer.

She shrugged and moved toward the front door. "You dress like the landscape around here. Drab."

"I like to think of my wardrobe as steady and conservative."

"Fuddy-duddy."

"Conventional."

"Unimaginative."

"Safe." The word slipped out before I could stop it.

Mary gave me a strange look. "Oookay. Do you want to talk about it?"

"No."

FIFTEEN

Dutch trotted up to his room to drop off his coat and take more aspirin. He knew he should feel elated. He'd finally gotten rid of that final stone. He'd faced fire, a burning building. And he'd actually saved someone this time. He could move on, move out, and get on with his life.

He needed to share this with Dr. Brùn. He reached into the drawer of his desk and pulled out a small, dark cherrywood box and placed it on the blotter. He hadn't looked inside the box in more than a year. Now he should be able to look at it without pain. Taking a deep breath, he opened the lid.

The contents blurred in his vision for a moment. He blinked, then reached for the gold and red firefighter's challenge coin resting on top. Originally a military tradition, the challenge coin was a small token of obligation to his fellow firefighters. He held it a moment, then whispered a prayer for his former firefighting partner and best friend. The friend who'd gotten separated from him during that fire in the apartment complex, who raced into that doomed building to find him, who became trapped by a collapsed wall.

The friend who died trying to save him.

Dutch had found another way out. Only later, when he discovered what happened, did his life spiral out of control.

Underneath the coin was the invitation to Clan Firinn, which had saved his life for the second time. After completing the rehab program, he'd been allowed to continue his education, gaining his PhD and staying on to work with new candidates in the program as an adviser. With his advanced degree, he could still support public safety without returning to firefighting.

Clan Firinn, Dr. Brùn, needed to go on, to continue to help others.

Beatrice was the one threatened by the blackmail notes, but the entire program was under fire. He felt this truth in his gut. It was no coincidence that those bodies had been found in a place important to Clan Firinn's success. Someone wanted Dr. Brùn to fail.

The library downstairs was one place he hadn't looked for answers. He grabbed a yellow legal pad and headed out.

He took the main staircase down the two flights of stairs to the foyer of the lodge. A few guests were scattered around the spacious room reading or quietly talking. He crossed to the stairs going down to the basement level, where his lab and the library were located. The motion-activated lights flickered on as he clattered down the metal steps. No lights were on in the library, indicating that he was alone. *Good.*

Some records about Clan Firinn wouldn't be found on any computer search.

The library, on his left at the bottom of the stairs, was separated from the hall by windows. He could easily see the room was empty. The directory of materials resided on the computer located just inside the door. Although the room had a selection of books and magazines, he was after the microfilm—stored in a large set of metal drawers on rolls, like film—and microfiche filed in envelopes in another set of drawers. The microfilm machine could read either format.

He looked up Clan Firinn's history. Most of it seemed to be on microfilm in the form of newspaper articles from the Colfax paper. He searched for Dr. Brùn and Beatrice Greer, found a couple of articles, then pulled the related boxes from the files. The plans for Clan Firinn's buildings, articles of incorporation, business license, and other documents were in the microfiche section. He pulled them from the files and set them aside, wanting to start with the newspapers. On the first reel, he found a brief note that Dr. Brùn purchased 640 acres near the town of LaCrosse.

The next few articles tracked the construction of the buildings, culminating in the ribbon-cutting ceremony a year after construction began. Dr. Brùn held the scissors, but he must have turned his head just as the camera snapped. His face was blurred. Behind him on the steps were a number of people identified as his staff. *Left to right. V. Hansen, N. Smith, P. Duke, B. Green, R. Dalton, F. Laicher, M. Bankus.* One of the people behind Dr. Brùn's shoulder was looking down, but the hat she wore looked familiar. Dutch sent the article to the printer.

The motion-activated lights in the hall went out. He stood and moved to the printer to make sure the library lights wouldn't do the same.

The printout wasn't much more helpful. The woman wore a wide sun hat that resembled one he'd seen Beatrice Greer wear. He counted over the names listed underneath. *B. Green.*

If that was Beatrice, had she married? Divorced? Was Green a newspaper typo? Some of the folks going through the Clan Firinn rehab had so ruined their lives that they changed their names. Dr. Brùn had said Beatrice was the reason for the program, so maybe her name change had to do with what brought her here. But it was a big jump to deduce from a sun hat who was wearing it.

So assume it's Beatrice. The paper only confirmed that Beatrice was involved with Clan Firinn from the beginning.

Whatever brought her to here, Dr. Brùn wasn't going to share that knowledge with Dutch. Maybe it was time to show those notes to both Dr. Brùn and the police.

The lights came on in the hall. Dutch moved to the windows, searching for whoever had activated the lights.

The hall was empty.

A prickly feeling danced between his shoulder blades. *Don't be silly. There's a rational explanation for the lights coming on.* They might be on a timer. Or maybe someone opened a door farther up the hall, spotted him working, and decided to not to disturb him. Or he was being watched.

———

158

The phone rang and I answered. "Samantha Williams."

"Yes, hi, this is Norman Bottoms."

My thoughts were still full of hidden negatives, the missing year of my life, and the fatal fire. I had no idea who Norman Bottoms was until he coughed. The man from the library.

"Yes, Mr. Bottoms. What can I do for you?" I had to concentrate to understand what he was saying.

"I thought about Suttonville all day. I mean, I hadn't thought about it for a long time, but your questions today made me"—he coughed—"made me go over some things." More coughing. "I think you should look at Kyshtym, K-Y-S-H—" *Click*.

The phone went dead. I clicked the switch hook several times but couldn't even get a dial tone.

I hung up, then wrote *Kyshtym* on a pad of paper.

Mary had already gone to her room. I could go into the main lodge and see if one of those phones worked. Peeking out the door, I saw no sign of the dogs.

I'd only used the rear entrance of the lodge, so I trotted in that direction. The sun was setting and the evening was chilly. My teeth were chattering—only partly from the temperature—by the time I reached my destination. Lights gleamed from the lower floor windows. The basement door was unlocked.

Dutch's lab was dark, but the hall and library were brightly lit. Dutch was just sitting down at an oversize machine when he spotted me. He walked over and opened the door. "What a nice surprise. Come on in."

I entered.

"Did you, by any chance, peek in earlier and set off the lights?"

"No. The lights were already on. Why?"

"Nothing. How are you doing?"

I wanted to blurt out my latest discovery, but years of keeping to myself prevailed. "As well as can be expected. Thank you for saving my life."

Dutch looked down and awkwardly patted me on the shoulder.

"I wanted to say that earlier and I don't remember if I did, but I also came over here because the phone in Highland House is out."

Dutch picked up a nearby phone, listened for a moment, then hung up. "Seems all the phones are down."

"Is that normal?"

"It happens. Who did you need to call?"

"A man I met today named Norman Bottoms. He just called because he wanted me to look into something having to do with Suttonville."

"Did he say what?"

"He was spelling out a word when the phone went dead."

"What word?"

"I believe he was spelling out Kyshtym."

"What does it mean?"

"It's an event. The Kyshtym disaster, in the midfifties in the former Soviet Union, was an explosion in a cooling tank holding radioactive materials."

Dutch rubbed his mouth for a moment, then began pacing.

"What's wrong?" I finally asked.

"That's the problem. I don't know what's wrong. I've been trying to put some things together, but I'm not getting very far."

Now it was my turn to want to pace. "Dutch . . ."

He paused and looked at me. I was suddenly aware that we were alone and no one knew we were here. I'd avoided putting myself in this situation ever since . . . I scrambled to put a brick over that memory. On the other hand, I really did need someone to talk to, someone who could look at the puzzle I'd been assembling. "I need to show you something."

"Okay."

"It's in Beatrice's studio."

Without speaking, Dutch left the library and grabbed a jacket from his lab. Once outside, he pointed to the side of Highland House. "You can get into the studio without going through the house."

It was as if he could read my mind. I didn't want to run into Mary nor have Dutch in my bedroom.

Inside the studio, I pulled out the foam board that held my own research.

"Nice job, Samantha."

The heat ran up my neck and onto my face. I turned away and pretended to look for a marker so he couldn't see how much his approval touched me. "I, um, well, the two people who seem to be connected to all that's going on—Beatrice and Ryan—are both dead."

"True. But Ryan's death was a terrible accident." He reached into his pocket and pulled out a folded piece of paper. "I found this in the library." Taking a piece of tape, he placed a printout on the board of an article on Clan Firinn with a photo.

I moved closer to see. "What's important about this?"

He took the marker, his fingers lightly brushing my hand.

I'm in real trouble here. I like Dutch. A lot. And I swore I'd never trust a man again. I stepped away.

If Dutch noticed, he didn't say anything. "This person." He circled someone behind Dr. Brùn. "Might, just might, be Beatrice."

"So? She's lived here a long time."

"Look at the names." He tapped the names listed under the photo.

"B. Green." I looked at him. "I don't understand."

"*If* that's Beatrice, she may have changed her name."

"Or the paper got it wrong. And if she did, I suppose there could be a lot of reasons." I sat in the drafting chair. Dutch leaned against a craft table. "Is there any connection between Beatrice and Suttonville?" I asked.

"Not that I know of. This fellow who called earlier . . ."

"Norman Bottoms."

"Norman. You said you spoke to him in Pasco. What did he say then?"

I closed my eyes and thought about our meeting. "He mentioned the fence they put up. The town was blocked off with a guard to keep people out."

"That makes sense."

"Um, the people working there wore biohazard suits."

Dutch nodded.

"Oh, and the vehicles had no markings on them, like to identify they were the police or sheriff's department."

Dutch straightened. "That part is strange. There should have been a few marked cars. Anything else?"

"He was coughing a lot, poor man. Said he had cancer—"

"What kind of cancer?" Dutch stared at me with an intense gaze.

"I think he said throat. Or thyroid. Why?"

"How old do you think he was?"

I raised my eyebrows. "Maybe in his seventies. What are you thinking?"

Instead of answering, Dutch leaned forward and wrote *Norman, Hanford, Kyshtym,* and *nuclear* on separate sheets of paper, then taped them on the board below *Suttonville.*

The wind outside rattled the windows, followed by the tapping of rain.

"Why did you write *Hanford*?" I asked.

Dutch walked to the window, stared out for a moment, then returned and looked at the board. "I don't know if any of this is connected, but I think I have a place to start looking." He tapped the word *Hanford,* then glanced at his watch. "I need to dig deeper. The phones should be working by morning. I need you to give your friend Norman a call. I'll meet you here tomorrow at ten."

"Is there anything I can do?"

"Find a map of Washington State."

SIXTEEN

Dutch raced through the rain squall to the library. He usually didn't mind the lack of internet access, but tonight he really needed it. He'd find what he could in the microfilm and microfiche records and tomorrow he'd take a trip to find out the rest and see if it all made sense.

When he finally finished his research, it was after three in the morning. Norman's thyroid cancer combined with the biosuits opened a new possibility. His eyelids felt like sandpaper. He'd ended up with more questions than answers, but nothing more could be gleaned from the Clan Firinn library. *Tomorrow.* He glanced at his watch. *Make that later today, I'll try to put it all together.*

After Dutch left I moved to my room. The steady rain lulled me to sleep.

I was alone in a big, echoing house with bare floors. It was dimly lit, even though it was broad daylight outside. I was in my usual hiding place under the piano in the corner of the room. I had my favorite books there, though my father had made me bring them out so he could see what I was reading. He kept them for a couple of days until I asked for them again. He even bought three new Dr. Seuss books for me because he was sorry he forgot.

After I read my new books for the third time, I closed my eyes.

I stood in a field with a small stream. The stream ran through a large culvert, then dropped into a shimmering pool. I wanted to go wading, but the pool turned black and smelled awful. The black water got on my hands and I tried to wipe it off.

I opened my eyes. It was dark, but I could see through a narrow opening. Legs moved in front of the piano, and voices called out, but I didn't know what they were saying.

I tried to sneak out of my hiding place, but everything had changed. The house was full of strangers.

As I tried to get to my room, a big policeman saw me. He reached for me, but I screamed. I screamed again—

I jerked upright, soaked in sweat. The remains of the dream clung to my mind like gauzy cobwebs. For years, the memory of the day my parents died haunted my sleep. It had taken a worse nightmare to erase it.

Going back to sleep would be out of the question. I got up and moved to the kitchen to brew some coffee.

The rain had stopped earlier in the morning, leaving a tepid sunlight to peek through drab clouds. The weather matched my mood. I took my cup of coffee into the living room, where Beatrice's Bible still lay. After praying for my students, their parents, and the new friends I'd made here at Clan Firinn, I opened the Bible to Matthew. "Therefore do not worry about tomorrow, for tomorrow will worry about itself. Each day has enough trouble of its own." I leaned back into the sofa and closed my eyes. *Each day has enough trouble of its own.* "So true, so true."

"What's true?" Mary walked into the room and settled into a chair with her cup of coffee.

"You're up early."

"Restless night. I kept thinking about Ryan. What a horrible way to die."

I nodded.

"So what's true?"

"Matthew chapter 6 verse 34." I read it to her.

"Oh, that. Religious stuff."

"Mary, it's not religion. It's a walk—"

She held up her hand. "Don't. You can't convince me there's a loving God up in the clouds somewhere."

"I'm sorry. My faith gives me comfort when things aren't going right or easy in my life. It's described as a peace that surpasses all understanding."

"Peace? Really? Look around you. Death, war, disease. Where's God in all that?"

"I think God allows us to go through some things in order to help others going through the same—"

"Don't."

I closed the Bible.

She stared at me a moment, then blinked. "I'm sorry. I just have had too rough a life to believe in anything or anyone."

"You believe in your husband, believe enough to go looking for him. And you have a baby on—"

"Don't," she said louder than before, then took a deep breath. "What's with the board in the studio?"

"You were in my studio?" I tried to keep the annoyance out of my voice.

"Cool your jets. I was just looking for you."

"I'm sorry. Like you, I had a bad night."

"I thought you had that peace beyond understanding?"

"That's why I pray."

Mary stiffened. "Apology accepted. The board?"

"I was just trying to put all the pieces together, rather like my own jigsaw puzzle."

"And did you?" She took a sip of coffee.

"No, but Dutch might have."

"Dutch was here last night? Really?" She stared at me over the rim of her cup.

My face warmed. "I got a phone call last night, but the phone went dead, so I walked over to the lodge to return the call and ran into Dutch—"

"You don't need to explain. You're a big girl and entitled to entertain men if you choose."

The warmth turned into a burn. "I . . . I need to get dressed." I got up and headed for my room. *I'm back to being a coward.* I should have told her . . . what? That I'm not interested in Dutch? That would be a lie. I reached my room and shut the door. "What's the matter with me?" *What's the matter is Mary struck a nerve.*

But I'm not ready. I may never be ready.

After taking a shower, I inspected my meager outfits from Pullman. Even after washing, they still smelled faintly of mildew. In the closet I found jeans, a great rope belt, a navy long-sleeved top, and a blue-and-cream cardigan. When I finally found a place to live, I'd take notes on this wardrobe.

Dutch had arrived and was sitting in the living room talking to Mary when I entered. He stood. "You look nice."

"Thank you." I dug my nails into my palm to distract me from blushing. "I was about to make breakfast. May I make some for you?"

"Actually, I'm here to talk to you about . . ." He glanced at Mary.

"Don't worry. If it's about my chart, she's already seen it."

He pulled up a chair and placed a file folder on his lap. "I did some digging last night. It was when you mentioned the fellow who called you had thyroid cancer that something clicked in my mind. I just need to talk to Norman to ask him a few questions."

"Let me get his card."

"While you're at it, did you find a map of Washington State?"

"I have one in my car." Mary stood and left to retrieve it.

I returned first with Norman's card and the foam-board chart. "Would you like some coffee?"

"Please." He followed me into the kitchen. "Samantha, once you find another apartment and get settled, I was wondering if I—"

Mary trotted into the room. "Here's your map."

"Thanks." Dutch took it and moved to the dining room table, which, for once, wasn't covered with Mary's clutter.

I wanted to ask him what he was about to say, but the moment had passed. I dialed Norman's number. After he answered, I reminded him of who I was, then said, "I have someone here who wants to ask you a few questions."

Dutch took the handset from me. "Hi, Norman, this is Dr. Van Seters. Samantha mentioned to me you had thyroid cancer. I was wondering if—" He listened for a moment. "I see. Yes, I've heard of it. Where did you grow up?" He listened for a minute. "Yes. Thank you so much for the information. If I learn anything new, of course I'll share with you. Goodbye." He hung up. "Why don't you both sit down."

Mary and I both sat at the table on either side of Dutch.

He placed the file folder on the table, then spread out the map. "This is just speculation, but it might also tie some things together. When you mentioned Norman has thyroid cancer, Samantha, and he told you about the biohazard unit in unmarked vehicles in Suttonville, I had a theory." Under where he'd written Norman's name, he wrote *Green Run*. "There are several reasons for someone to develop thyroid cancer. Certain inherited genetic predispositions, being female, and exposure to high levels of radiation." Dutch shifted his sling and winced.

I'd almost forgotten his broken arm. It must have been bothering him this morning. "Can I bring you an aspirin?"

"Thank you. I'll be fine." He circled a city on the map. "Norman was born in the 1940s and raised here in Kennewick, part of the tri-cities of Richland, Pasco, and Kennewick."

Mary rolled her eyes. "You cling to as much useless information as Sam does."

"Maybe. But for now, we'll have a little history lesson." Dutch glanced at both of us. "Part of my research from last night. In World War II, the United States created the Manhattan Project, a highly secret effort to end the war. The physicists who invented the nuclear bomb were in Los Alamos, New Mexico, but the largest plutonium production work was done here." He circled an area south and west of Clan Firinn along the Columbia River. "Hanford, Washington."

Cold fingers of fear tripped up my spine. "I knew that, but I guess I never really thought about it," I said slowly. Hanford and Kennewick were less than thirty miles apart.

"The Hanford Nuclear Reservation created more than half the plutonium used for the United States' arsenal." He opened the file and shuffled his notes for a moment. "In 1949, the United States was at the front end of the Cold War. The Soviet Union detonated their first atomic bomb in August of that year. That sent the US into a tailspin to keep up, and the best place to work out possible weapons was Hanford. Also, because of the site's remote location, Hanford was a perfect place to experiment with radiation."

Mary's lips were tightly pressed into a line. I made a point to relax my hands, currently gripping the edge of the table with a white-knuckled clasp.

"Over the next several decades, Hanford's radiation fallout found its way into the air, water, and soil, with the largest intentional release in 1949, known as the Green Run. The idea was to test equipment that could track the radioactive plume so the US could monitor similar Soviet activity. The public downwind of the plume was not warned, nor evacuated. The highest levels of iodine-131, almost one thousand times higher than the acceptable limit, were found on vegetation samples taken from Kennewick."

My mouth had dried. I got up and went to the refrigerator for some bottled water. I held up the bottle to see if anyone else wanted one. Mary nodded. I brought two waters to the table.

Once I was seated again, Dutch continued. "Green Run released several hundred times more radioactive iodine than the 1979 Three Mile Island accident. Three Mile Island, ironically, is listed as the most significant accident in US commercial nuclear power plant history. Green Run doesn't even appear on the list."

"Because it wasn't an accident," I said quietly.

"Right. The radioactive materials settled on the pastures and ground in a two-hundred-mile radius where cattle were grazing. It passed into the milk as well as food supply. The children living downwind were the most affected."

"Norman," I said.

Dutch nodded and looked at a page of written notes. "In 1986, the Department of Energy released nineteen thousand pages of carefully redacted documents relating to Hanford. That's when the information about Green Run became public."

"I'm guessing that not everything became public," Mary said.

"Good guess." Dutch made a mark on the map. "Which brings us to Suttonville, less than fifty miles from Hanford." Dutch placed three printed images in front of us, all of people in white coveralls, hoods, and masks. "Can you tell which photo is from Hanford and which are from other biohazard events?"

"All the suits look very similar. No, I couldn't tell you. So you think that those people that Norman saw cleaning up Suttonville may have been workers from Hanford?" I asked.

"Not necessarily," Dutch said. "Contractors have always worked on the Hanford Site and could have been hired for this. The contracted companies are almost a who's who of American businesses. General Electric, DuPont, ARCO, Westinghouse— rumor had it Hanford subcontracted practically everything."

"Do you think Hanford was somehow responsible for the deaths at Suttonville?" I finally asked.

"Another Green Run situation?" Dutch shook his head. "All but one reactor was shut down between 1964 and 1971. N Reactor was shut down in January of 1987, fully ten months before the incident at Suttonville. It couldn't have released any contaminated fallout."

"How does all this fit in with Beatrice's blackmail notes, death, or Clan Firinn, or . . . or . . ." Mary shrugged.

We were silent for a few minutes, each studying the board. I touched each mounted image, trying to find something new. When I came to the apple varieties, printed in alphabetical order,

I scanned the list. My gaze stopped partway down the first page. "Well . . ." They both looked at me. "This may be a connection. The apple paperweight in the blackmail notes is similar to the one discovered at Alderman Acres buried with human remains from Suttonville."

"Yes, but—" Dutch began.

I pointed to the taped list of apples. "Alderman is the name of a member of city government, but it's also a type of apple imported from Scotland. A gold-colored apple."

SEVENTEEN

We sat in silence after my statement. "Who . . ." I cleared my throat, then took a swallow of water. "Who named the new construction site?"

"I don't remember," Dutch said.

Someone knocked at the front door.

I gasped, then jumped to my feet.

"Would you get that, Sam?" Mary stood and patted her stomach. "Someone's pushing on my bladder. I need to go powder my nose, in a manner of speaking."

I walked to the front door and opened it.

A Whitman County sheriff's deputy wearing a badge with a black mourning band greeted me. "Samantha Williams and Dr. Van Seters?" His gaze went over my shoulder.

"Yes."

"Dr. Van Seters here," Dutch walked up next to me.

"I'm here to get your signed statements about Deputy Ryan Adams. I also have this for you." He held out my wallet.

"I can't believe it showed up. Thank you!"

"What is it, Sam?" Dutch asked.

"My wallet." I looked inside. No driver's license, but my cash and credit cards were inside. "Where did you find it?"

"At the Rose Cottage. The owner found it and called because she didn't know how to reach you. I had to come over here to get your statement, so I picked it up. May I come in?"

"Of course, excuse me. Come in."

Dutch shook hands with the deputy, then picked up the foam board. "I'll put this in the studio."

By the time Dutch returned, I'd given the officer all that I knew. Dutch added his portion.

I wanted to ask the officer about Ryan, but his drawn and pale face kept me silent. I finally murmured my condolences.

He nodded. "Good man." He checked his watch. "I have to get going. I still need to talk to a couple more people." He left, followed by Dutch.

I looked at my tattered wallet. For the first time since Dutch's SUV crashed into the school, I felt I had a tiny part of my life back. With my credit card, I could now order a replacement driver's license. I could go shopping. I could get a hotel room. Leave here. Move to another town. Another state. Forget Suttonville, golden apples, bodies, Ryan's death, Beatrice's blackmail notes. Hidden negatives. Missing year.

Forget my students, my children. Forget Dutch.

The back of my throat burned.

Mary came into the room. "Were you making breakfast? I'm starving."

I shook off my spiraling thoughts. "Sure. What do you want?"

"How's your french toast?"

"I'll tell you after I check out our supplies. You were gone a long time. You okay?"

Mary poured another cup of coffee. "This will sound morbid I guess, but I used that phone to call the news station to find out if any John Does showed up over the past two days."

"You're right. That's morbid. Mary, maybe you should rethink this whole thing, just wait for news."

"Funny you should say that. I'd already pretty much decided to do just that, but they recovered a body in Lake Chelan."

"And you're going up there."

"I have to . . . but this will be the last." She lowered herself to a chair. "Do you want to come along?"

I placed a loaf of french bread on the counter, then took milk and eggs out of the refrigerator. "I really need to start looking for a place to live. And a car. And a replacement license. Maybe you could drop me somewhere so I can access the internet and look at listings. I should also pick up my mail and figure out a forwarding address."

"If you'd like," Mary said slowly.

"Actually, never mind." I mixed the eggs, milk, and a splash of vanilla together in a bowl. "I think I can get Leroy to take me. That is, if Dutch doesn't need a driver. That way I won't slow you down."

She smiled. "Perfect."

After breakfast, Mary offered to clean off the table while I called the main lodge to find Dutch. He came to the phone shortly. "I'd like to have Leroy drive me to Pullman to try and locate a new apartment and so on, but if you need transportation . . . ?"

"That's a great idea. Would you mind if I went with you? I need to pick up a few things. We can get it all done in one trip."

"Sounds good."

"I'll call him and set it up."

I barely had time to wash the dishes and make a list before Leroy arrived. He was driving his red Ford Taurus, recently washed. He grinned at my expression. "Not bad, right?" he said. "Not only do you have your own personal driver, but we'll be in a clean car."

"Very nice. Dutch has asked to go along. Is that okay?"

Leroy's brows drew together for a moment, then he smiled. "Why not? Is Mary coming too?"

"She's heading up north for a bit. Let me let Dutch know you're here." I returned to the house and picked up the phone. "Hi. Could you tell Dutch that Leroy's here?"

Mary followed me outside. "I guess we'll meet again later." She strolled toward the garage.

"Mary?"

She turned.

"You'll call me if there's anything . . . You know."

"I know. I will." She waved.

"Where to?" Leroy asked.

I pulled out the list I'd made. "I think I need to get to a library and find a computer, then find a phone—"

"Whoa. Wait," Leroy said. "You need to come into the modern

age. You need a smartphone so you can do your own internet surfing and calling."

"I guess. I've never owned one."

Leroy took a step back. "You're kidding. I've never met anyone who doesn't own a cell."

"Expand your horizons. We're out there."

Dutch joined us. "Ready?"

I insisted Dutch ride in the front with more leg room. I knew the route well as I'd driven it several times a week to go to work. We were silent for the first few miles before I asked, "Dutch, do you think your boss, Dr. Brùn, is behind any of this?"

He turned in his seat. "I've never known him to be anything other than generous, caring, and kind. To think he'd do anything like what we're finding is beyond belief."

"What about someone close to him?" I asked.

"Like Scotty?" Dutch chewed his lip for a moment. "I understand their friendship goes way back. He's retired from the air force and head of security. He's loyal, trustworthy, and totally devoted to both Clan Firinn and Dr. Brùn."

"Why?" Leroy asked. "Did the doc save him or something? Was he one of the inmates?"

"Guests," Dutch said automatically. "I don't know."

"So you don't know the background of either Beatrice or Scotty?" Leroy asked.

"I did find out she funded an educational foundation, so she must have had money." Dutch shook his head. "Here's the thing. I just feel that the blackmail—"

Leroy jerked the wheel and the car swerved before he got it

back under control. "Blackmail? Now there's blackmail in addition to Beatrice's death? Anything else you want to tell me?"

I narrowed my eyes at Dutch and shook my head.

"Sorry, Sam." Dutch twisted his lips. "Cat out of the bag."

"Bound to happen." I took a deep breath. "I keep thinking the problem we have is like a big jigsaw puzzle. Each piece has a shape, pattern, and color that fits with the whole, but we could be dealing with a couple of puzzles mixed together, and we don't have a clear picture on the box to show what the end results should look like."

"Then we should look at anyone involved," Dutch said. "Maybe we can at least eliminate suspects."

"What about your friend, Mary?" Leroy asked. "She's been hanging around all this time."

I watched the scenery for a few moments. We'd slowed to a crawl behind a green-and-gold John Deere tractor. "I've thought of her. I really don't know much about her, but she doesn't seem to have any connection to Clan Firinn, Alderman Acres, or Beatrice. She couldn't have stolen my purse, then driven over to Pullman to sabotage my apartment and still make it to the Airbnb for dinner. Nor, as far as I can see, does she seem to benefit from any of the actions. And she's pregnant."

The tractor pulled over far enough to allow us to pass him.

"If Ryan was involved, he's out of the picture now." Leroy shot a quick glance at me through the rearview mirror. "Sorry, Sam. Didn't mean to be so blunt."

I gave a half shrug. "We also have whoever is driving that black SUV and seemingly following us."

"Black SUV and dark suits. Sounds like the government. FBI," Leroy said. "The feds always drive black SUVs on television."

"If the government was interested in keeping what really happened at Suttonville out of the news and off people's radar," Dutch said, "they'd do things such as install cameras and check out anyone snooping around."

No one spoke as the significance of his statement sank in. Leroy's gaze darted to the rearview mirror, then the side mirror. "I don't see anyone following us right now."

"They've probably already installed a tracking device on this car," Dutch said with a straight face, then winked at me.

Leroy put on the brakes and pulled onto the shoulder of the road.

"What are you doing?" I asked.

"Checking." Leroy put the car into Park.

"I was just kidding, Leroy." Dutch reached out to keep the other man from getting out of the car.

Leroy shook off Dutch's hand. "I know about these things." He turned off the engine. "The Illuminati. New World Order. I should have seen it as soon as we went to Suttonville. That was their practice. And now we're next." He got out of the car and slammed the door.

"Do you have any idea what he's talking about?" I asked Dutch.

"I suspect he's been reading something other than Dr. Seuss."

"And he said *our* conversation about *The Wizard of Oz* was stupid."

Dutch got out and walked over to where Leroy was now

inspecting the front end of the car. The two spoke for a few moments, then Dutch came to my side of the car and opened the door. "It would appear that I've opened the proverbial can of worms," he said quietly. "If you'd get out and help us check the car for tracking devices or bugs, we'll get to Pullman that much faster."

"Do I need tinfoil to make a hat?"

"Maybe."

I stepped out and made a show of examining the nearest wheel well. The tractor caught up with us, slowed, then pulled over. Leaving his tractor running, the driver got out. "Need help, folks? Car trouble?"

I groaned inwardly. Now I needed a paper bag to put over my head.

Dutch walked over to the man and spoke for a moment. The driver nodded, returned to his tractor, and drove away.

Dutch got into the car. I joined him. After one final look under the chassis, Leroy got in and started the engine.

Leroy and Dutch talked about college sports for the rest of the journey. Pullman was home to Washington State's second largest university, dubbed Wazzu by locals, and nestled between the Palouse hills. Less than nine miles away was Moscow, Idaho, home of the University of Idaho.

I wasn't a sports fan, and their conversation about the relative merits of Pac-12 compared to Big Sky Conferences was easy to tune out. At least Leroy seemed to move beyond his bizarre conspiracy theories. His intensity left me uneasy.

Once in Pullman, I was able to set up a post office box and

pick up my mail without running into my former landlord. We headed to a mall outside of Moscow to buy a phone for me. I convinced the two men to leave me at a coffee shop while Leroy ran Dutch around town.

I had to admit having internet access at my fingertips was a welcome change. With Leroy's quirks, I decided to take a quick look at his background. He was the one to find the bodies and the paperweight and currently was staying at Alderman Acres in his trailer.

Next I turned to Miller Construction, the company employed to develop Alderman Acres, and immediately hit pay dirt. Leroy Miller was the only son of the owner of the company, but the article I found in the Spokane Paper was about Leroy's father.

Spokane Man Dies in Fiery Accident

Jack Miller, owner of Miller Construction, died yesterday in a one-car accident on Highway 195 near Colfax. Miller built a contracting empire but was recently in the news in a breach-of-contract suit involving alleged illegal labor practices. The company filed a Chapter 11 bankruptcy in July.

Miller's obituary added a few more details.

MILLER, Jack L. Jack L. Miller died in a car accident on September 29, 2014. He was born February 15, 1957, in Spokane, the only child of Leroy and Ruth (King) Miller. He attended grade schools in the Pacific

Northwest, graduated from high school in Spokane and attended . . .

The article went on to note he'd completed his master's degree in chemical engineering at Stanford and had been married four times. Leroy was his only offspring. What was most interesting was the gap between his graduation from Stanford in 1980 and starting Miller Construction four years later. The obit listed no job history until he started his company.

It seemed strange to me that Dr. Brùn would hire Miller Construction to work on his development. I suspected Dutch would simply say that was in keeping with his opinion of the man as being generous, caring, and kind. A collector of lost souls in need of a second chance.

Like me.

The thought leaped into my mind and I shook my head to shove it aside. I didn't need a second chance.

A half hour and a latte later, I'd identified a few possibilities for an apartment and some promising used cars. My job search was less successful. For at least the next year until my teaching position reopened, unless I wanted to be a waitress, clean houses, or sell something, job options were a bit limited. I'd done all three in the past, but a master's degree in fine art should at least bring more than a minimum wage.

The overcast day gave way to rain, fitting my mood. "What would Kipling say? Something about paint tubes? *When . . . painted . . . ?*"

"What is making you so pensive?" Dutch pulled out a chair

on one side of me while Leroy sat across from me. "Wait. Don't tell me. A Dr. Seuss quote," Dutch said.

"Actually, Kipling. Um . . . when, when . . . oh yeah. 'When Earth's last picture is painted, and the tubes are twisted and dried, when the oldest colours have faded, and the youngest critic has died, we shall rest, and, faith, we shall need it—lie down for an æon or two, till the Master of All Good Workmen shall set us to work anew!'"

"Very nice."

I dropped my gaze to my spoon and stared at it as if it were the Cheshire cat and would soon disappear from sight.

"Did you get 'er done?" Leroy asked.

I looked up and frowned. "Excuse me?"

"Accomplish what you needed to do?" Dutch asked.

"Oh, yes, well, as much as I can do for now."

"Dutch and I thought we'd chow down here in Pullman before heading back. Okay with you?" Leroy asked.

"Sure."

Halfway through dinner, Dutch's phone rang. "Dr. Van Seters. Oh, hi, Mary. Yes, she's right here." He handed me the phone.

Mary sounded a bit breathless. "I'm sorry to bother you. I won't be back tonight. I'm running into the same foot-dragging here, but I'm persistent. I'll probably be back tomorrow. Either way, I'll call."

"I have my own phone now. Call me direct." I gave her the number, disconnected, and handed the phone back to Dutch. "Mary's . . . detained for the night."

"What's wrong?" Leroy leaned forward. "No, wait. Don't tell me. Female things, right?"

"Mmmm. Female things. Right." I ducked my head so he couldn't see my grin.

By the time we'd finished dinner and started back to Clan Firinn, the rain had settled into a steady drumming and night had arrived.

I was sleepy and content to lean back and listen to the drone of the men's voices.

Headlights blasting into the car shook me from my rest.

"Oh boy, someone's in a hurry." Leroy adjusted his rearview mirror to shield his eyes.

The headlights grew closer. Closer. The driver hit his brights.

I gasped and grabbed the armrest.

Leroy floored the accelerator. We gained a little before the driver caught up and slammed into us.

We spun. My head smashed into the window. I bit my lip and tasted blood.

Leroy twisted the wheel, trying to get control of the car on the slick pavement.

I caught a glimpse of our tormentor before he raced ahead. A black SUV. His headlights disappeared around a corner.

"Did you see that?" Leroy asked.

"Black SUV," Dutch said. "Are you okay, Sam?"

"Yes, but we have to get off this road!" I didn't seem to have enough air to get the words out. "He could be waiting up ahead to try and T-bone us."

"No cell service." Dutch held up his phone.

I looked around, trying to figure out where we were. The rain streamed down the windows and the night was inky black. "Have you passed Highway 127 yet?"

"We just passed it." Leroy slammed on the brakes, put the car into Reverse, then spun the wheel, turning the car around. He shifted gears and shot forward.

I turned to watch for headlights.

We drove a short distance before coming to a few buildings. He turned right, barely slowing down. "Do you know where this goes?"

"Yes. A few turns and we'll end up on Highway 26 on the other side of LaCrosse."

"Why do you think the guys in the black SUV are suddenly, violently after us?" Dutch asked.

"Maybe we're getting too close to discovering . . . something." Just as I thought we'd gotten away, headlights appeared. "Please don't let this—"

The bright beams came on and grew closer.

Leroy let out a string of curses.

The SUV caught up with us and slammed into the car.

I screamed.

We lurched forward. Leroy fought to maintain control.

The driver backed away, then smashed into us again.

Our car jerked, reeled to the side, then straightened.

Once again the SUV slowed.

I braced for the next onslaught. *Please, Lord.*

Leroy twisted the wheel to the right. We slid on the pavement, hurtled against a guardrail, scraped against it, then charged up a small road, gaining speed.

The headlights disappeared.

Dutch leaned slightly forward. "Where does this—"

A white gate appeared, blocking the road.

I clapped my hand over my mouth, muffling another scream.

The inside of the car lit up as the bright beams lanced into the cab.

Leroy accelerated, jerked his car to the left, and flew off the pavement before running into a fence. One headlight must have been broken. We seemed to be in an overgrown field. We smashed into sagebrush and piles of tumbleweed. The windshield wipers couldn't keep up with the deluge of rain. We hit invisible potholes, sending neck-cracking jolts through our bodies. Only our seat belts kept us from smashing against the ceiling. A grove of trees now blocked us. Leroy swung around them, lighting up more trees. A park bench flashed by.

I knew where we were. Central Ferry State Park. Closed for many years.

The SUV grew closer. Closer.

"Leroy—"

The rear window shattered. Glass covered me. The rain flew in.

"Get down!" Dutch screamed. "He's shooting—"

"Leroy, stop! We're in—"

Too late. We were airborne. Straight into the Snake River.

EIGHTEEN

We hit the river's surface with a spine-snapping jolt.

Frigid water began pouring into the car.

"Where are we? What's this?" Leroy's voice was shrill.

"Snake River." I unsnapped my seat belt. "Dutch?"

Dutch's head rested against the window next to him.

"Dutch?" I shook his shoulder.

"I can't swim!" Leroy screeched.

"Help me get Dutch out." I touched the side of his head. My hand came way wet. He must have been knocked out when we hit. "Leroy, calm down. I'll help you, but we have to get Dutch out."

"Get him out yourself! I might die! Didn't you hear me? I can't swim."

"Leroy," I made my voice as calm as I could. The icy water rushed over my feet. "Listen to my voice, Leroy. The water isn't deep here. Only a foot or two. You can just step out and walk to shore. We're about six feet lower than the park. Behind us is a small beach. You can walk to the beach, then climb up. We're fine." *Assuming the current doesn't move the car into deeper water.*

"I'm getting out—"

Craaaaack! A bullet pinged the trunk of the car.

Adrenaline flooded my system. I ducked. "Turn off the headlights!" He plunged us into darkness. I risked a peek over the seat.

A set of headlights aimed down at us at the edge of the river.

Craaaaack! Another bullet hit the trunk. The car slid forward and gently bounced as the current shoved us farther into the river.

"Leroy, the water is still less than waist deep. We just have to figure out how to keep from getting shot while we get to shore. I don't think—"

Thump. Thump. The front end shifted right.

"I'm getting out of here!" Before I could stop him, Leroy twisted the wheel and stepped on the gas.

The spinning rear wheels disengaged us from the river bottom. We floated forward. Leroy started cussing without taking his foot off the gas. "No! No! No!"

Craaaaack! This bullet hit the side of the car.

Another quick peek. The headlights were receding as we moved downriver.

"The water's getting deeper!" Leroy's voice blasted within the confined space of the cab.

"Stop the engine, Leroy. You're forcing us into the center of the river."

Leroy continued his cursing in a lower voice and turned off the engine. "What do we do now? I don't want to die!"

"We're not going to die, but you have to calm down. Unsnap your seat belt, then unsnap Dutch's belt."

Leroy's panicked breathing almost covered the *click* of his belt, then Dutch's. "Now what? It's getting deeper!"

The frigid water lapped up my legs. "We're still not in really deep water." *I hope.* "We'll make you a life preserver, but you have to do as I say."

Only his rapid breathing answered me.

"Slip off your jeans. Tie the cuffs together tightly to trap air. Zip up your fly." I kept my voice soothing and low. I did the same with my jeans. The arctic water on my bare legs sent my teeth chattering. "Now open the waist over your shoulder and scoop air, then drive the waist opening into the water to trap the air. Hold the waist closed underwater with one hand and put your head between the pant legs."

The slap of denim hitting the water let me know he was following directions. My jeans had a rope belt. If I could tie that belt underwater to Dutch's belt, it might be enough to keep him afloat. I snapped my jeans, inflating them, then pulled the waist underwater and tied the rope with rapidly numbing fingers. I just needed to get the pants around Dutch. "Leroy, I need you to—"

The front of the car started to tilt downward.

Leroy yelled once, then crawled over the seat heading for the shattered rear window, knocking me aside. His leg caught my cheek and I saw dancing stars.

The car tilted farther forward.

I slipped over the seat back into the almost submerged front of the car next to Dutch. With the shock of the cold water, I started hyperventilating and my chest muscles tightened. I forced myself to relax and seek his head in the inky-black cab. I found it and pulled the inflated pants over his head.

The water was to my shoulders and rising fast. *Oh, Lord, please help me. Help me.*

My hands could barely move. I fumbled with tying the rope to his belt. Once. Twice. On the third try, I tied the knot.

Dutch's body lifted, then rose with the water. I guided him toward the rear window, feeling his body as he cleared the car. With the water to my chin, I pushed off the dashboard to follow.

I was stuck.

My sweater had caught on something. I yanked. Nothing.

The car went under.

I twisted and pulled to get loose. I couldn't see. Couldn't breathe. Freezing water covered me. My hands wouldn't work.

I braced against something solid, tugged my arms out of the sleeves, then shoved the sweater down my body and off. I put my hand on the ceiling of the car and pushed away from the dashboard toward the submerged, shattered rear window. The remaining glass scraping against my back let me know I was on my way out.

The current grabbed me. I hoped I was swimming upward. No air. *Please, God, help me.*

I reached the surface and sucked in a huge gasp of air. Blinking rapidly, I tried to see something. Anything. Dutch. Leroy. Land. Only darkness. If I called out, would the driver hear me and shoot again? Possibly spotlight me? *Father Abba. Help me. Please.*

My strength was draining fast with the cold. *Decide on a direction. Swim perpendicular to the current.* But which direction? The river was over half a mile wide here. I wouldn't make it if I swam the wrong way. Hypothermia was a ticking clock.

Turning in the water, I looked for light. I couldn't even see the headlights from the SUV.

Then I spotted it. Up high. Probably a home on top of a bluff. I swam toward the light. What was that light? Headlights? No. I knew I was growing confused. "One-two-three-four-five-seven-eight-ten-nine-five." I sounded drunk.

My arms splashed rather than propelled me forward. I wasn't going to make it. I wasn't—

Something cracked against my knee. Then again. A raw, stabbing pain shot up my leg. *What? Land.* Banging against the rocks. *Get out of the water.*

I grabbed for the slimy boulders, fingers numb. Slipped. Scrabbled for a purchase. The current relentlessly tugged me. I finally found a small slip of land that projected into the river. I crawled out on hands and knees. I knew I had to keep moving, but I wanted to just sleep. *Keep moving. Find that light. Lord, show me that light. Guide me. Help me.* Looking up, I spotted it. *I can make it.* Reaching out, I found a steep incline. I crawled forward. I'd somehow lost my shoes. The thin cotton blouse clung to my wet body. The rocks were sharp, stabbing into my knees.

The ground leveled. I stepped forward and stubbed my toe on something hard. I fell.

Liquid fire shot up my foot, hands, and knees. I couldn't stop the muted scream.

Did he hear me? Would I be spotlighted by headlights and shot like an animal? I tried to calculate how far downriver we'd drifted, but my brain wasn't working right. The only light I saw was ahead on top of a hill. Single light. Not headlights.

Reaching out, I touched my throbbing foot. I could have broken a toe. Maybe all my toes. My hands and knees burned from the abrading rocks. Curling up, I wrapped my arms around my legs and cried. *This is too hard. Give up and die.*

"'*The Lord is my light and my salvation; Whom shall I fear?*'" My aunt's voice came clearly into my head. "'*The Lord is the strength of my life; Of whom shall I be afraid?*'"

I stopped crying. "Scaredy-cat." I would have continued with names, but I couldn't think of any more. Taking a deep breath, I reached over and felt a board under my hip. Behind me was a thick metal bar. *This means something.* I forced my brain to concentrate. Not a bar, a rail. Railroad tracks. I'd tripped over the first rail.

Now what? Stay on the tracks and head toward Central Ferry State Park? The shooter could still be there. Head for the light? I sounded like the woman in *Poltergeist*. "Carol Anne, go into the light." I whispered, then huffed. "I'm losing it. Lord, help me."

I listened. The river splashed to my right. On my left, more rushing water, like a small stream. And panting. Growing louder.

NINETEEN

I couldn't run. I'd just fall or end up in the river. Ebony blackness surrounded me.

The panting got closer.

Maybe I could throw rocks at it . . . whatever "it" was. *Do bears pant? Cougars? Wolves probably do.* I could scream. Startle the creature.

Let the shooter know where I was.

I'd have to fight. But if it was a bear, I should play dead.

The panting now had a slight whine in it. Anticipation of a good meal?

The panting stopped. Now the soft *crunch* of footsteps came from behind me.

My heart hammered in my head. I tried to reach for a rock, but I couldn't move.

The creature was right behind me, its hot breath on my back. It sniffed, then circled me.

I remained still, arms around my legs.

The beast suddenly thrust its head under my arm, lifted it up, and licked me on the face.

I found my arms around his massive shoulders. It had long, soft fur. Warm fur. I knew it was a dog, but I had no fear. I soaked in the warmth of his body.

He waited a moment, then lay beside me. I don't know how long we stayed there, but the dog finally stood, lifting me up with him. He was huge, his head level with my waist. He wore a collar and I grabbed on.

The ground trembled under my feet. Or were my legs shaking?

The dog moved forward, pulling me along. I limped and stumbled. "Not so fast."

The shaking increased, now with a low rumble. In the distance, a light appeared.

Railroad tracks. Train.

The dog's speed increased. I stumbled.

The train was coming straight at us. The headlight lit up the tracks in front of me. The land on either side of the tracks disappeared.

The conductor must have spotted us. An ear-piercing warning horn blasted several times.

I grabbed the dog's collar with both hands just as he leaped off the tracks, pulling me with him. We landed on hard-packed earth. I let go and rolled down a slight incline.

The train thundered past.

I covered my head to block some of the sound. The ground rumbled under me. The train seemed to go on forever before it finally passed.

The dog again found me and nudged me to my feet. My legs were cooked pasta. I just wanted to go to sleep. Instead, I again grabbed the dog's collar with both hands and leaned on him. We started to climb. The ground was packed earth, like a game trail. The light above appeared and the dog moved toward it. We climbed. I pushed one leg in front of the other. *Just one more step. One more. One more.*

The ground leveled and I sank down. I couldn't move. Everything hurt. Or was cold. I would have to die here. So close to the light.

The light blinded me. Then spoke. "Oh, mercy, child!" Hands tugged on my arm.

"Laymaslaeep," I muttered.

"Child, you have to get up. I can't lift you."

Now the dog got involved. He stuck his head under my armpit and shoved me.

"Ggooway." Didn't they get it? I needed to be left alone.

"Okay, Fonzie, you push and I'll pull," a woman's voice said.

Fonzie? I'd dropped into a *Happy Days* rerun?

The dog shoved again as the hands tugged on my arm. I staggered to my feet, my arm wrapped around the woman's shoulder while she supported my waist. We moved forward, our path lit by her flashlight. We came to some stairs.

"Lift your foot, girl. Higher. A bit higher. Now up." We repeated that three times before she opened a door. Inside it was warm. I wanted to sit down, but she held me upright. "You have to get out of those wet things. Stand here."

I swayed, blinked, and looked around. I was in a living room softly lit by several lamps. The dog, a large, black beast with hair over his eyes, sat beside me so I could hang on to him.

The woman returned with a comforter and other items and placed them on the nearest chair. She then unbuttoned my blouse and bra, then pulled off my wet panties, leaving me in my all-together birthday suit. "Now put your hands up."

If she's thinking about robbing me naked . . . I giggled and put my hands in the air.

She pulled a flannel nightgown over my head. "I'm glad your sense of humor is intact. Now lie down on the couch."

I lay down.

She covered me in the soft down comforter, which she tucked around my legs, then disappeared. *Maybe I died back in the Snake River and this is heaven.*

Fonzie sat in front of me, apparently making sure I wasn't going to wander off to get lost or hit by a train.

I drifted off. A gentle shake on the shoulder woke me.

"Drink this." She helped me up, handed me a mug of hot, sweet herbal tea, then placed a fleece-covered hot-water bottle at my feet.

She waited until I'd finished the tea and nodded with satisfaction when I handed her the empty cup. "Before I call the sheriff to report an almost-naked woman just showed up at my door, I'm hoping you can enlighten me as to how you got here."

"A black SUV chased us into the river at Central Ferry State Park. Please don't mention me. But Dutch and Leroy . . ."

She sat in a chair across from me. "Are they still in the car?"

"No."

"Okay, but why shouldn't I mention you? Are you in some kind of trouble?"

"Probably, but not what you think." I sighed. "It's a long story."

"I'll call the sheriff about your two friends."

"Be careful. Maybe just say you heard a crash and people shouting."

"If you say so. I'm Janet, by the way."

"Samantha Williams. Everyone calls me Sam."

"Well, Sam, I'll make that call, you get some sleep, and we'll talk in the morning." She stood, took my cup, and patted Fonzie on the head. "Keep an eye on her for me."

I don't remember her leaving the room.

The smell of bacon and coffee lured me from sleep. When I opened my eyes, nothing looked familiar.

My stomach tightened. I shot upward.

A big black dog leaped to his feet and barked.

Fonzie. The train. River. Cold. I was at . . . Janet . . . That was her name. Janet's house.

Janet came into the living room with a mug. Now that I could clearly see her, she looked pleasant enough. She was tall and lean, with a remarkably unlined face and long gray hair braided and coiled on the back of her head. "Here, drink some coffee, then come have some breakfast. No word of your friends." After placing the mug next to me, she left.

The coffee tasted good. Standing proved to be more problematic. My big toe sported a split covered in crusted blood, my knees were scraped, and my hip surely had the grandaddy of all bruises. I hobbled to the kitchen table. Fonzie followed me and sprawled across the floor like a giant bear rug.

"Is Fonzie a big schnauzer?"

Janet set a plate of scrambled eggs, bacon, toast, and a slice of orange in front of me. "Isn't he beautiful? He's a Black Russian Terrier."

"I've never heard of them."

"They're fairly rare. They have Giant Schnauzer, Airedale, Rottweiler, and Newfoundland behind them."

"He looks like an . . . oversize plush toy."

"A plush toy bred to be a guard dog for the Russian army."

Fonzie let out a long, grunting sigh.

I closed my eyes. *Thank you, Lord, and bless this kind soul.*

When I opened them, Janet sat in front of me with her own cup of coffee. She didn't speak as I scarfed up every bite of breakfast.

"You've had a good night's sleep and eaten a big breakfast." Janet added some cream to her coffee. "It's time to enlighten me on how you ended up frozen and half naked in the middle of the night and in the middle of nowhere."

"I suppose that doesn't happen every day. I do owe you an explanation. And a huge amount of gratitude." I thought about it for a few moments. *Where to start?* Does she need to know about the bodies, Suttonville, blackmail, and apple paperweights? I finally decided to keep to the most recent events. I told her the details about our car being driven off the road and shot at—Leroy and Dutch, the black SUV, the river. "I don't know who's driving the SUV, but if they're from the government, or—"

"The government? So you believe some kind of conspiracy is going on?" She lowered her head, then looked at me with raised eyebrows.

"Right now I don't know what to think, except Dutch is gone." My vision blurred and a lump grew in my throat. How could he have survived being in that water for any length of time?

"Just so I understand. Dutch is your husband? Boyfriend?"

"No. I . . . I just . . . he was kind to me. He was unconscious, and in that cold river . . ."

"You did all that you could. That cold water may have revived him. Do you want me to call—"

"No!"

She straightened.

"I mean, no thank you. Right now no one but you knows I'm alive." *And no one would care except whoever wants me dead.* I shoved the unwelcome thought down. "I have to somehow unravel what's been going on. If everyone thinks I drowned, or just disappeared, they'll forget about me and—"

"Oh, Sam, people won't forget about you. Your family, friends . . ."

I shook my head. "No one would miss me, Janet."

"What about your child?"

TWENTY

The room twirled around me. My heart raced. I couldn't move. I tried to speak. "How . . . how . . ."

"Last night, when I got you out of your wet clothes, I saw you have stretch marks and an old C-section scar. That's why I asked if Dutch was your husband or boyfriend."

The last walls around my carefully guarded life crumbled. I clenched my hands together to keep them from shaking.

"You can't convince me your child wouldn't miss you. Children need their mothers."

"She . . . doesn't know. She has a mother. I put her up for adoption." My breakfast threatened to come up.

"What about her father?"

I gulped air. I knew someday, somehow, someone would find out and ask me about it. I'd never confided in anyone. I looked into her kind face.

"You're safe here, Samantha."

Maybe it's time. I nodded slowly. "My parents died when I was five. Or I think they did. I'm still sorting things out. I was sent to live with an aunt, my mother's sister, and her husband." I sucked in more air. "I'd been living there nine years when Aunt Shirley had a massive heart attack. She died. I was devastated. Her husband left the funeral arrangements to me . . ." I looked down at my clasped hands. "That night, the night of her funeral, he came into my bedroom." I took a deep breath, then let it out slowly. "I ran away that night. I stole his truck and drove it to Spokane, then walked away, leaving the keys in it. I never looked back."

Janet stared out the window, her finger absently running around the rim of her coffee cup. "You were fifteen."

That didn't seem to need any response from me.

"What happened after you reached Spokane?"

"I found a women's shelter and began looking for work. I didn't know I was pregnant yet. I'd been there about two weeks when I met Mrs. Gimble. She was posting a position on the bulletin board, looking for a house-sitter. I told her my aunt had just died and I was looking for work. I lied about my age and told her I was eighteen. When we shook hands, I knew she'd feel the calluses on them and figure I was a hard worker. We hit it off and I moved to the house she'd recently purchased on the South Hill. It was perfect for me." The words poured out of my mouth as if they'd been waiting to escape. "She traveled a lot and didn't want to leave an empty house, especially in winter. It was an older home, you know." I snapped my mouth shut.

"Go on."

"When the baby was born, I . . . , well, I couldn't raise her, but I really didn't want to let her go. I had nothing to offer her."

She nodded encouragement.

"The adoptive parents agreed to let me watch her grow up. They also agreed to never tell her—" I clapped my hand over my mouth.

"It's okay to talk about it."

"I've already talked too much." I stood. "Thank you for breakfast. I wonder if I might use the bathroom and maybe borrow some clothes?"

"Of course." She rose and moved to a door off the kitchen. "Follow me."

The door led to a bedroom clearly belonging to a teenager. Snapshots, a church program, and several blue ribbons from the county fair were pinned to a cork bulletin board. A shelf ran around the walls near the ceiling and was filled with dolls and stuffed animals. A collection of track trophies and medals covered the white dresser. In the corner of the room was a sewing machine with an antique wire dress form next to it. An open cube shelving unit held folded fabrics separated by color.

Janet opened the dresser drawer and pulled out jeans, underwear, and a navy-blue T-shirt with Gonzaga Bulldogs on the front.

"Your daughter is going to Gonzaga?"

She handed me the clothes. "She was accepted, but . . . a drunk driver . . ." She looked down, then at me. "The bathroom is over there." She pointed.

I wanted to say something, reach out to her, let her know I understood. *But I don't. Not really.* Not this kind of pain and loss. I had a daughter too, but I never raised her. Never got a chance to help her with her homework. Watch her play sports. Go to church and worship with her. But I did give her a chance to live, to have a family who would love her. That was enough, wasn't it?

I slowly found my way to the bathroom. The mirror informed me that I badly needed a shower. The hot water was heavenly, but reminded me of the numerous dings and cuts all over my body. I took the time to wash my hair. Pulling on the borrowed jeans and T-shirt, I found Janet's daughter was slightly larger than me, probably muscular from her athletics. The clothes smelled recently laundered.

I found my host in the kitchen with a box of pears, canning jars, and lids, and several big pots. Without saying anything, I found a paring knife and began washing the fruit.

"I meant to ask you. How did you find your way here from the river?" She pulled out a bag of sugar. "There's no road from the Snake to here."

"Fonzie found me and led me up a trail. At least I think it was a trail. It was dark and I wasn't in any condition to pay attention."

She measured out the sugar. "And that's another funny thing. Fonzie has never gone to the railroad tracks. He doesn't stray far at all. You must have made some noise that he heard."

"Probably when I fell on the rail. I was trying to get to the light from your house."

She stopped working and looked at me. "Sam, you can't see any lights from my house from the river or the railroad tracks."

The hairs on my neck prickled. "Oh." I thought about my prayers. My aunt's voice in my head. "My aunt used to say, 'For he shall give his angels charge over thee, to keep thee in all thy ways.'"

"So it would seem, though when Fonzie rolls in a dead ground squirrel, he hardly seems like a guardian angel."

"Duly noted."

"She was a smart lady, your aunt. What else did she say?"

"She often told me to learn and read and grow as a person, because I'd never know what could prove to be useful." I smiled. "That was one she'd say just before giving me more chores." I thought for a minute. "Janet, if I could borrow your phone, I'd like to call and see if anyone else reported our car going into the river. Maybe I can find out what happened to Dutch and Leroy."

"Of course, but if you call, they might want to find out more about us. I thought you didn't want anyone to know where you are."

"True."

"I do have a computer. You could check the local news. It's slow, but it works."

I followed her into the living room, where a laptop sat on an end table next to a wingback chair.

"I'll be in the kitchen if you need me."

Janet was correct. The internet speed was slow. I was eventually able to access all the local news stations but discovered no word of what happened to Dutch or Leroy.

Janet returned, wiping her hands on a dishtowel. "Well?"

"Nothing."

She sat opposite me. "Samantha, did it ever occur to you that . . . maybe a lot of this . . . being followed around by strange men in black suits . . . is . . . well, really not all true? Maybe it was just a drunk driver or something?"

"Unfortunately, it's all true. I should start at the beginning." I moved to the sofa so she could sit next to me. "Here's the article on the crash into the school." I turned the screen so she could read it, then typed a bit more. "Here's the article on the body they found at Alderman Acres." Again I turned the computer toward her.

"I think I remember something about that. Wasn't there a second body?"

"Yes." Thinking I could find proof in the images, I tapped on that link. Instead, I found a photo of the ground-breaking ceremony that was slightly clearer than the one Dutch had shown me. Next to it was a second photo snapped at the same time from a different angle, this one taken by the *Spokesman-Review*.

I blinked, then clicked on the hyperlink to the corresponding article.

"What is it, Samantha? You're shaking."

"I . . . I'm not sure."

The article loaded.

I enlarged the photo. Behind Dr. Brùn was the woman Dutch had identified as Beatrice Greer. Like the Colfax paper, this one also identified the woman as B. Green.

I'd known her as Mrs. Gimble. The woman in Spokane who hired me to housesit while she traveled with her accounting job.

TWENTY-ONE

"What is it, Samantha?"

I couldn't speak over the lump in my throat. Mrs. Gimble. The woman who'd literally saved me from the streets, provided a home, took care of me through the darkest time of my life, had been living just a short distance from me for years.

I covered my mouth but couldn't hold back the gut-wrenching sob.

"Samantha, sweetheart, what is it?" Janet rubbed my back.

I just shook my head. I'd tried to find her after I left for college, but she'd sold the house and left no forwarding address. Over the years, I'd gone online and searched, but to no avail. Now I'd never be able to tell her thank you.

Janet stood, left the room, and returned with a box of tissues. I grabbed a handful. When the original flood of tears passed and I could speak, I pointed to the screen. "Mmmrs. Gimble . . . is dead . . . and . . ." My voice gave out. I couldn't catch my breath. A brick settled on my chest. I gave up trying to make sense and just cried.

Janet left again, this time returning with a cup of hot herbal tea.

The tea helped. I forced myself to drink the whole thing at once, then clutched the cup with both hands. "Thank you," I finally whispered. My throat hurt.

She patiently waited until I could regain my composure. The crying jag had left me drained. "Mrs. Gimble, or the woman I knew as Mrs. Gimble, was in that car accident I told you about. She was living at Clan Firinn and going by a different name. Oh no!"

"What?"

"I have her Bible. B. G. Beatrice Greer. Bonnie Gimble."

"Then you have something special of hers."

I nodded mutely for a moment, then took a deep breath.

"What do you know about her from when you lived in Spokane?"

"That's just it. She never talked about herself. She just . . ." A thought pushed into my brain.

"What are you thinking?"

I looked at her. "Don't you think it was convenient that I just *happened* to walk by as Mrs. Gimble was placing that ad on the shelter's bulletin board? What if . . . what if she wasn't there as a coincidence, but was waiting for me to walk by?"

"So . . . ?"

"Clan Firinn."

Her brows furrowed. "What about it?"

I typed the name into the computer. The same article Mary showed me loaded. "Listen. 'While participating in the program, members experience therapeutic work, educational opportunities, physical training, a structured schedule, personalized feedback, nutritious meals, and spiritual guidance. Graduates are assisted with career counseling, job referrals, and relocation.'"

"Okay," Janet said slowly.

"That's what Mrs. Gimble did for me. She gave me work, the chance to finish school, a home, guidance, and a safe place to have my baby. When the time came for me to go to college, she made sure I made the right choices and even helped me move to Pullman. Then she sold the house and disappeared."

"Why? Why would someone do that for you?"

"I don't know. I don't know what to think." I leaned back in my chair and thought for a moment, then typed in +*Clan* +*Firinn* +*Beatrice* +*Greer*. No results. I did it again but changed the name to +*B.* +*Green*. Still no results. I tried one more time, trying +*Clan* +*Firinn* +*ground-breaking* +*LaCrosse*. Several articles appeared along with images. Again I chose the images. Most were of a group of people holding shovels and posing for the camera. I selected one and enlarged it, poring over each face in the background. I knew this time what to look for and found it. No name appeared under the photo, just a blurry face.

"Here." I pointed. "Here she is in a photo of Clan Firinn's ground breaking in 1990. She showed up in 2007 as Bonnie Gimble, then again more recently as Beatrice Greer. There's no record of a Beatrice Greer and I'm guessing . . ." I typed *Bonnie Gimble* into the computer. No results. "Maybe she was . . . like a traveling Clan Firinn angel—"

Fonzie, previously sprawled across the floor, suddenly leaped to his feet and charged to the front door, barking.

I took a quick peek.

A black SUV parked in front of the house.

"Oh no!"

Janet looked, then shoved me toward her daughter's room. "Stay put."

Someone knocked.

I leaned against the closed bedroom door.

"Fonzie, sit." Janet's voice came clearly, followed by the squeak of hinges. "How can I help you gentlemen?"

"We're trying to find this woman. Have you seen her?"

Fonzie growled.

I held my breath.

A pause. "What's she done?"

"It's nothing to be alarmed at. She escaped from the women's correctional facility."

Are they talking about me?

"Why do you think she'd be around here?"

"We've had reports. If you do see her, lock your door and give us a call." He gave a phone number.

"I'll write that down. Who should I ask for?"

"Don't worry. It's my personal cell." He gave the number again.

"Got it. Thank you."

"Thank you, ma'am. It's a good thing you have that big dog."

A couple of car doors slammed, followed by the sound of an engine, then the crunch of gravel, fading.

"You can come out now, Sam." Janet's face was pale.

"Who were they?" My voice came out squeaky.

"They never identified themselves, but they have a photo of you. They were wearing suits. Washington State license plates."

"And they told you a phone number rather than give you a card."

"Yes."

"I've got to get out of here." I quickly looked around the kitchen, hoping for inspiration.

"Sit down, Samantha." She pulled out a chair and sat opposite me. "When you first told me about these agents from the government hunting you down, I confess I found it hard to believe."

"You believe me now."

"Yes. But I don't know what you're going to do."

I was grateful that she didn't point out the obvious: I was without transportation, money, or identification. I didn't even own the clothes on my back. I felt for the key still on a chain around my neck.

"You're welcome to look up anything on the computer."

"Thank you. You've been so kind to me, but I think I need to leave. It isn't safe for either you or me. Those men may return."

Janet reluctantly nodded her head.

"And I can't keep running around playing hide-and-seek with some unknown suits bent on harming me."

"Why do they want to hurt you?"

I traced the oak grain on the tabletop. "I don't know." I said slowly. "I'm no one. Invisible. Nothing in my present life—teaching an after-school art class in a tiny farming community, reading books, assembling puzzles, attending lectures . . ." I looked up. "Nothing should have put me in the crosshairs of anyone, let alone killers."

"Whoever is behind this, or so it seems to me, has some powerful motives. Money? Are you rich, or do you have a big life-insurance policy?"

"No."

"Revenge?"

"I would have had to do something horrible to someone for them to want revenge, right?" I looked at her. "Like I said, I'm a nobody."

"Think about it anyway. Some of the strongest reasons for someone to try to kill another person are money, revenge, and jealousy."

"That's really good insight, Janet. I've never wanted or needed to return to my past, but now I think it's time."

"Is that possible?"

"Everything my parents owned is in storage. I've never gone through any of it."

Her gaze tracked to my hand holding the key. "So you're going to open up the storage facility—"

"No. Their things are at my aunt's farm."

If possible, Janet's face grew paler.

"I have to go back."

"You're going to where that man—"

"He died. Several years ago. I was the only one left in the family, so I inherited the farm. I sold off most of the acreage but held on to the house. It wouldn't bring much, but land usually is a fair investment. I didn't want to sell the house until I had a chance to pick up my parents' possessions."

"You could have had them picked up at any time."

I looked away. "Maybe I should have said I was waiting until I could deal with them, and with that part of my past."

"That's reasonable. After that, you can return here."

"No. I'll have to look . . . elsewhere."

"Where?"

"I don't want to tell you. I don't want you in any more danger."

She stood, moved to the sink, and started filling a pot with water. "How can I help you?"

I got up and walked to the front door to check for the return of the black SUV. I thought I was calm, but I was unsteady on my feet. When I returned, Janet was measuring out sugar and pouring it into the pot.

"I'll need to borrow some clothes and money, but I'll pay you back. If you could drive me to the bus station, I'll be fine."

"You'll hardly be fine looking like that. With your distinctive hair color and good looks, you'll be noticed." She placed the pot on the stove, turned on the heat, and stirred. "I could drive to town and pick up some hair dye. That would help."

"Good idea." I thought for a minute. "Would it be possible . . . um . . . to borrow your daughter's sewing machine and some fabric?"

She raised her eyebrows. "Of course. But you're welcome to my daughter's clothes. It's . . . time."

"Thank you. I have an idea that might work, but I have to make the clothing."

She looked at the wooden crate of pears for a moment, then took the pot off the burner and turned it off. "I'll get ready—"

"Wait. Why don't I help you can these pears, then I can sew while you head to town."

"Maybe I should ask if you've ever canned pears."

"Yes, and apples, tomatoes, peaches—you name it."

For the next several hours we worked silently in tandem. The repetitive actions allowed me to think about my next moves. As we finished, I said, "You know, I've been thinking . . . Those two men . . . I mean, this place is pretty remote . . . Why do you think they came here?"

She picked up her purse and car keys, then paused. "Good question. The river is south of here, and only a trail that's difficult to see leads to my house. There would be no reason to think you'd walked up here. My road comes in from the north. We're miles from Hay, the nearest community." She shrugged. "Maybe they found the car and looked at the area with a program like Google Earth, checking what places were near the river. Or your friends made it to shore and said something. Maybe they followed up on my report. Maybe they even somehow tracked you."

"Well, as you pointed out, I arrived practically naked . . ." *Except for the shirt I borrowed from the wardrobe at Clan Firinn.* "Beatrice, or whatever her name was, had a connection to both Clan Firinn and me." *At this point, I'm probably as paranoid as Leroy. Bugs, tracking devices, New World Order . . .* "Janet, there may be a possibility those men will be watching here, watching you, following you."

She stood still. "I hadn't thought about that. What should I do?"

"Ignore them. Drive to the grocery store as if nothing is going on, but don't just buy hair coloring. Can you shop for a number of items so that one purchase is hidden?"

"Good idea."

"One more thing. Take my blouse. Wad it up to its smallest size. When you get to the parking lot, look for a pickup with stuff already in the back. Park next to it and when the coast is clear, toss the blouse in. If it has a tracking device in it, they may think I'm on the move and we may buy some time while they follow the truck."

"We could search the blouse . . ."

"What if we find something? If we destroyed it, they'd know. It's better to assume a device and take proactive measures."

"It's worth a try." She shook her head. "This all seems so . . . I don't know . . . furtive, undercover . . ."

"No. It's just being cautious and prepared."

Still shaking her head, she brought me the blouse already twisted into a small ball. "Such a shame. A lovely top."

She left Fonzie with me. After she drove away, I locked the doors and began work, though frequently Fonzie and I walked to the front of the house to look for black SUVs or men in suits.

Working in the bedroom, I tried not to think about Janet's daughter, but evidence of her loss was all around me. The bedding was fresh, no dust covered any surface, and all of her clothes still hung in the closet.

Time passed and it grew dark outside. The dog napped. It had been years since I'd sewn my own clothes, and I was creating an outfit without a pattern, so I worked slower than usual. I finally stood and stretched, then wandered around the bedroom. I didn't mean to snoop, but I couldn't help myself. *I'm sure Dr. Seuss wrote something noble about exploring. If not, he should have.*

I found out her daughter's name was Sydney and she'd probably been killed shortly before her birthday. Several unopened birthday gifts were in the closet. She'd graduated from high school valedictorian of her class. She was also a budding artist. Her closet held boxes of art supplies—watercolors, colored pencils, charcoal. In one plastic container I found ink and calligraphy pens. *Perfect.* In the kitchen, I found a glass bowl along with rubber gloves and paper towels. In the bathroom, I found a drawer holding old toothbrushes. I tucked the paper towels into my top to protect it, pulled on the rubber gloves, then placed ink in the bowl. After dipping the toothbrush into the ink, I closed my eyes and spattered the ink across my face with the toothbrush. It was a watercolor technique for creating textured foliage, but it could also create freckles.

The results looked pretty good—a spray of tiny brown freckles across my nose and cheeks. Along with the outfit and colored hair, I would be far less recognizable as my true self.

Finally I had to turn on the lights. I had no idea how far the nearest town was that would have a store carrying hair dyes.

Fonzie started barking at the crunch of gravel and car engine.

Heart thudding, I raced to a window.

Janet parked near the kitchen door.

216

I waited a moment, watching for anyone following her, before unlocking the door and helping her unload the car.

Leaving the groceries on the kitchen table, she turned and looked at me. "When did you develop freckles?"

"When I found the ink in your daughter's closet. I hope you don't mind."

"Clever." She strolled toward her daughter's room. "How did you do?" She stopped dead when she saw my work.

The dress hung on the dress form, a plain, dark, two-piece navy plaid dirndl with a matching apron over a white elbow-length-sleeved blouse. I hadn't finished hemming the ankle-length skirt. Sitting on the sewing machine was a large black scarf with tiny white dots.

"Um, Sam, maybe I can help you with this. Perhaps add some darts and take it in a bit."

"It needs to hang like a sack."

"I realize you want to hide your figure—"

I laughed. "You said I'd be noticed the way I look. That means they'll be looking for someone trying to hide. I plan on being obvious. A Dariusleut Hutterite woman."

"Dariusleut Hutterite as opposed to . . . ?"

"A Schmiedeleut or Lehrerleut, of course. You can tell by the size of the dots on the scarf."

Janet slowly sank down to the bed. "Of course. Dots."

"My aunt and I would go to the Hutterite colony near Ritzville to buy potatoes. There are at least five Hutterite colonies in Washington State, and one just across the border in Oregon. This scarf, the Tiechl, will help cover my hair."

"Would a Hutterite be traveling by car or bus? Don't they go by buggy or . . . ?"

"That's the Amish."

"How do you know so much about them?"

I moved back to the kitchen to unpack the groceries and she followed. "As Mary would say, I'm a plethora of useless information. When I went to the colony, it was . . ." I waved my hand, grabbing for the right word. "They live a communal life. Like a big family. Happy . . . sharing." The hollowness I became aware of during that visit returned. "Anyway." I put a carton of milk into the refrigerator. "How did your disposal of the blouse go?"

She grinned. "I felt like a secret agent. I drove to one of the largest stores in the area and parked next to a ratty-looking pickup with the truck bed filled with household items. I doubt they'll find that small parcel for weeks. I couldn't tell if anyone followed me in either direction."

"If what I believe about the tracking device is true, they'll turn their attention to that truck. They'll work that out soon enough, so we don't have much time."

She unloaded one of the bags of groceries, placing two boxes of Clairol medium-brown hair coloring on the table. "I bought two boxes because of all your hair, and this color should dull that reddish-blonde. We can start in the morning—"

"No, Janet, I have to leave as soon as possible to get a head start."

In the silence that followed, the refrigerator kicked on and the kitchen clock *tick, tick, ticked* down the seconds. "Okay," she finally said. "Do you need help with your hair?"

I picked up the nearest box, opened it, and read the directions. "I think I can do this alone. It takes about twenty-five minutes to process. I should be able to do a fast hem of the skirt—"

"I'll hem your skirt, then make you some dinner."

"Compromise? If you could hem the skirt, I'll just take a sandwich to go. And if you could drive me to a bus stop?"

"Further compromise?" Janet walked to a cabinet near the door to the living room, pulled out a drawer, and took out a set of keys. "I have an old pickup truck you can use. Just return it when you're done."

"Thank you." I gave her an impromptu hug, then stepped away, suddenly aware that I was hugging a virtual stranger.

She turned her back to me and finished arranging the groceries. "You'd better get started with your hair," she said in a muffled voice.

It took longer than the projected twenty-five minutes, but the results were amazing. Instead of my distinctive copper-blonde hair, I had unremarkable brown hair. I parted it in the middle and french braided it, then pinned it up in back. The Hutterite outfit, now neatly hemmed and pressed, was hanging in Sydney's room with a pair of clunky black shoes and black leotards nearby. I pulled on the dress, stockings, and shoes, tied the scarf around my head and under my chin, then clipped it into place. The scarf reached to my shoulders and halfway down my back.

The mirror showed me a demure, modest Hutterite. *This might work. As long as I don't run into a real Hutterite speaking German.* My entire vocabulary consisted of *ich liebe dich, ja,* and *darf ich Ihnen einen Keks anbieten?*

I love you, yes, and *may I offer you a cookie?*

I found Janet in the living room darning a sock. She looked up.

"I have to leave now."

Wordlessly she stood and walked to the kitchen, where she handed me a pair of reading glasses. "Finish off the look. They're not very strong and you don't have to wear them all the time." She picked up a small cooler and held it out. "Dinner."

I took it.

She opened her purse and handed me a handful of cash. "I went to the ATM."

"I don't know how I can thank—"

"Just let me say goodbye to you. This time, I want a chance to say goodbye."

TWENTY-TWO

The tan 1997 Ford F-150 was perfect for my purposes. Small, nondescript—the type of farm vehicle someone from a Hutterite colony would use to drive to another colony. Janet had placed a blanket and small flashlight next to me on the seat.

Our goodbyes already said in the kitchen, Janet didn't leave the house to see me off. Fonzie pressed against me until I slid into the truck. "Okay, big guy. You saved my life. I don't know if you're an exceptional dog or I've completely misjudged your species, but thank you either way." I lifted the fur draped over his eyes so I could see them. "Watch Janet for me."

I caught a glimpse of Janet through her daughter's window as I drove past. The lump in my throat made it hard to swallow as I followed that dusty, one-lane road. My headlights were the only light I could see in the vast expanse of this sparsely populated region.

I brought the boxes of hair color and any other evidence I'd been at Janet's house. On a map she gave me, I'd studied and plotted out a route to Pullman, my first stop. Even though I lived in the city for a number of years, I'd never returned to the house I shared with my parents. Though my aunt said nothing was left at the house, at this point, I didn't trust anything anyone had ever told me.

After driving for over an hour, I reached the edge of town. When I attended WSU, I'd lived near the campus in the northeast part of town. I had no idea of my first address and recalled only that the house was older, painted ivory, and had similar houses nearby. I also remembered it was set back from the road with a high fence and near a water tower. Not a lot to go on and many years had passed. This was a stupid idea, but I had to try.

It was after midnight and most of the town had gone to sleep. Few vehicles were driving on the street. The quiet night was split by the high-pitched wail of a fire truck, growing louder as it approached.

Fire truck. I remembered a fire station close enough that I could hear its vehicles at night. I pulled over and waited until the truck passed, then continued up the road, looking for the station. I spotted it on my left. Beyond was a street climbing a hill into the southeast part of town. I turned left.

Pullman was very hilly, ranging from slight inclines to streets worthy of San Francisco or Seattle, and many of the neighborhoods were narrow and tree lined. I drove around aimlessly, looking for something familiar.

I finally found the water tower. Turning, I circled the nearby blocks. *Let that fence still be standing . . .*

Apparently in this part of town, wooden fences were pretty common. I'd just about given up when I found it.

I parked in front of the familiar wooden fence and turned off the lights. Before I could get out, a patrol car appeared at the end of the street, driving in my direction.

I ducked.

I listened for the sirens, lights, any sign that they were suspicious of me.

They drove past without slowing down.

Leaving the truck's lights off, I pulled into the driveway.

Now what? The present owner of the house was sure to notice a strange pickup in his driveway. Whatever was here, I needed to work quickly.

I grabbed the flashlight and slipped from the truck. No lights showed from my old home, but a small porch light on the house to my right flickered between the thick foliage.

"Well, you namby-pamby, pantywaist, milksop wussy poltroon, see if anything triggers a memory."

Shielding the flashlight with my hand, I took a quick look around. The backyard was as I remembered it. Exactly as I remembered it. The swings were rusty, the grass could use a good watering, and the new owner had made no effort to stamp their personal style on the yard. The driveway ended at a detached garage. A quick peek would tell me if the owners were home.

Creeping to the nearest garage window, I shone my light through.

Empty.

I let out a breath. Of course, they could be out for a night on the town, but . . .

The beam of my flashlight caught a bicycle in the corner.

A girl's pink bicycle, with a matching pink basket, covered in dust. My bike.

I rubbed my arms as I felt the tingling of sweat forming between my shoulder blades. *There's a simple explanation. They've just never cleaned out the garage. Right.*

The purr of a car engine made me douse my light and wait for the car to pass. I switched it back on and made my way to the back door of the house. A window next to the door allowed me to shine my light inside.

The kitchen looked the same. My beam picked up the edge of a white sheet thrown over something beyond it.

It wasn't possible, was it?

With trembling hands, I felt along the outside edge of a metal trellis on my left. My father had kept a key in a small box with a magnet holding it to the trellis.

My fingers encountered the box.

I tugged it free and slid it open. The key was still inside.

I removed it and opened the door.

The house smelled stale. The floor had a slight layer of dust, uninterrupted by footprints. I passed through the kitchen to the dining room, my clunky borrowed shoes clacking loudly on the bare oak floors. To my left were the empty, built-in sideboards painted a familiar light cream color. White sheets covered all the furniture like shrouds.

The living room was papered with the same light-blue floral wallpaper, with slightly lighter rectangles where photos had hung. I looked under a couple of sheets, finding the sofa and chairs from my childhood.

The grand piano stood in the corner, pushed up against built-in bookshelves. I remembered my mother playing all the time. My dad said she played by ear. I didn't know what that meant at the time. I told my dad I only saw her play with her hands. He'd laughed and hugged me.

I removed the dust cover and looked underneath.

My dream returned, only this time I was awake.

I was alone in a big, echoing house with bare floors. It was dimly lit, even though it was broad daylight outside. I was in my usual hiding place under the piano in the corner of the room.

I shook my head violently and flashed the light around. No books, but there were two doors to a built-in cabinet under the shelf. Of course. I used to crawl into the cabinet to hide. My parents had tried to stop me, but finally gave up and placed a pillow and blanket in there. I was getting too big to fit but still squeezed inside on occasion. I'd been there, sleeping, that last day in this house. A dream within a dream. I'd dreamed of the field and stream.

What about the pool that turned black and stank?

I straightened. Maybe that was just a part of the dream I had while hiding.

Then what woke me up?

A shout . . . my father's voice. He'd said . . . "No!" Then thumping. Silence.

A voice. Male. "You might as well come out now."

Then slams as a few doors opened and closed. "If you don't come out, Samantha, I'll bring a dog to find you."

More thumping and banging. A door opened and closed. "Your last chance, Samantha. The dog will rip you to pieces." An anxious whine, toenails on the back steps, panting.

Sirens.

A string of cursing. The back door slammed.

Now, I was shaking so hard I almost dropped the flashlight. The sirens in my mind faded. I'd stayed in the cupboard for hours after that, finally falling asleep in exhaustion.

My aunt told me my parents died in a car accident that day, and I'd accepted it. I'd never thought about it. They wouldn't have gone for a drive and left me alone. Not a five-year-old.

My folks had been here. With a man and a dog.

I walked toward the dining room, searching for something, anything that would enlighten me. This time I noticed the area rug that had been in the dining room was missing. Slowly I walked around the table.

I wanted to go wading, but the pool turned black and smelled awful. The black water got on my hands and I tried to wipe it off.

Black pool. Pool of blood? My parents'?

My flashlight illuminated a large dark stain on the oak floor.

I turned and vomited. Grasping the table, I held on to keep from falling.

Another car drove by on the street before I could shield my flashlight. Had they seen my light? Did they know this is an empty house?

I couldn't stay here. Someone might call the police about a prowler, or a neighbor might be walking a dog and spot the truck. And the ghosts of my past were way too real.

Trying not to run, I left the house, returning the key to its hiding spot. Confident the street was quiet, I quickly backed the truck from the driveway. I turned toward the Washington State University campus, stopping briefly at an all-night store to purchase a brush, deodorant, toothbrush, toothpaste, and baby wipes. The store was almost deserted, and though the few shoppers and workers glanced at my garb, they just as quickly looked away. I figured they'd gawk once my back was turned but wouldn't be rude enough to stare at my face.

I could park, at least for tonight, in my parking area behind the house where I'd had the apartment. In the morning—I glanced at the clock on the dash; make that in a few hours—the stores would be open. I'd purchase another cell phone and see what more I could find out about my past. And learn whether Leroy and Dutch had survived the icy Snake River.

TWENTY-THREE

The dream came again, more vivid than before. My muffled scream shook me from its gauzy clutches. *Now. I must go over the dream now.*

I was alone in a big, echoing house with bare floors.

I hadn't been alone. My parents were . . . where? Not in the living room. Outside? Yes, they'd gone outside.

It was dimly lit, even though it was broad daylight.

That was easy. I'd been under the piano, in the corner where it was dark.

After I read my new books for the third time, I closed my eyes.

I wouldn't have fallen asleep on the cold oak floor. I'd crawled into the cabinet under the bookshelves. Something woke me. My father's shout? But that didn't wake me. I heard it when I was already awake. What did I hear before that?

Yelling. Someone was yelling. What were the words? I shook my head.

I must have crawled from my hiding place and gone looking for my folks. I must have found the black pool. I had no direct memory of that moment.

I opened my eyes. It was dark, but I could see through a narrow opening. Legs moved in front of the piano, and voices called out, but I didn't know what they were saying.

I'd gone back into the cabinet. The narrow opening was the door slightly ajar. I *did* know what they were saying.

They were calling my name.

I tried to sneak out of my hiding place, but everything had changed. The house was full of strangers.

As I tried to get to my room, a big policeman saw me. He reached for me, but I screamed. I screamed again—

I wasn't screaming because of the policeman. I was covered in blood.

What had happened next? A blank. Whatever came after the death of my parents, I'd walled it up in my memory. The first thing I remembered after that was my aunt's farm. How I got there was a blank.

The dashboard clock let me know the stores would be open soon. I'd buy a cell and search for more answers online. I started the truck and headed to a nearby park. I knew they had bathrooms where I could freshen up.

Moms and dads with their young children, students playing with Frisbees, and a group of folks doing tai chi had already filled the park. I drew the usual curious glances as I made my way to the public restrooms with my bag of toiletries.

A little girl came in while I was refastening my scarf.

"Why are you dressed so funny?"

Please, Lord, don't let her parents be German language professors at the university.

"Darf ich Ihnen einen Keks anbieten?"

She didn't take me up on the cookie offer.

The next stop was the store where I could purchase a cell phone. The same salesclerk that had sold me a phone less than two days before waited on me again. I held my breath in case he recognized me, but his expression remained pleasantly blank.

"I didn't think you were allowed modern things like this." He waved at the cell display.

"That's the Amish."

"Oh. What's the difference?"

I pointed to my scarf. "The size of the dots."

His brow furrowed, but he sold me a phone. I gave a fictional address and paid in cash.

I knew the McDonald's had Wi-Fi and decent coffee, so I drove over, parked, and ordered breakfast. I took my tray to the table in the farthest corner. While I ate, I looked for news of Dutch and Leroy's rescue from the Snake River.

No mention of the two men, nor of a car accident, nor even recovery of bodies.

Did that mean their bodies hadn't shown up? My breakfast congealed in my stomach and I pushed the tray away. No mention of the three of us missing. Janet had reported the accident. Maybe authorities didn't believe her. The car was somewhere floating along the bottom of the Snake River, so no evidence of the wreck.

Wouldn't someone have noticed we were gone? Dr. Brùn should have noticed.

Because of Beatrice's death, I knew Clan Firinn, and by extension, Dr. Brùn, were on my do-not-trust list.

A thought struck me. No one really knew why Beatrice was driving in that part of town when she'd been shot. What if she had been on her way to meet me, to reconnect? She hadn't just been near the school. She'd been on the one side where only that portable classroom was located.

I drummed my fingers on the table. I'd been working in LaCrosse for some time before the accident. Beatrice could have come by at any time.

But she hadn't sought me out. Why? Did someone recently discover our connection and use that to lure her to a specific place and time? How would they have found out?

"Grrrrr." I quietly snarled at my coffee cup, then quickly

glanced around to see if anyone noticed. A little boy was staring at me, but he was too far away to hear.

What about the empty house? My dream? I looked up my parents, Phillip and Ruth Williams, on the internet.

Nothing.

I blinked at the screen. If both of them died in the house that day, it would have been in the news.

No wonder Mary hadn't found anything when she'd checked.

But that didn't make sense. I saw them dead.

Maybe. I didn't really remember what I saw except blood. And even that was an assumption. My memory was just a stinking dark pool.

I sat very still, trying to figure out another way to search. Maybe the address of the house?

I scrolled to the Whitman County Assessor's Office and typed *Williams* in the tax sifter. Three pages of Williams loaded, but none were at the right address.

Of course, you idiot. If they sold the house . . .

I typed in the address.

"McWilliams, Samantha Trust" came up in the results.

The clattering and chattering of the diners receded. McWilliams?

Once again that feeling of being tossed about and rudderless returned. Had I forgotten my own name? What had happened in the house on the quiet side street so long ago?

I typed in Phillip and Ruth McWilliams.

My hand remained posed above the screen, frozen by the words.

April 7, 1997. Pullman, Washington. Dr. Phillip McWilliams and his wife of fifteen years were found dead this afternoon in an apparent murder-suicide. The bodies of the popular professor of physics and his wife were discovered by Dr. Andrew Lee, a fellow professor and friend. Police were initially concerned that their five-year-old daughter had also been killed but discovered her shortly after they arrived. An investigation is pending.

Easter 1997. Just as I'd remembered. I found a calendar from 1997. April 7 was one week after that holiday. One final memory.

I reread the news report three times before I saw it. It confirmed that I was five. I'd arrived at my aunt's farm when I was six.

Are you sure?

I closed my eyes and thought back to my earliest memory of the farm. The house. Chickens wandering around the lawn. A border collie named Tipi. No memory of being taken to the farm. Just my aunt explaining where my room was, when we ate meals, what time to go to bed. As if she'd been saying all that over and over.

I'd said, "Okay."

She'd hugged me and cried. "The doctors said you might eventually recover. Do you know your name?"

"That's silly. I'm Samantha."

Had I spent a year with my aunt, walking around like a zombie? Or had they put me in a hospital? Maybe I'd never know where that time went. Only that when I woke up, I was a year older, terrified of dogs, and prone to nightmares.

"Are you all right, lady?"

I jerked, opened my eyes, and looked up. A man in a light-blue shirt and tie stood above me. Several people around me were staring at me.

I stood. "I'm sorry. Just . . . I'm sorry." I got up and rushed to the door. So much for not being noticed. I must have been making some sound to draw the manager's attention.

I ran to the truck, got in, and drove out of the parking lot. No one seemed to follow me, but to be sure, I drove around the nearest block before pulling into a coffee shop where I knew they had free Wi-Fi.

Once I parked behind the shop, I rolled down the windows and made a point of just getting my breathing under control.

Every new fact of my past was worse than the previous piece, as if I were putting together a jigsaw puzzle and the emerging picture was some horrible vision of the artist Hieronymus Bosch.

I wasn't Dorothy Gale in *The Wizard of Oz*, longing for a place where I had no problems, where my world wasn't drab and ordinary. I wanted to go *back* to where my life was organized, neat, tidy, and under control.

That was impossible. And I had to know where the road ahead would lead.

I typed in *Dr. Phillip McWilliams*. I found his obituary. Date of birth and death. Marriage to my mother. My birth. Undergraduate degree from the University of Idaho. PhD from the Massachusetts Institute of Technology. He worked at the Oak Ridge National Laboratory and the Lawrence Livermore Labs before ending up at Hanford Nuclear Site. He left Hanford in 1985 and took the teaching position at WSU.

Hanford again. But the dates didn't line up with Green Run or Suttonville.

Dr. Andrew Lee's name had appeared in the article as the friend who'd found my parents' bodies. Maybe he was still alive.

I typed in Andrew Lee's name. His obituary came up.

I slumped in my seat and stared out the windshield for a few minutes. A tiny voice whispered in my brain. *Why don't you just go back to being nobody?*

Because somebody seemed bent on destroying this nobody.

Lifting the cell, I typed in *Mrs. Andrew Lee, Pullman*. Maybe, just maybe, he had a widow.

He did. Her address appeared on one of those sites that would also give me family members, arrest records, job history, and a whole frightening list of personal information, for a fee. I could call her, but I decided to see if a personal approach might get me further.

I drove to the address listed. It proved to be a neatly maintained older home fairly near my parents' home. A car in the driveway looked promising.

I parked in front, walked to the front door, and rang the bell.

A tiny older woman with a round face and black hair answered. "I'm sorry. I'm not interested in donating—"

"I'm here about your husband."

She started to close the door. "He's gone. Go away."

I blurted, "I'm Samantha Will . . . um . . . Samantha McWilliams. Your husband knew my parents, Phillip and Ruth."

She stopped, then peered at me. "Sam?"

My heart jumped. "Yes."

"You were sent to an Amish community?"

I'd forgotten my disguise. "Hutterite. But no. I'm . . . trying to sort of hide . . ."

She reached out, grabbed my arm with a surprisingly strong grip, and pulled me inside. A quick glance toward the street, then she slammed the door shut. "Were you followed?"

"Um . . . not that I know of."

"Good." She pointed to the living room, then moved around from window to window, pulling down the shades.

A crawling chill snaked around my neck.

Room darkened, she pointed to a chair. "Sit."

I sat. "Why did you ask if I was followed?"

"Because the truth always finds its way to the surface. Your father tried to reveal it because it was eating him up. And it did kill my husband."

"I don't understand."

She took a seat across from me. "No one believed me when I said both my husband and your father were murdered."

TWENTY-FOUR

The cold I'd felt intensified, raising the tiny hairs on my arms. "You believe your husband was murdered?"

"I don't believe. I know."

"How? Why?"

"Why? Because your father would never have killed himself, let alone his lovely wife. And then those men came to see my Andrew after he found your parents. He called them Mr. Stick and Mr. Carrot. They wanted to know if your father gave him anything. They offered him money, the carrot, or they'd do something bad to him, the stick. Of course he couldn't give them anything—he had nothing in his possession. So they killed him."

I wanted to ask her if the men drove a black car and wore suits, but I didn't want to stop her flow of words.

"And how? How did they murder him? An 'accident.'" Mrs. Lee made quotes in the air with her fingers. "They said he fell asleep at the wheel and drove off the road. But I know better."

"Because?"

"He told me."

I licked my lips. "He told you?"

"Yes." She took a sip from a glass of clear liquid sitting on a coaster next to her.

For the first time I noticed crystals lined the top of a bookshelf. A stylized painting of a Hindu goddess hung on the wall. A photo of an older man sat on the dining room table. I cleared my throat. "You speak to him—"

"He communicates through a Ouija board. A spiritualist told me to get one."

I stood. "Look at the time. I must be going."

"My Andrew told me they work under contract, you know."

"Thank you so much for seeing me." I walked as fast as I politely could toward the door.

She didn't move. "That way there's plausible deniability."

At the door I paused. "By any chance do you remember if my dad owned an apple-shaped paperweight?"

She thought for a moment. "I believe he did. He kept it on his desk. Why?"

Instead of answering her question, I ran to the truck, jumped in, and drove down the street. The meeting left me restless and uneasy. How much truth was wrapped within her delusions?

I drove around aimlessly until a glance at my gas gauge reminded me of my limited funds. "Admit it," I whispered. "You don't want to check out what's left of your parents' possessions."

Dutch was aware of voices, movement, smells, lights, and shadows, but it seemed too much effort to work out what everything meant. He was warm. That was all that mattered.

"Dr. Van Seters?"

That same annoying voice poked at him. *Go away.*

"Dr. Van Seters, can you hear me?"

Obviously I hear you. Go away.

"Dr. Van Seters, this is Dr. Harris. Can you open your eyes?"

Dutch opened them a slit. The light was very bright. He closed them again.

"Very good. Dr. Van Seters, you're in a hospital. You were airlifted here from where you were fished out of the Snake River. You've had a tremendous shock to your system, but we expect you to fully recover. Do you understand me?"

Dutch nodded, then drifted into darkness.

"Dr. Van Seters?"

Another annoying voice. A different one. He opened his eyes, then blinked at the face above him, trying to bring it into focus. "Yes," he croaked.

The face resolved into a female police officer. "I'm Deputy Montez of the Whitman County Sheriff's Office. I need to ask you a few questions."

"How long have I been here?" Dutch cleared his throat.

"A day or so. Someone called in your accident. We discounted it at first because we couldn't find anything. Eventually we found a car had gone off the road at Central Ferry State Park. Were you alone in the vehicle?"

Was he alone? He couldn't remember. He closed his eyes.

"Dr. Van Seters, please stay with me and concentrate. You had a makeshift life preserver. A pair of small woman's jeans. Could those have belonged to Samantha Williams? She's missing."

Samantha Williams. The name sounded familiar. Samantha. Sam. "Sam?" He opened his eyes. "Sam was there? Sam must have been there. Did she call in the accident?"

"Not that we know of."

"We were . . . were . . ." Why couldn't he remember? "Maybe. Headlights?" He saw flashes of lights in his mind. Headlights. And . . . "Gunshots?"

Silence followed his comment. He gazed at the faces around him before focusing on one. "Dr. Brùn?"

"I'm here, Dutch. I'll be taking you back to Clan Firinn as soon as you're released."

"What about Sam?"

Dr. Brùn didn't answer.

He threw back the covers and tried to get up. "I need to find her—"

"Oh no you don't." His mentor pushed him gently back into bed. "The only thing you need to do is get well and try and remember what happened."

Dutch clutched the sheet. *And if I can't remember, what will happen to Sam?*

———

From Pullman, the farm near Washtucna was a bit over an hour and a half away. If anyone was looking for me, that might be someplace they'd watch.

I didn't think I'd remember how to get back to the farm, but I found my way without any trouble. Washtucna had a population of slightly over two hundred, but we'd lived well outside of town. It was midafternoon by the time I arrived. The same green metal gate, now covered with rust and held fast by an ancient lock, blocked the driveway. The mailbox that had stood next to the gate was history. It didn't look as if anyone had been up this road in a long time. From here, I could easily walk to the house, but I didn't want to leave Janet's truck near the driveway nor along the road.

I drove past the turnoff and up the road about a mile. Assuming there hadn't been too much change, I knew a place where I could pull off the road and tuck the truck out of sight. Just to be cautious, after I parked, I walked to where I'd turned off the pavement and used a branch to sweep away my tire tracks. I set off toward the house.

The air was filled with the aromas of plowed earth and dried grasses. A mourning dove cooed from a nearby tree. I knew these fields. I'd spent many hours roaming when not consumed by the endless chores of farm life. In the spring, these same fields looked as if a huge bolt of green velvet had tumbled across the landscape interspaced with bands of fluorescent-yellow canola blooms.

I slowed as I approached the final hill. The house would be in a tree-lined area, with a barn used to house the tractors, two outbuildings, and a chicken coop. I wiped my hands on my skirt and forced myself to continue forward. I hadn't seen the place for years.

The trees came into view, black skeletal branches rattling in the slight breeze. Dead. Like the lawn and old garden. As if God had wiped life from the area in punishment. No birds chirruped. Nothing moved except the branches.

White paint peeled from the house in strips. The once neatly painted dark-green shutters were either gone or hanging by a single hinge. The white propane tank next to the kitchen was covered with gray-green moss and streaked with rust. The front porch sagged and the screen door lay on its side next to a pile of sagebrush.

The outbuildings had fared even worse. The walls of one listed like a drunk, and the roof of the other had collapsed. The barn must have been torn down years earlier.

As I approached, I fumbled the key from my blouse. I stopped when I reached the first porch step. I wouldn't need the key. The door was ajar.

A quick check showed no sign of any intruders, at least for a long time. The dust was undisturbed.

My aunt had stored my parents' personal things in an unused room the size of a small bedroom off a hallway. I shoved the front door open with my foot.

The cold living room smelled of dead rodents and mildew. Trash spilled from the kitchen and covered all but a single easy chair. Stained paper plates, bags of garbage, clothing, boxes, books, and open cans stacked up shoulder high. Apparently my aunt's husband had turned into a hoarder after her death. I followed the only cleared path through the house to the hallway leading to the bedrooms. All but one of the doors stood open. I kept my eyes forward, unwilling to look toward my old bedroom or my aunt's room.

The hall was in darkness. To avoid stepping on any moldering garbage, I pulled out the small flashlight Janet gave me. The storage room door opened with a shrieking protest of rusty hinges.

The windowless room had been filled with boxes when I left, each one labeled as to which room it had come from, along with my aunt's Christmas decorations. Now the boxes were shredded, the contents strewn or shattered on the floor and piled up to the ceiling. Any fabric or clothing was ripped, books torn apart, and art slashed. A thick layer of dust covered everything and the prevailing stench of rodent feces filled the air.

Had my aunt's husband gone through their things when I fled? Or someone else after the house was abandoned? I should have expected that. I studied the debris. A sharp object such as a box cutter or knife had been used to rip open everything. The slashing suggested anger, yes, but also methodical action. Searching.

I backed from the room, turned, and picked my way to the living room.

Two men in dark suits stood there. One held a gun.

I clapped my hands over my mouth to cover the scream. How could they have found me so quickly? My gaze darted around the room, looking for an escape. Instead I spotted the tiny camera mounted near the ceiling, almost hidden by the debris.

"So we finally meet, Samantha." The man holding the gun showed his teeth in what might pass for a smile. His gaze raked me from head to foot. "Nice disguise. Original."

Go for it. "*Ich liebe dich. Darf ich Ihnen einen Keks anbieten?*"

The man's grin widened. "*Ich liebe dich nicht, und ich will auch kein Keks.* Thanks for the offer. I think it's time we talked."

I can throw my flashlight at him. Run.

The other man stepped toward the door as if reading my mind, blocking my exit.

"Who . . . who are you and what are you doing in my house?" I was grateful my voice didn't break. Much.

"Very good. Going on offense. No, we're not leaving until we come to some kind of understanding."

"How about you start by showing me some kind of identification?"

"We are." He held up his pistol. "This is all you need to know."

My heart pounded so hard I thought they could hear it. "Why have you been following me?"

Mr. Gun's brows furrowed. "Stop with the questions. We need some answers. Where is it?"

"It? What is *it*?"

"Don't play games. You know. That's why you're here." His eyes were slits and lips thinned.

"I assume you mean the paperweight. I don't know. I thought it might be here."

The two men exchanged glances. "It was here, Sam. We found it. But it had been opened and the contents removed. We need the contents. Or should I say, we need you to find and destroy the contents, and I think you *do* know where that is." The man nearest the door took a step toward me. "And you're going to tell us."

"Or what? You're going to shoot me?" *Brilliant, Sam, taunt them into pulling the trigger.*

"Everyone has their price, Sam." The man lifted his gun. "It's just a matter of figuring out what it is. Money? You'd be surprised what people will do for a great deal of money."

I shook my head.

"How about we lock you in here for a week or two? Or forever? No one has been here for years, and no one will hear your screams."

I grew dizzy. I folded my hands into fists, digging my nails into my palms to help me focus. *The carrot and the stick.* These guys were too young to have talked to Dr. Lee after he found my parents, but the message hadn't changed. "I already destroyed it." I tried to sound convincing, but I just sounded lame.

"What? What did you destroy?"

My mind blanked. What could have been hidden in a brass apple paperweight? Photos? Film? A flash drive? *No, the paperweight was around before flash drives.*

I hesitated too long.

"I think you need to go over your choices, Sam. Ponder them. Come to the right decision. Turn around."

They were going to shoot me in the back. Sweat beaded across my spine and slithered down my back.

"Now walk forward." He directed me toward the window-less storage room. "Give me the flashlight."

Reluctantly I turned around and handed it to him.

"Now empty your pockets."

"They're empty."

"Do you want me to search you?"

My muscles tightened. The thought of his hands touching me made me sick. I took out my cell phone and held it out.

"Maybe I'll search you anyway."

Vomit burned the back of my throat.

He took the cell phone, letting his fingers stroke my hand. I snatched it away.

"Go on." He motioned me farther into the storage room, shutting the door firmly behind me.

I knew there wasn't a key to lock the room. I'd just wait for them to leave—

Bang! Bang! Bang!

He'd nailed the door shut.

The room was inky black, with only a sliver of anemic light coming from under the door.

I turned and pounded on the door. "Let me out! You can't do this! I'll help you! Open up!"

No sound came from the other side. I put my ear against the door but couldn't hear anything. Were they waiting for me to break? Or had they gone already, content that a few hours, or even days, would be the "stick" I needed to do their bidding. In darkness. In this room that reeked of mouse droppings.

I again pounded on the door, then listened. I thought I heard something, but it might have just been my heartbeat. I clenched my teeth, then kicked the door. Hard.

The jarring pain shot up my leg. It felt like I broke a toe. Or smashed the same toe I'd injured on the railroad tracks.

I sat and rocked my aching leg while burning tears rolled down my cheeks. I gave in and sobbed for a few moments. *Idiot.* I knew how to kick for self-defense. Why didn't I think first?

I swiped my hand across my eyes. Maybe that's just what they wanted—psychological torture to get me to break. Once again I listened at the door. I thought I heard a sound.

I banged on the door again. "Don't leave me here! Help!" *Bang, bang, bang!*

No response. The men had gone.

All isn't lost. Dutch will . . . will what? I didn't even know if he was alive.

Other than the two suits, no one knew I was here.

The light under the door grew even more faint. I wasn't going to spend the night in this stinking room in this evil house. No! *Not. One. Night.*

By now the pain in my foot had subsided somewhat and helped me focus. I stood and looked around me, then pictured what the room had looked like before they took away the flashlight. Was there anything I could use? A handy cell phone, gun, or hammer?

All I remembered were shredded clothes, a few ripped books, emptied and torn boxes.

The faint, skittering sounds of mice dashed around me.

The sound made my skin crawl.

Those creeps had locked me into this horrible place to break me. They wouldn't succeed. I felt for the wall on my left, the only place where trash wasn't piled high, and punched the surface. "Scum." Now my hand hurt. "Disgusting goons." I kicked the wall with my good foot. "Loathsome, festering thugs!" Kick. "Putrid, noxious bullies!" Kick.

Crack! The plasterboard shifted slightly.

"Barbaric gorillas!" Kick.

The Sheetrock bent inward.

"Brutish, hateful punks!" Kick.

Something crumbled.

I reached down and felt the surface. I'd punched a hole in the wall. I grasped an edge and pulled. A chunk came off in my hand. If I could make a big enough hole . . .

I put my foot flat against the wall and shoved hard. "Penurious, sadistic hooligans!" The wall moved. It took two more kicks to free a small opening. I was out of names, so grunts accompanied the kicks.

No light came from the opening. I'd punched through to the living room. Piled with garbage.

TWENTY-FIVE

I pictured the house layout. If I could get through, I could get out by aiming right and going down the hall and exit to the back side of the building, where there probably weren't any cameras.

I kicked a few more times and found I was breathing hard. Too hard. And that smell . . .

Propane.

They must have opened the gas stove in the kitchen.

Don't worry. The tank must be nearly empty.

Are you sure? How much gas would it take to fill this house? I tried to concentrate, but I was feeling lightheaded.

Don't stop and think about it. The two men must have decided they no longer needed me. Whatever had been in the golden apple, I didn't have it, nor did I know about it.

Poor girl. Went to look at her parents' things and inadvertently got stuck. By the time someone found my body . . . tsk, tsk, a terrible way to die.

I attacked the wall with renewed strength, pulling more

away, enlarging the hole on both sides until I'd reached the two-by-fours. The air reeked of gas and I gagged. My nails tore to the quick.

I'll make it. The trash had been stacked shoulder high against the wall in the living room. I only had to crawl up and through a few feet to be clear. The camera was aimed at the cleared path through the living room. I'd need to stay away from that.

Better yet, keep pulling the wall away until I was even with the top of the garbage.

I grabbed, grunted, coughed, and tore upward until I reached a horizontal two-by-four. I couldn't get the leverage to pull the plasterboard higher. I stopped and tried to catch my breath. *Do gas fumes rise or sink?* I couldn't remember, couldn't think. I dropped to all fours, then placed my face near the floor. The air was slightly fresher.

With renewed strength, I returned to my assault on the wall. As I'd removed the chunks, the trash started sliding into the room, covering my feet, then my legs. I could no longer drop down to breathe. *Keep going.*

I kept imaging rats, or spiders, skittering across my body. Every time something tapped against my leg, I wanted to kick out or flail at it. *Conserve strength.*

Lord Jesus, please help me. Give me courage.

I removed my scarf, then wrapped it around my nose and mouth. *Don't hesitate. It won't get any better.* I pushed through the opening using a breaststroke-like movement, trying to shove the debris aside or compress it.

Things dropped, poked, slithered, and jabbed at me. I

couldn't help the words tumbling from my chattering teeth. "No. No. Nonononono." The stench seeped through the scarf. Squeaks, crackling, and crunching assaulted my ears. I kept my hands in fists so as not to touch anything with my fingers. I wanted to vomit from the gas. Darkness swirled around my brain. *Stop and you'll die.*

One final shove and my head was free of the filth. I scrambled forward, staggering from the muck, until I could stand on the floor.

I staggered away from the front of the house, down the hall, toward my old bedroom. Once inside, I slammed the door shut to keep out the gas, then turned and blinked.

The room was almost exactly as I'd left it so long ago. Only the dust on every surface showed a passage of time.

No time. No time. I lurched to the grimy window and yanked upward. The frame wouldn't budge.

I picked up the small metal chair beside the bed and heaved it at the glass.

The window shattered.

I grabbed the dust-covered bedspread and threw it over the sill, then climbed out, landing on my hands and knees. I stayed there, sucking in fresh air.

Still dizzy, I finally stood and ran—at least, I ran as fast as I could with my injured foot and fuzzy brain—toward the hills on my left. Not until I'd gotten some distance from the house and out of sight did I stop and begin shaking out my clothes, swatting at anything that may have hitched a ride. I yanked off the scarf and used it to whack at my hair.

The stench clung to my clothes and body.

My stomach churned and I vomited.

This isn't enough. I yanked off the dress and blouse, then shook them violently.

The sun was setting and temperatures dropping. I pulled my blouse and dress on, then continued hobbling toward the truck. If the two men had stationed any kind of lookout, they'd do it on one of the few highways. I could drive in a completely different direction by heading to I-90, loop around through Spokane, then Idaho, then head south again. Somewhere along the way I could stop and clean up.

Whatever those slimy creeps wanted—and were willing to kill for—I would stop them. I would find "it," along with the terrible secret behind Beatrice, Clan Firinn, the death of my parents, and me.

Driving around the back roads, it took me several hours to reach Spokane. I used the time to formulate a plan. I wouldn't be caught and cornered like before.

I stopped to gas up and used the ladies' room to clean up the best I could. I managed to find a pay phone in Ritzville and called the Woods' home.

Mrs. Woods answered.

"Hi, this is Sam. I'm sorry about the time."

"We're still up. You sound a bit . . . breathless. Is everything okay? Have you recovered from the close call at the school?"

"Um, yes." My mind went blank.

After a moment, she said, "If you wanted to speak to Bethany, she's already gone to bed. I could take a message?"

"Yes. A message . . ." *What to say?*

"Sam—"

"I'm sorry, Mrs. Woods. Things have been a bit crazy for me. I didn't mean to bother you. I'll let you go. I'll be in touch." I gently hung up the phone.

I knew what I had to do. *Don't think about it. Just do it.*

I needed clothes, a place to sleep, and food. I could get a motel room for the night, but the only places that would take cash for the room would probably charge by the hour. There wasn't anything at the house in Pullman that would help—I'm sure that was the first place the two men looked. They'd also stake it out.

That gave me an idea. If we were going to play cat-and-mouse, I was going to be the cat.

I found a Walmart in Spokane. My funds were getting low, but since the two men knew I was dressed like a Hutterite, I needed a change of clothing. I ignored the curious glances from the middle-of-the-night shoppers and found a small pair of binoculars, notebook and pen, black hooded sweatshirt, T-shirt, sweat pants, bandages for my still aching toes, and cheap running shoes. I added a greeting card and bow.

The checker blinked at my appearance.

I smiled. "*Darf ich Ihnen einen Keks anbieten.* Presents."

If I survived this, I would learn another German phrase.

I found a dark street and changed clothes. It felt good to put on something that didn't reek of ancient garbage or gas.

The highway from Coeur d'Alene to Pullman was virtually empty in the early morning hours and I made good time.

Once there, I parked two blocks from my old house. Pulling the sweatshirt hood over my hair, I quietly got out. I kept to the velvety-black shadows under the trees, avoiding streetlights. A patrol cruiser drove past, but I was able to keep a good-sized tree between his headlights and me.

Once near the house, I took out the binoculars and found a good line of sight. Methodically I examined the house and surrounding trees. I looked for red lights—infrared light—which would pick up images at night. It didn't take long to find it.

If I'd been more aware, I might have found numerous similar cameras around the farmhouse.

The shape of the camera looked like one other I'd recently seen—the game camera in Suttonville. Not conclusive, but worth adding to my puzzle pieces.

I found my way back to the pickup. Daylight would be coming in a few hours. I needed to find a pay phone where I could have a fast exit.

I finally found the perfect setup just off the Washington State University campus. I parked on a side street. I got as comfortable as I could and closed my eyes.

The roar of a garbage truck woke me up. I hadn't meant to fall asleep. The sun was just rising and traffic, even on this side street, had picked up. Time for that call.

I pulled up the hood of my sweatshirt to hide my hair and face, then jogged to the pay phone.

"Nine-one-one, what's your emergency?"

"I just passed a house." I gave the address. "It looks like someone's trying to break in." I quickly hung up, then trotted back to my truck and checked the time. Law enforcement should show up pretty quickly. I drove slowly over to the house, giving the police plenty of time to arrive. They'd just pulled up to the front of the house when I cruised past. I kept my gaze on the street, then parked in the next block, checked the time, and waited.

The police left after fifteen minutes.

The black SUV showed up five minutes later.

I slid down in the seat and watched through my side mirror. *Twenty minutes.* The two men wouldn't have wanted to appear while the police were here, so they had to be staying in Pullman itself. That made sense. If they wanted to keep an eye on Alderman Acres, the farm at Washtucna, the town of Suttonville, and this house, Pullman would be a logical choice.

A chilling thought whispered into my mind. They had to have known I came by the house yesterday and decided not to confront me until I was in a more remote location.

It took the men even less time than the police to check the house. They returned to their car and drove by me.

I slid even farther down in my seat until they reached the corner. Once they turned right, I started the truck and followed. As I'd expected, they drove to a large chain motel next to the university campus. Stopping on the street, I waited until they'd parked and gone inside, then watched the windows for any sign of which room they'd taken. None of the sheer curtains moved.

I tapped the steering wheel with my nail. Not good. Just because they hadn't touched the curtains didn't mean they weren't overlooking the parking lot.

I'd have to take that chance.

They'd parked at the end slot in the front of the motel. The lot was relatively busy with guests checking out and leaving. I turned in and parked next to their SUV.

The muscles in my midsection tightened. I was so close to their car. And so exposed.

Now what? On television, the heroine would call her buddy at the police department to look up the license plate.

I got out and walked around to the rear of my truck, then stared at the SUV, looking for inspiration. Nothing. They didn't even have a scratch from sending us off the road. How could that be? I made another circuit, this time peering inside.

"Excuse me?"

I turned so fast I almost fell.

A man wearing a patch with a security company logo was standing nearby. "Are you looking for something?"

"Um. I was. Well, to be honest, I was driving to work and thought I saw my husband's SUV parked here." I knew my face would be bright red. I'd have to trust that my story would explain it. "We . . . um . . . have been having problems and I've suspected . . . well, when I saw his rig in front of a motel in broad daylight, well . . . I . . ."

The security guard nodded knowingly. "Of course. We don't want any trouble here. Are you sure this is his SUV?"

"I thought it was."

He walked around the vehicle. I risked a glance at the windows overlooking the parking lot. If the men looked out . . .

He returned to me. "Does your husband work for Hanford?"

I sucked in a quick breath at the name. My father had worked at Hanford. Another link? "Um, no. He's a . . . an insurance sales-man. Thank you for your help." I moved to my truck and got in before he had any more questions. I was trying to fit my key into the ignition with a shaking hand when he tapped on the window.

Slowly I rolled down the window.

"You really need to give your husband a break. Don't assume the worst."

"Than . . . thank you, officer. Good advice." This time I was able to jam the key in and did my best not to spin my wheels getting out of the lot.

I drove carefully, mindful that I didn't have a driver's license and a traffic violation would be a very bad idea. I finally pulled into a grocery store lot to go over my options.

The two men in the SUV had a Hanford parking permit, linking them indirectly to my father, who had worked at Hanford until 1985. Mrs. Lee and the two men confirmed my father had owned a golden apple paperweight. That paperweight meant something to Beatrice Greer—or my own Mrs. Gimble—whatever her name was, because she was being blackmailed by someone who knew of it. Beatrice, under the name of Mrs. Gimble, had provided me a home after I ran away from the farm. Beatrice had also lived at Clan Firinn. The new housing development owned by Clan Firinn was named Alderman Acres, perhaps after a golden apple. Bodies from Suttonville had been placed at Alderman Acres along with an apple paperweight.

I felt like I'd found most of the edge pieces of the puzzle. Now to fill in the center.

And not die in the process.

TWENTY-SIX

By afternoon Dutch was restless and ready to leave. He used the bedside phone to call Dr. Brùn. "Spring me out of here."

"I'll see what I can do."

Dutch swung his legs over the side of the bed, then waited for the dizziness to pass. He still had only a blank where the events of the previous day should have been. *Had* Sam been in the car? If she had, her quick thinking in creating a life jacket from her jeans had saved his life.

His face warmed and he gritted his teeth. *Not again.* After his friend and partner had died trying to save Dutch from the fire, it had taken years to work through that.

If Sam had rescued him . . . if she died because of that . . .

I hate her.

The fierceness of the thought left him shaken.

Dr. Brùn entered his room. "All set." He stopped when he saw Dutch's face. "What?"

"Nothing."

Dr. Brùn moved to a chair and sat.

"I'm ready to go."

Dr. Brùn crossed his legs and leaned back.

"I said I'm ready to go. I need to get out of here."

Dr. Brùn straightened his pant leg.

Dutch punched his pillow. "It's just . . . how do I . . . I don't . . ." He looked at the older man. "Are you sure Sam . . . ?"

"Ah. I see. You're thinking Sam died trying to save you, just as your partner did so long ago. Two debts you'll never be able to repay. And you're not worthy of the cost."

"No. Maybe. I don't know."

"How does that make you feel?"

Dutch couldn't answer.

Dr. Brùn waited for a moment. "Dutch, you're stronger than you think. You're not the same broken man that arrived at Clan Firinn years ago. You recently faced fire again. You'll be able to work through whatever this outcome is. Do you hear me?"

Dutch stared out the window, then slowly stood. "I hear you."

"Good. The doctor said you can go as long as you rest when you get home."

"I'm not making any promises."

———

I couldn't remember the last time I'd eaten. I counted the money I had left, then went into the grocery store and purchased a couple of water bottles and a sandwich. Back in the truck, I tried to put together my next steps. I could hardly drive to the Hanford Site and ask them if they had a couple of goons working for them and going around threatening people, driving them off the road, shooting at them, locking them up and trying to kill them with gas, looking for . . . whatever it was . . . stuffed into a golden apple paperweight. That sounded one step removed from making a tinfoil hat to keep out the space-alien mind probes coming from Area 51.

I had no idea of Dutch's fate, nor how deeply he was involved in Clan Firinn. Clan Firinn itself held too many questions.

I didn't have the card or phone number of my resident expert on Suttonville, Norman Bottoms. I could go back to the library in Pasco to see if he came there daily. "Right. Pasco library isn't *that* far."

A woman passing by the truck heading for the store gave me a glance that almost had me checking for that tinfoil hat. *Important observation—no more speaking out loud.*

Leroy was driving the car when we went into the Snake River. Maybe I should drive over to Alderman Acres and see if he'd returned to his trailer. Of course, he may have simply gone home with work stalled. But if he was missing along with Dutch, that meant . . .

I don't want to think about it.

Alderman Acres was much closer than Pasco. And the Woods' home, and Bethany, was on the way.

I'd driven the route between Pullman and LaCrosse several times a week for the past few years and could do it blindfolded. The problem was that I didn't have to concentrate on my driving. All the thoughts I wanted to keep walled up in my brain danced around in my head in abandon. *Do I really want to know what happened to that missing year after my parents died? Why did my name change? What actually happened to my parents? Who was Beatrice and why did she help me?*

When I finally corralled those thoughts, a new battery assaulted me. I was running out of time, money, resources, and answers.

And I had no idea where to go.

"Stop it!" I slapped the steering wheel. I'd been in worse shape when I'd fled the farm—homeless, pregnant, and without a dime. That first morning at the homeless shelter, a woman had read a verse from the Bible. It had been like God Himself spoke to me. *"For I am the* LORD *your God who takes hold of your right hand and says to you, Do not fear; I will help you."*

I rolled down the window and let the fresh air cool my face. "I'm not afraid, God," I whispered. "I'm just not sure how much longer I can stay alive."

Before I knew it, I'd arrived in LaCrosse. After parking on a side street, I took out the notebook and pen and wrote for a few minutes. I tucked the note into the greeting card, wrote *Mrs. Woods* on the front, and attached a bow. Janet's words echoed in my ears. *"This time, I want a chance to say goodbye."*

The Woods' mailbox was attached to an outside fence. I popped the card inside, turned, and headed straight to the construction site. Leroy's camper was still parked there, but no other vehicles were anywhere around. Considering his car was somewhere in the Snake River, that wasn't surprising.

I parked next to the scruffy barbed-wire fence at the edge of the site and walked to the camper, then looked around. The silence was disturbed only by a distant call of a falcon as it was being pursued by a small black bird. The breeze kicked up dust devils in the recently graded ground and brought the scent of cut grass. On a far hillside, a tractor created a dust trail as it worked the soil. I tapped on the door.

No answer.

I opened the door. "Leroy? It's me. Samantha. Are you here?"

The stench of old garbage wafted from inside, followed by a number of flies. "Leroy?"

That answered my question. Leroy hadn't returned.

Of course, he could have made it back here from the river, then gone somewhere else. All I *really* knew was this place was empty.

I stepped inside. The stink was worse. A nasty-looking something on a plate sat on the counter and the sink was full. To my left was a partially open pocket door leading to a bathroom with dirty clothes on the floor. More stomach-churning odors came from that direction. Another pocket door on my right probably led to the bedroom.

Most of the cupboard doors were partially ajar and the contents spilled out. I opened the nearest door and found numerous cans of pasta and tuna. The next cupboard held paper plates jammed in at all angles. The final door revealed a box of latex gloves, paper towels, a jar of rubber cement, a ream of paper, envelopes, a coffee mug of pens, pencils, and scissors, and printer ink. The computer and printer must be in the bedroom. Three steps took me to the bedroom door. I slid the door open.

A cloud of flies flew past. A gut-wrenching stench enveloped me.

Leroy lay on the bed. Dead.

The world twirled and grew dark. I couldn't get any air into my lungs to scream. I spun and tore from the camper. I missed the bottom step and fell. Stumbling to my feet, I blindly ran into a pair of arms.

I did scream this time.

"Whoa there. Calm down." A Whitman County sheriff's deputy gave me a small shake.

"H-he . . . he's dead!"

"Who's dead?" The deputy let go of my arms.

"L-l-le-r . . . roy. Leroy. In there." I pointed.

"Wait here." The deputy unsnapped his pistol as he walked toward the camper.

I didn't want to wait. I wanted to be far away from any more dead bodies or people who made them dead.

I trotted toward the pickup.

"Hold up there!" The deputy obviously had seen Leroy.

I ran faster.

"Stop or I'll shoot!"

I jerked to a halt.

"Put your hands behind your head."

Stupid, stupid, stupid. I locked my fingers together behind my head. "I've just had—"

"Get on your knees."

I knelt. He couldn't think I had anything to do with—

He grabbed my arm, twisted it behind my back, snapped on a handcuff, then repeated the action on the other arm. He lifted me to my feet and, still holding on to one arm, radioed dispatch.

"Look, I—"

"Shhhh." He finished speaking to his department and turned to me. Quickly he searched my pockets, then said, "You have the right to remain silent. Anything you say can be used against you in court. You have the right to speak to an attorney for advice before we ask you any questions. You have the right to have an attorney with you during questioning. If you cannot afford a lawyer, one will be appointed for you before any questioning if you wish. If you decide to answer questions now without a lawyer present, you have the right to stop answering at any time. Do you understand each of these rights I have explained to you?"

"What?"

"I said, do you understand?"

"Yes, but—"

"Having these rights in mind, do you wish to talk to me now?"

This can't be happening. "I just found him. That's all." I finally looked at his face. "What are you doing here? You must have known he was dead."

He had a deeply creased, pockmarked face and wore black-framed sunglasses. His lips were compressed into a thin line. "I was doing a welfare check. Why did you run?"

"I don't know. To get away from yet another body."

"What do you mean by 'yet another body'?"

Before I had a chance to answer, another patrol car arrived. The officer holding my arm walked me over to his SUV and placed me in the back seat, then slammed the door shut.

I closed my eyes and slumped.

TWENTY-SEVEN

The doctor X-rayed Dutch's arm again and said the swelling was sufficiently reduced to cast it. Dutch just wanted to leave, but that would mean a separate trip to Colfax to get the cast done. Once the fiberglass cast was finished, the nurse placed him in a wheelchair to leave the hospital. Dutch felt ridiculous being pushed to the car, but no one would listen to him.

Dr. Brùn, apparently sensing his mood, didn't try to make conversation once they got on the highway.

Dr. Brùn's cell rang.

Dutch jerked. He must have drifted off.

Dr. Brùn answered. "She is?" He glanced at Dutch.

Dutch mouthed, "Sam?"

Dr. Brùn shook his head. "Of course Mary is welcome to stay tonight. But please keep her away from the guests. Right. That would work. We'll be there soon." He disconnected. "Looks like you'll have company as you recuperate. I'm having you moved

266

to the front ground-floor bedroom at Highland House for a couple of days. No steps."

"I'd much rather—"

"I know. I had to agree to a few concessions to get you out of the hospital."

"In that case, thank you. I take it Mary doesn't know where Sam is either?"

"I didn't talk directly to her, just Scotty. He says she's pretty upset—something about her husband—and needs a few days to rest. I doubt she knows what's happened since she left." Dr. Brùn cleared his throat. "Have you been able to recall anything that occurred after you left Clan Firinn?"

"No. I know I wouldn't have been driving anywhere, nor would Sam without a driver's license. What about Leroy? Have you contacted him?"

"We haven't been able to get hold of him. I've asked the sheriff to do a welfare check at Alderman Acres. I would have checked myself, but I wanted to make sure you were going to be okay. We'll swing by there before going to Clan Firinn."

Dutch closed his eyes. *Black SUV.* The words echoed in his brain as clearly as if someone had shouted them. "Black SUV," he said out loud.

"What's that?"

"It just came to me. Black SUV. A black SUV with two men in suits has been following us—at least that's what Sam believed. I did see them in Suttonville, parked at the edge of the coulee. Maybe they were following us and . . . I don't know . . . did something to the car . . . I remember lights . . ."

Dr. Brùn's jaw clenched. "I see."

Something in the way he said that made Dutch turn to look at the older man. "Do you know something about that?"

"No. But I can call around." He patted Dutch on the shoulder. "Everything will be fine."

———

Alderman Acres soon filled with official vehicles from the sheriff's office. The handcuffs chaffed my wrists, and the car's interior was heating up. I was about to lie on my back and kick at the windows when the deputy returned and opened the door.

"What's your name?"

"Samantha Will . . . McWilliams."

"You're not sure?"

"Long story."

"Do you have any identification?"

"You searched my pockets—"

"Don't get smart. Just answer my question."

"No. Another long story."

"Where have you been the last twelve hours?"

"Ano—"

"Don't tell me another long story."

I didn't answer.

He rubbed his chin. "Where do you live?"

"I'm staying at Clan Firinn."

"So you're one of Dr. Brùn's refugees. That explains it. Stand up."

I stood. He turned me around and uncuffed me.

I rubbed my aching wrists. "Did you decide I didn't kill Leroy?"

"I'm still investigating. I need you to stay put. I'm going to have someone drive you over to Clan Firinn for now."

"Then I'm not under arrest?"

"Just wait here."

I waited until he moved away, then walked over to a tree to get out of the sun. *Now what?* Clan Firinn could be the epicenter of this whole tornado of events. I didn't want to be under house arrest there.

Where else could I go? I didn't want to put Janet in any more danger. I was homeless, broke, hungry, tired, and being pursued by people who seemed to want me dead. I needed a place to hide until I had a plan.

A white Escalade pulled into the excavation site, parked, and Dr. Brùn stepped out.

I retreated farther into the tree's shadow.

Dutch, now sporting a blue fiberglass cast, got out of the passenger side.

I grew breathless. *He's alive!* I wanted to launch myself at him, have him wrap his arms around me and say everything would be fine. I started forward, then stopped. An idea formed in my brain. What if I disappeared again? Went someplace where they'd never suspect me of hiding.

Clan Firinn.

None of the buildings were ever locked and most seemed empty. All my notes were there. I could stay out of sight, invisible, at least for a few days. It was crazy, bold, and just might work.

Several deputies, Dr. Brùn, and Dutch gathered near the camper.

Crouching and keeping various vehicles between the group and me, I raced to the SUV, opened the back door, slipped inside, and crawled quickly to the cargo area in the rear. The windows were heavily tinted, so I was pretty sure I wouldn't be spotted by someone walking by.

I'd barely settled when Dr. Brùn and Dutch returned to the SUV.

". . . believe someone shot him," Dutch was saying.

Dr. Brùn started the car, effectively making it difficult to overhear the conversation.

We drove for a few minutes. The crunch of gravel and rattle of the cattle guard oriented me to our location. All the gates must have been left open, because we didn't stop until we pulled into a garage.

The two men got out and walked away, leaving me curled up in the back. So far, so good. I thought the garage was to the right of the main lodge, fairly near Beatrice's studio.

Heart pounding, I listened for any sounds before rising and peering out the window. The cedar-and-glass garage door was down. Good. I crawled to the side door and opened it.

The car alarm blared, smashing into my eardrums in the small space.

I slammed the door and frantically looked around the spotless garage. A row of plastic garbage bins along the front wall seemed to be the only hiding spot. I jerked the lid off the first one, then the second, before finding the third with only one black bag in the bottom. I jumped in, pulling the lid over my head just as the garage door opened.

The stench in the confined space made me cover my nose and try to breathe as little as possible. *What's with me and garbage?*

Footsteps sounded as someone entered. The clamor ceased, leaving my ears still ringing. A voice called out, "Nothing. Maybe a small quake or a glitch. If it happens again, I'll take it in."

The footsteps left, then the garage door shut.

I couldn't get out of the garbage can fast enough.

There were two side doors. I was pretty sure the one on the left led to the main lodge. I gingerly opened the door on the right. No one was in sight. I started toward Beatrice's studio.

The two Scottish Deerhounds rounded the corner next to Highland House, spotted me, and raced in my direction.

I jerked to a stop. I'd made my peace with Fonzie, but how would it feel to be near these two monsters?

The dogs slowed their approach, staring at me. No, not at me. They were staring at my hair.

"What do you think of the color?" I bent forward so they could smell.

Both dogs did a thorough exam, with one giving a loud sniff in my ear. It tickled. When I stood upright, the dogs sat in front of me. "Have we come to an understanding?" I gingerly reached forward and stroked each dog on the head.

Apparently we had. The dogs trotted away.

I was inordinately proud of myself.

271

Sliding through the studio doors, I entered Highland House and listened. The room was heavily insulated. No sound penetrated.

I needed to figure out if anyone was in the house.

I checked Beatrice's bedroom first. It appeared as I left it, but it felt different this time. I'd known her, loved her like a caring friend. It didn't seem fair that I'd finally located her only to permanently lose her again. Had they held a funeral for her?

The bedroom door was closed to the rest of the house. I listened, ear pressed against the surface for a few moments. Voices.

Cracking the door, I peeked through the opening.

Dr. Brùn was speaking to Dutch. "... so like I said, I've heard from the sheriff's department. Samantha was detained outside of Leroy's camper shortly before we arrived. The truck she was driving is still there, so she's either on foot or got a ride with someone. They have an all-points bulletin out on her."

"Why would she run?" Dutch's voice was high pitched. "There's no way she could have killed Leroy. She's not safe on her own."

"Don't worry about it now. We're doing all we can to find her. You need to rest."

"I need to—"

"No, you don't, unless you want to return to the hospital." Both men came into view as Dr. Brùn, hand on Dutch's back, urged him toward the bedroom. "You're over there. Mary will be arriving soon and will be in her old room."

Dutch paused. "What's that smell?"

Dr. Brùn stopped.

I ducked back into the room.

"It smells like old garbage," Dr. Brùn said. "I'll get someone to clean out the kitchen. Go lie down now."

Dutch's bedroom door shut, followed by the front door.

Smell? I sniffed my sweatshirt. Hard to be invisible when I smell like failed deodorant, trash can, and a hoarder's rotting house.

TWENTY-EIGHT

I risked a quick shower and found a welcome change of clothes. After bundling up the stinky ones, I stashed them in an oversize drawer in the studio.

With Dutch, and soon Mary, in the same house, my grand idea of hiding out didn't seem so great anymore. Once again my aunt's voice came into my head. "*The* LORD *is my light and my salvation; Whom shall I fear? The* LORD *is the strength of my life; Of whom shall I be afraid?*"

"Okay, God, now would be a good time to drop in with a little boost," I whispered. I was really hoping for a beam of light to illuminate . . . something. A choir of angels would be nice.

The board with my notes lay where I'd placed it. The sooner I figured out the riddle, the sooner I could . . . what? Call the police? FBI? DHS?

Somebody.

Worry about who to call when you figure out what everyone wanted. I'd already formed some connections. Ryan Adams had been the officer responding to the bones at Alderman Acres and had a family connection to Suttonville. Mrs. Gimble/Beatrice was connected to Clan Firinn, the paperweight, the summons from the fake coroner, and me. The two suits were connected to Hanford, the paperweight—or whatever had been hidden inside—and my parents. My father had worked at Hanford.

I didn't want to fall victim to false reasoning by linking things together that had no association. *I have ears, and an elephant has ears; therefore, I am an elephant.*

Maybe a timeline would help.

Beatrice had been connected to Clan Firinn since at least 1990. Could this week's events go back to the beginning of this place?

I studied the board again. I had no idea when the blackmail notes were delivered to her.

Returning to my bedroom, I pulled the notes from their hiding place in the cushion and brought them into the studio. Nothing on them gave me any idea of when they had been sent.

I was about to tape them to the board when again I noticed the glue holding the scanned photo to the paper. Someone had done a sloppy job. I rubbed a small area. *Rubber cement.*

Leroy had rubber cement in his camper, along with a box of latex gloves, a ream of paper, envelopes, and printer ink. Everything he would need to create blackmail notes.

It could be just a coincidence.

Leroy supposedly "found" the golden apple. What if he didn't? What if he owned a golden apple paperweight and knew about the contents?

Guesswork. Leroy had no known connection to Clan Firinn, Beatrice, or me. At least on the surface.

My connection to the paperweight was through my parents, who supposedly died by murder and suicide. What if Leroy was connected in the same way? I had thought it strange that Dr. Brùn had hired Leroy's dad, who was in bankruptcy and involved in an illegal labor practices suit. His dad had been a chemical engineer with a degree from Stanford with a gap in his history between 1980 and 1985.

My father had worked as a physicist at Hanford until 1985.

I jotted my thoughts on a piece of paper and added it to the board. There still wasn't a direct link between Hanford, Clan Firinn, the paperweight, and Beatrice—only an intriguing possibility at this point.

My gaze drifted to the newspaper article Dutch had discovered. I kept returning to Beatrice.

A white space near her name drew my attention. It was where Dutch had written *Hanford, nuclear,* and *Norman* and had taped them below *Suttonville.* I could just barely see the evidence of where the tape had been. *Maybe the note just fell off.* I looked around the floor and underneath the board.

Someone must have removed that piece of paper. He'd written . . . I closed my eyes and pictured him working on the chart. *Kyshtym.* He'd written Kyshtym, the name Norman gave me in our interrupted phone call. That had triggered Dutch to look up Green Run and Norman's thyroid cancer.

What if Norman had mentioned Kyshtym for a reason other than the cancerous fallout? What if . . . ?

I wanted to bang my head against a wall. Or maybe my sore toe. Think, think. What had those two men said about the golden apple paperweight at the farmhouse? *"It was here, Sam. We found it. But it had been opened and the contents removed. We need the contents, or should I say, we need you to find and destroy the contents, and I think you do know where that is."*

If the golden apple held something like a microdocument or photos, who removed them, and why? Anyone might have found them after my parents died. Before that, who knew what the apple held? Mom and Dad, of course. But why hide the contents and then remove them?

Because . . . because . . . they found someplace else to hide them? I found myself pacing, ending up in front of the lightbox holding the negatives I'd found in my Dr. Seuss book.

I decided to examine the images again. A quick search of the art room turned up a magnifying glass.

Only one useful slide showed me my Easter basket, piano, bench, sheet music, bookshelves, and the edge of a vase. No handy reflection of a face in the piano wood or vase, a gun sitting on the shelf, or a golden apple.

I sat on the rolling drafting chair.

Maybe there simply isn't anything to find, the contents of the apple forever lost. How could I convince anyone of that? The two men in suits seemed perfectly happy to eliminate anyone who was even remotely connected to that apple.

I leaned against the drafting table and rested my head on my hands, staring at the board. *What am I missing?*

Look again, the little voice in my head whispered.

Green Run was in 1949, Kyshtym was in 1957. Parents worked at Hanford until 1985, Suttonville was in 1987.

I wasn't born when this all started. Come to think of it, my parents weren't even born.

Start again. Someone wanted to bring attention to Alderman Acres, Suttonville, and the golden apple paperweights. Not just bring attention, but connect the three things.

Each of these elements—the bodies from the doomed town, the paperweight, and the location where they were placed—represented something.

A message. A warning? A threat? Meaningful to someone.

What if the warning was ignored or not understood? Two bodies had been placed in the same location a week apart. I'd bet there was an apple there also. The forensic anthropologist had not confirmed or denied a second paperweight, but Leroy had said there was one.

Explore the possibilities.

I stood and paced again.

What if you sent a message twice and the recipient ignored both? And what if you were . . . angry? Vengeful? What had Janet said were the strongest motives for crime? Money. Jealousy. Revenge.

Keep going. The next event was the murder of Beatrice. Beatrice died shortly after the second body was found. Was the messenger . . . *don't forget the suits* . . . or the group getting desperate? Were they running out of time? If there was a specific date or day that was important, that would make sense. I'd been teaching at the school for some time. Beatrice had been at Clan

Firinn for a lot longer. Why choose *this* time to start the chain of events?

Timing. Timing and messages. My gaze drifted to the lightbox. Why would my father have placed this particular set of negatives in a place that only I would look? Why would they have made such a fuss about *that* particular Easter? And why would he write in only one book?

Our dearest daughter,

Should you ever need any guidance in your life, note the gifts given to you this Easter, 1997.

All our love,

Mommy and Daddy

It's always easiest to remember something when it's connected to an emotionally powerful moment. We remember where we were when we heard about the events of September 11. When the space shuttle *Columbia* disintegrated after takeoff. When Hurricane Katrina devastated New Orleans and much of the coastline in Louisiana, Mississippi, and Alabama.

Standing, I moved to the lightbox and picked up the magnifying glass again. My dad had written *gifts*, so I concentrated on the Easter basket: *Bible. Dr. Seuss. Plastic eggs. Enough yellow Peeps to keep me wired for a month.*

Guidance suggested the Bible, but he'd also written *note*. Not look to the Bible, turn to the Bible, or any other logical word. *Note.*

As in musical note?

Shifting to the sheet music on the piano behind me, I could

make out musical notes on classically lined sheet music with the words underneath. There wasn't a title at the top of the page, and the words were too tiny to read. I jerked upright.

Sheet music? Mom didn't use sheet music. She played by ear.

This is ridiculous. There was nothing to see.

Not with the magnifying glass.

"What could I use to enlarge—" *Dutch's microscope.*

I could kill the proverbial two birds with one stone. Look up more on Kyshtym in the library *and* see if I could read more in the negative.

I checked the time. Dinner would be served soon at the main lodge, and residents would be wandering over to eat. I crept outside and watched for a few moments. No one seemed to be moving about. I crossed to the other building unnoticed.

The outside door leading to the library was unlocked, as was the library itself. The computer showed two articles on Kyshtym, both on microfiche. I straightened when I read the name of the second article. "Kyshtym and the Hanford Tank Farms."

I pulled the article.

At the Mayak plutonium production site in the former Soviet Union, the cooling system in a tank holding waste similar to that found at the Hanford Tank Farms exploded. Known as the Kyshtym disaster, the explosion sent radioactive fallout over 200 miles downwind. The September 29, 1957, tragedy was one of the largest nuclear accidents until the April 26, 1986, Chernobyl meltdown.

A Soviet study showed the Kyshtym disaster re-
sulted in the deaths of over 8,000 people. While this
carnage is unimaginable, this was from a single storage
unit. Hanford has 177 such tanks in close proximity to
each other. Additionally, there is no effective security
or containment at the Hanford Tank Farms. A determined terrorist could set off a series of events that
would be catastrophic beyond our imagination.

Terrorism? I found myself clutching the microfiche knob
with a white-knuckled grip. I pushed the Print button, turned
off the machine, and collected the printout.

I also had a possible link between Kyshtym and Suttonville.
September 29.

Today was September 29.

Now for a closer look at the film negatives. I just hoped
Dutch's lab was unlocked. It was.

The lab smelled vaguely of disinfectant, with everything
labeled and orderly. On closer examination I discovered the
microscope I'd seen on my earlier visit was set up to view on
a nearby laptop. Powering up the computer, I found I needed a
password. The hall lights went off, leaving me in a dimly lit room.
Soon it would be too dark to see. *What else could enlarge the
print on this negative?* The microfiche unit in the library would
magnify too much. What I needed was—

The light came on in the hall, indicating someone had
entered.

I ducked under the desk and held my breath.

281

Steps moved down the hallway, then I heard a *click* as the outside door opened and closed. If someone were outside, they'd see if I turned the light on in the lab. I slipped from my hiding spot and looked out the window. Clear.

I turned and reassessed the lab, hoping for inspiration.

The display case across the room held an antique microscope.

I crossed to the case. Locked.

Looking around the room, I spotted a metal lamp on Dutch's desk. I unplugged it, brought it to the display case, and smashed the glass.

Crash!

The sound was ear-splitting.

Not waiting to see if I had drawn attention, I grabbed the microscope and moved it to a raised table. I'd need to use the same lamp I'd just smashed into the glass to illuminate the microscope's stage and take the chance that whoever had gone outside wasn't going to return through the same door. I found a pair of scissors and cut the good negative apart from the damaged ones. A box of microscope slides and cover slips were in a drawer.

I placed the film on the slide, then covered it to keep it flat. Shortly I had the words to the sheet music in focus. Because this was a negative, the words were white against the black of the paper.

There were four of us contracted by Hanford to work as a team, code named Golden Apple. We were told we were assisting the US government in providing vital assistance to win the Cold War. We reported, of course, to a military commander.

We concentrated our research on green slugs—uranium fuel rods—and possible use

The words ended there.

If I'd hoped for a full explanation, confession, or detailed message, the water damage in my apartment had forever wiped out that opportunity. But I did know more, maybe even enough to put some things together. And if the date September 29 was significant, I was almost out of time.

Dutch's lab, however, was not the best place to stay. Too many people could see in or walk by. I needed to act quickly.

I peeked out the window to check for anyone wandering about, then ran back to the studio and taped the new facts to the board. I had no idea what this had to do with anything that had happened. I hoped, and prayed, that Golden Apple was just one more piece of useless information. Any other conclusion was unthinkable.

I found my way into the bedroom, rubbing my arms. Did the apples contain instructions for a bomb? Were my father and others thinking about sabotaging the Tank Farms?

A door shut somewhere in the house.

I moved to the bedroom door and peered out.

Mary walked in and flopped onto the sofa.

Dutch's voice came from near his room. "Mary! Are you okay?"

"Tired. Discouraged."

"Did you want to talk about it?"

"No." She sighed. "I asked Dr. Brùn if I could stay here for a couple of days. I tried calling Leroy to see if he'd pick me up, then left him some text messages, but he doesn't seem to be picking up."

I sensed movement in the kitchen, heard water running, then Dutch appeared bringing Mary a glass of water.

"You're being so good to me." Mary said. "What happened to you while I was in Chelan? Was Sam successful in finding another apartment in Pullman and getting a car lined up?"

"Sam . . . um . . . Sam may be looking for a place to stay as we speak."

Thump.

"What's wrong, Mary? Are you okay? Let me get a towel to wipe that up." Dutch moved to the kitchen, returning with a kitchen towel.

"Clumsy of me," Mary said. "I haven't been able to call her, either. Have you actually seen Sam?"

"No. She apparently showed up . . . let me catch you up on what's been going on." He explained the black SUV forcing us into the river and Leroy's murder.

"That's terrible. Are you sure Sam is okay? Are those two men still after her?"

I retreated to the studio. I needed to stay out of sight.

Beatrice's prayer closet. I needed divine intervention to unravel the final threads.

Before retreating, I grabbed Beatrice's Bible from the bedroom, then entered the small space and closed the doors. I lit the candles with the lighter, then let the Bible fall open to the verse Beatrice had turned to so often. Psalm 38:4: "For my iniquities have gone over my head; Like a heavy burden they are too heavy for me."

"Lord, help me." I whispered my prayer. "And if it isn't too much trouble, please help me quickly."

"Are those two men still after her?" Mary's words spun in my brain. What if—

The doors next to me flew open. Dr. Brùn smiled at me. "Come, Samantha, we need to talk."

Behind him were the two men in suits.

TWENTY-NINE

Dutch took a seat on the sofa and closed his eyes, but his brain wouldn't stop going over the events. He finally gave up, rose, and walked into the kitchen for a bottle of water.

Mary was still at the dining room table, now sipping a glass of something dark. "Would you like a glass of grape juice?" She held up her goblet.

"No thanks." He opened the refrigerator and grabbed some spring water.

A noise came from Beatrice's bedroom. He strolled in and looked around.

The noise came again.

He crossed the room and entered the studio.

Two men in suits were holding Sam by the arms. Dr. Brùn stood nearby.

Dutch jerked to a halt. "What's going on here?"

"It's nothing, Dutch." Dr. Brùn smiled. "These two gentlemen have some questions for Samantha, that's all."

Sam shook her head, then winced and tried to pull away.

"Let go of her," Dutch said.

Dr. Brùn shook his head. "Really, Dutch—"

"I said let go of her!" Dutch stepped forward.

Dr. Brùn gave a signal and the men let go.

Sam backed away and pointed at the men. "Call the sheriff." Her face was red. "Those two men tried to kill me!"

"Samantha," Dr. Brùn said. "I assure you no one tried to hurt you. Like I said, they just want to have a little chat with you."

Sam turned to Dr. Brùn. "I don't know what they told you, or what you think happened, but they drove us off the road and into the Snake River. Then they used us as target practice. When I returned to the farm, they demanded I give them the contents of the apple paperweight, then nailed me into a room and turned on propane gas."

The men's eyes widened and one said, "We didn't touch you, let alone try to kill you." The other man shook his head. "We returned to the farm and found the broken window. We didn't smell any gas."

Dr. Brùn stepped to the nearest phone, dialed, and spoke, "Have Scotty come over to the studio. Have him put the rest of security on alert." He hung up and turned to Sam. "Now I have some questions."

"Questions." Sam became very still. Slowly she looked to one side of the room. Dutch followed her gaze. She was staring at the foam board chart she'd made. "Money, revenge, *and* jealousy. Not one, but all three," She finally looked at Dr. Brùn as Scotty arrived. "Dr. Brùn, what kind of a doctor are you?"

Dr. Brùn's eyebrows shot up.

"Dr. Brùn has a PhD," Scotty said.

"In what?" Sam asked.

Dr. Brùn shook his head and mouthed the word *no* at Scotty, but Scotty was looking at Samantha and missed it. "Project management. Why?"

Instead of answering, Sam turned to the men. "And you two. What's the term for someone hired by a company to do the dirty work?"

"Hatchet men." Dutch said.

"That's it." Samantha nodded. "Your job is to do unpleasant things that other people don't want to do. You're hatchet men working for Hanford."

One man shrugged. "What's in your pocket, Sam?"

"Nothing."

"Show me or I'll remove it."

Sam pulled something out.

Dutch recognized Sam's negatives from her Dr. Seuss book.

The man picked up an empty metal container, grabbed the negatives, dropped them in, then lit a match and threw it on top. He then looked at Sam. "We've found what we were looking for. I assume there were no other forms of communication from your father?"

Sam's jaw tightened and shook her head.

The men turned toward the door. "Then we're done here. For now." One looked at Dr. Brùn. "Nothing has changed. If necessary, we'll be back."

"Wait," Samantha said. "I think someone might be planning an attack on Hanford. Today, tonight—"

One man paused at the door. "Proof?"

"You need to talk to Norman Bottoms—"

"That nut? He's been spouting nonsense for years. Got anything else?"

"You just have to put it all together—"

"Call us when you do." The man waved a dismissive hand. They left.

Dutch turned Samantha toward him so he could see her face. "What is going on here?

"That's just what I was about to ask." Mary, still holding her glass, had entered the room.

"Ah, Mary my dear," Dr. Brùn said. "Shouldn't you be resting?"

Mary smiled at him and set the drink down on a nearby table. "You're always thinking about others."

Sam glanced at her watch. "I couldn't stop them, but maybe I can convince all of you. If we don't act fast, none of us will be alive soon."

THIRTY

My statement made Dutch, Dr. Brùn, Scotty, and Mary gawk at me. "Did you just let out a Sneetch?" Mary asked.

I shook my head. The expression on the hatchet men's faces couldn't have been faked. The foam board chart held most of the answers. All I had to do was to put everything together with the words Janet had said to me. *"Some of the strongest reasons for someone to try to kill another person are money, revenge, and jealousy."*

"Are you okay, Samantha?" Dr. Brùn asked. "I think this has all been too much for you."

"Money, revenge, and jealousy," I said. "What if it were all three?"

"Sam?" Dutch took a step toward me.

I moved across the room so I could easily see everyone. "I'm fine, but like I said, we haven't much time." I waved my hand at the foam board. "I did have all the pieces. I just didn't have the whole picture." I turned to Dr. Brùn. "My dad, a nuclear physicist, worked with you at Hanford between 1980 and 1985 as part of Operation Golden Apple."

Dr. Brùn stared intently at me.

"Also part of your team were Beatrice Green and Jack Miller, a chemical engineer. Jack was Leroy's father. The four of you were to come up with different solutions to the massive nuclear waste generated by the Hanford Site. Either a commercial or, preferably, a military application much like Green Run, where radioactive material was released over a populated area."

"You've figured out quite a bit." Dr. Brùn nodded at me. "That, shall we say, mistake in 1949 stopped all intentional radioactive releases until 1962."

"But in 1980 the Cold War was in full swing." I took a deep breath. "So you were recruited to come up with alternatives. Your team decided to concentrate on green slugs, uranium fuel rods fresh from the reactor."

"I don't understand," Dutch said.

Dr. Brùn explained. "Normal processing for the uranium takes between 83 and 101 days after removal from the reactor—"

"Dr. Brùn!" Scotty's face had drained of blood. "No!"

Dr. Brùn glanced at his friend. "It's time, Scotty. The fallout from our work has destroyed or killed too many people."

I remembered what Mrs. Lee had said, words that seemed like so much babble at the time. *"The truth always finds its way to the surface."*

Dr. Brùn nodded at me. "You always were a bright child."

"You knew me?"

"I knew *of* you. Your father was both a friend and colleague when we worked together. You were born several years after Operation Golden Apple." Dr. Brùn said. "I watched you grow from a distance and promised myself I'd look after you should anything happen to him. When you disappeared after your aunt died, I had to step in. Without you, or anyone, knowing about our past."

"You sent Beatrice to find me."

"Find you, provide a home for you, help you until you could get your degree."

My throat closed up for a moment. "And when Beatrice was murdered—"

"I knew you again needed my help." Dr. Brùn nodded at Scotty. "Scotty retrieved your purse and removed the contents, then made sure you'd need a place to stay—here at Clan Firinn—where I could protect you until I discovered who was after us."

I blinked. "You flooded my apartment too?"

"I didn't think your father would object."

"How did you figure all this out?" Scotty asked.

"The trigger was 'questions,' but I had to go back and rethink what questions were asked, and what questions were not asked. At dinner the first night you asked a lot about Mary's background, but not mine. You already knew."

"Clever," Mary said, "but why all the hush-hush, Dr. Brùn? Why didn't you just come out and take care of Sam?"

"He couldn't," I said. "That was part of the deal, right Dr. Brùn?"

Dr. Brùn nodded.

"Now I'm really lost," Dutch said. "What deal?"

"Our team finished the work in 1985." Dr. Brùn said. "We were paid well, very well indeed, and signed the usual government secrecy agreement. If we revealed any part of our activities, we could be arrested for treason. The government kept very close tabs on both Dr. McWilliams, Samantha's father, and me. We were not to have any contact with each other, but we were aware of what was going on in each other's lives. We changed our names and most of us changed our appearances somewhat.

"When the events of 1987 in Suttonville came to light, the four of us knew the military had somehow implemented our scenario." He glanced at Scotty, then quickly looked away.

"You planned to kill all those people?" Dutch's voice was strident.

"Of course not," Dr. Brùn said. "Our project outlined how green slugs could be placed near an enemy military site to incapacitate a large number of soldiers. We calculated how many, how far, possible side effects, probable success rate. By 1987 we didn't think it was even a possibility. Hanford's N reactor was shut down in January for routine maintenance but never reopened. We figured the window to carry out the plan ended when there weren't any fuel rods being produced and used by current operations. But we hadn't counted on the remaining irradiated fuel segments, fully one third of the total, that were now available to experiment with."

"So the plan *was* carried out," I said. "But your calculations were for adults. The first slugs placed near Suttonville killed babies."

Dr. Brùn reached for a chair and sat. "Yes, and some elderly," he said so quietly I could barely hear him. "We didn't know about that. We found out later. They dropped the next green slug in late September 1987."

"This time," I looked at each face, "the mistake was in not calculating the effects of a windstorm whipping across the radioactive rods."

"Let me guess," Mary said. "The coverup began, starting with eliminating any evidence by burning down the doctor's office in Suttonville with all the medical records. Then cleanup."

"Yes." Dr. Brùn seemed to age before my eyes. "The four of us from Golden Apple were paid a visit by men very much like the two you just saw, Samantha. They reminded us of the punishment for saying a word about what happened." He put his head down and dry washed his face.

"But you all knew the truth." Acid churned up the back of my throat. "And *that* fallout was a cancer eating at your souls."

"We thought that acknowledgment of our roles in the destruction of Suttonville," Dr. Brùn said, "would help somehow. We wrote out our confessions and had brass apple paperweights created with hollow centers. We placed the details into the paperweights."

"Putting your"—Mary paused for a moment—"'sin'"—she made quotation marks in the air—"on display, yet secret."

"You created Clan Firinn to help Beatrice." Dutch stared at his mentor, then at the board.

I walked over to the board and tapped the photo of Beatrice from the newspaper. "I saw this same photo taken from another angle. Beatrice was clearly recognizable."

Dutch slowly nodded his head. "It fits. But who would want to kill her? Were Sam's and Leroy's dads also murdered?" He shot a worried look at Dr. Brùn. "Are they after you too? Why now?"

"Let's talk about who and why," I said. "The Golden Apple team got a lot of money. Say money is just one motive. Someone didn't get any. If you're broke, full of anger, and want to get back at those who put you in that position—"

"You're not exactly rolling in money," Mary said under her breath. The remark startled me and I stared at her.

Dutch didn't hear her. "You put pressure on them," he said. "By putting a body from Suttonville at Alderman Acres along with a golden apple, then sending a blackmail note." He looked at me. "Do you know who?" He asked.

I tore my eyes away from Mary. "Leroy. His father had lost all his money, filed for bankruptcy. Leroy made the blackmail notes and sent them to Beatrice."

"Beatrice was being blackmailed?" Dr. Brùn asked.

I retrieved the pages for him to see. "When we went to the grain elevator, Leroy didn't join the search. He knew Beatrice hadn't delivered the money—because when she didn't respond to his first attempt he planted a second body. More pressure."

"I didn't know about the blackmail," Dr. Brùn said. "We'd hidden our identities hoping nothing like that would happen."

Dutch tapped the photo of the ground breaking at Alderman Acres. "You made a mistake. It was probably a Freudian slip that you named the development after the apple, and then let Beatrice's face appear in the paper."

I took a deep breath. "What about my father?"

"He couldn't live with the knowledge anymore." Dr. Brùn's voice shook slightly. "He and your mother had become Christians by then. He said something about a time when everything hidden would be revealed, and that even though he didn't actually carry out the plan, the fact that he could even think of it made him guilty before God. He was about confess. Face the consequences. Before he could go public, he was murdered."

THIRTY-ONE

I'd already figured out my parents were murdered, but to hear Dr. Brùn say it out loud left me shaken. "There's another guilty party to your plan. You said the military commissioned the work and executed it."

"I seriously doubt anyone had any remorse over carrying out a military plan," Dr. Brùn said. "It may have been called a *cold* war, but it was nonetheless war. And using American citizens for experimental purposes isn't new either. Green Run is just one example."

I gripped the edge of the drafting table. "But what if it wasn't the military in general, but *one* person in the military. A person who decided to move up the food chain and make a name for himself by carrying out an already approved plan."

No one moved.

"And what if"—I took a deep breath—"instead of receiving a hero's reward, that person was punished?"

"Thrown in prison?" Mary asked. "Then he got what he deserved."

"No." I shook my head. "That would involve a military tribunal and possible exposure. The government would keep this a secret at all costs. No, this person would be quietly removed. Forced to take a menial job. Instead of getting those stars on the collar, he got the boot."

"Go on," Scotty said.

"Money, revenge, and jealousy. The strongest motives for murder. Just think about how angry and vengeful this person would be," I said. "The four of you were handsomely rewarded for your role. Enough money for Beatrice to fund an educational foundation, Leroy's dad to start a construction company, and Dr. Brùn to create Clan Firinn. And my father . . ."

"Your father returned the money," Dr. Brùn said quietly.

My eyes burned. "In the eyes of this person, everyone else grew rich while he took the fall. It didn't matter that the guilt over the deaths of all the Suttonville babies and citizens drove Beatrice to the edge of reason, or you, Dr. Brùn, to devote your life to helping others, or Leroy's father to self-destruct. No. People had to pay. Even after my parents paid with their lives, it ate at this person. It was all there. The money. The jealousy. And his need for revenge."

"So he killed Beatrice?" Dutch asked. "But why Leroy—or you?"

"Next generation, so cleaning up loose ends. And to take attention away from the real revenge. The ultimate target."

"Which is?" Mary asked.

"Nuclear meltdown," I said.

Dr. Brùn cleared his throat. "Well now. Maybe we're all a bit tired and overwrought."

Sweat dampened my back. My mouth dried. They won't believe me. "Look . . ." My voice sounded desperate even to me. I pushed on. "Someone removed the scrap of paper where Dutch had written the word *Kyshtym*."

All four of them simply stared at me. "So?" Mary finally asked.

"Someone wanted me to forget Kyshtym, to concentrate on the other puzzle pieces," I said. "But what happened at Kyshtym is what could happen now."

Scotty glanced at Dr. Brùn and gave a slight shrug.

I pointed at the chart. "The Tank Farms at Hanford hold nuclear waste similar to that at Mayak, in the former Soviet Union. When the cooling system on one of the tanks failed, it caused an explosion known as the Kyshtym disaster. It was the largest nuclear disaster until the Chernobyl meltdown and explosion in 1986. But Kyshtym was just one tank. There are 177 tanks at Hanford, located beside each other, just under the ground."

"And you think someone is planning on blowing up the Tank Farms?" Dutch asked. "For revenge?"

"Yes," I said. "All he has to do is blow up one. And he could do that by simply sending a signal from a cell phone to explosives planted near the tank. Or flying a drone with a bomb to the right tank. Right, Mary?"

THIRTY-TWO

Mary stared at me, mouth open. A flush pink flush rushed up her neck and onto her face. "Have you gone loco? I have absolutely no connection to any of this!"

Everyone spoke at once.

"This has all been too—"

"You're not serious—"

"Name one thing—"

I held up one hand. "Not one thing. A whole bunch of small things. The first clue I almost missed. When I told Mary I'd received a closet full of clothes, she said as long as it wasn't Beatrice's clothes. Yet supposedly Mary had never seen Beatrice."

"I made a simple assumption," Mary said. "Beatrice was older—"

"Mary's father was in the military, the air force. He was passed over for promotion and delegated to running a drone around base to check the perimeter. You yourself told us he died a bitter and angry man."

300

"So?" Mary glared at me. "That doesn't make him a mass murderer."

"But *he* wasn't the one who was going to carry out the plan." I took a step toward her. "You were. You had a drone and what you called your work cell in your purse—"

"A lot of people have camera drones and work phones."

"You had a handgun to shoot Beatrice after you lured her to the school—"

"Again, lots of people have guns. You have a gun in your gun locker."

"I bet the state ballistics expert would love to look at your pistol. You knew we were going to Pullman and when we returned were able to run us off the road—"

"You said the men in suits did that."

"Yes, but I saw their SUV later. No damage to the front. I'd bet the rental car agency was upset at the damage to their vehicle. You were systematically going to kill everyone connected to Operation Golden Apple. Even poor Ryan—"

"Ryan died in an accident."

"But you set it up, hoping he'd kill both of us. You told each of us where to walk. You knew about grain dust, and Ryan was a chain smoker. You knew this from driving a truck during harvest for your uncle—"

"Ridiculous."

"You followed the men in suits when they followed me to the farm. You turned on the propane—"

"You're delusional."

"I saw their faces. They didn't have a clue what I was talking about when I mentioned the gas."

"I was at Lake Chelan."

"No, you were following me around."

"I can't follow anyone around while I'm pregnant." Mary said through gritted teeth. "In case you hadn't noticed."

"You aren't pregnant."

"Samantha!" Dr. Brùn said. "That's enough."

"You're not drinking grape juice. I can smell that glass of wine from here. Your pregnancy, like your imaginary husband and his sleazy friends, is a cover story. You lie so easily. Look how well you filled in the details of that imaginary book you're writing. When did your father die, Mary?"

"I'm not going to answer you. You're a sick woman." She half turned away from me.

"September 29?"

When she turned back around, she had a pistol in her hand. She aimed and pulled the trigger.

THIRTY-THREE

The pistol's concussion echoed in the studio, making my ears ring.

Scotty folded inward and dropped to the ground.

I stepped toward him.

"Don't move, Sam, or I'll shoot someone else." Mary turned the pistol on Dr. Brùn, then Dutch.

My stomach tightened to a hard knot. "Your plan isn't going to work, Mary."

"But it is going to work. I have four things that guarantee it. First of all, the phones here are out again. You can't call out. Second, you're afraid of dogs. You won't be able to leave. And third, the biggest guarantee. I know the identity of your daughter." She glanced over at Dutch, then showed her teeth in a parody of a smile at his expression. "Oh yes, your pure little maiden in distress had an illegitimate daughter. Bethany Woods. She looks just like her mother. I saw the resemblance the first time I saw them together. And it was an open adoption, so it didn't take a lot of

303

digging." She looked back at me. "You'll do anything to keep your daughter safe and your dirty little secret from coming out, right?"

I couldn't help myself. I looked at Dutch.

All the blood had drained from his face. He didn't take his eyes off Mary.

"What is your final guarantee?" I asked Mary through stiff lips.

"I don't exist. When I finish, no one alive will have seen me or known I was even here."

"Nonsense. You rented the Airbnb—"

"Online and in your name."

She had?

"When you reported the break-in—"

"Again in your name. The deputy saw only you. In every case, no one who isn't dead or here right now actually saw me. Mary Thompson isn't even my real name. Common. No way to track it down. I made sure no one got a good look at me when we were in public. A vague, dark haired, pregnant lady in a baseball hat and sunglasses."

Sweat beaded on my forehead and slithered down the side of my face. "But you do exist, Mary. Your fingerprints are all over the house."

"Not anymore. And it's your fingerprints on these bullets. You loaded the gun. Remember?"

"I have your hairbrush with your hair in it."

"Thank you for reminding me. I'll be sure to pick it up."

"You licked all those envelopes for Dutch."

She blinked.

I can talk her out of this—

Dr. Brùn reached for her. "Now, Mary, I'm sure—"

She whipped the revolver toward him. Her finger tightened on the trigger.

Dutch leaped between them.

She pulled the trigger.

Dutch crashed to the floor, blood rushing from his head.

Mary didn't hesitate. She fired again, this time at Dr. Brùn. She didn't miss.

Before my frozen limbs would thaw, she leveled the pistol at me. "What's that line from one of your kids' books? 'As for you, my pretty.' Here's what's going to happen. I'm going to leave here and head to Hanford. You will not stop me. You will stay here. If the police come, you will tell them you shot these three men." Her eyes were wide open, like white marbles, and spittle had formed in the corner of her mouth.

"Why would I do that?"

"Remember number three? I will kill your daughter. Slowly. And I will enjoy it."

"Mary . . . Mary, if you knew who I was, if you knew my father was one of the four, you could have killed me—"

"At first I wasn't sure. Once I knew, I tried. The car into your classroom. The grain elevator. The Snake River. The gas at the house. You're like a cat with nine lives. Or maybe that God you pray to is watching out for you. So I finally decided that death is too swift a punishment anyway. Knowing I could get to your daughter at any moment. Rotting in prison. Branded a murderer. Traitor . . ." She grinned.

I wiped my hands on my slacks. "'The LORD is my light and my salvation; Whom shall I fear? The LORD is the strength of my life; Of whom shall I be afraid?'"

"Your religion's worthless now, but go ahead and pray. It won't help."

I narrowed my eyes at her. "Now, Mary, I'm going to give *you* four guarantees that you won't succeed."

She shook her head. "What makes you think you can bargain with me? I hold all the cards. I'm going to leave here and, as you so cleverly figured out, use my phone and drone to drop a small charge at a certain location at the Tank Farms. The GPS location is already programmed into the drone. My father ranted in detail about what he would do to get even before he drank himself to death. He set the charges years ago. Bad luck kept him from pulling it off. At least he was able to take care of Leroy's dad, your parents, and that snoopy doctor who found the bodies. He left it to me to finish up with Beatrice, Dr. Brùn, Leroy, and you. Even if too much time has passed to activate the C-4, the charge will do irreparable damage to the monitors and regulators . . . well, irreparable in the time anyone would have to stop the meltdown."

"Nor will you carry it out. I promise you that."

"Then your daughter is dead."

"No. That's my first guarantee. You can't touch her. She's gone."

"What are you talking about?"

"I sold my aunt's land, almost a thousand acres of prime wheat fields, and put the money into a trust in Bethany's name.

I left a note for Mrs. Woods giving her the information. I told her to take Bethany and disappear." I squeezed my hands into fists. "And that leads me to guarantee number two. The Woods would move heaven and earth for that little girl. When I told her it was the only way to keep her safe, I knew they'd leave without a moment's hesitation. I've told them never to tell me where they've gone to . . ." My throat closed over the giant brick of emotion that welled up. I'd never see my daughter again. *Stop it. Don't think about it. Not now! The Lord is the strength of my life. The strength.*

Mary blinked. Her lips pulled back over her teeth.

"Guarantee three. I'm not afraid of dogs."

Her jaw tightened.

"Number four, your cell phone won't work here. And I'm going to make sure you don't make that call."

She raised the pistol and aimed at me. "I'm leaving now. You won't stop me."

I dived to the side as she pulled the trigger. A thousand bees stung my arm. I landed and rolled.

More shots sent slivers of wood from the easel above me.

I crawled on knees and elbows, keeping the furniture between us.

Mary fired again, striking the wall just above my head. *Click, click, click.*

She's out of ammunition. I jumped to my feet.

She threw the pistol at me, turned, and ran from the room.

I followed but tripped over a chair, reinjuring my foot. She was already out of the bedroom by the time I made it to the door. I ran as fast as I could, but I was limping. Her car roared to life and sped off, throwing gravel, by the time I hit the front door.

Charging toward the garage, I tried to ignore the pain in my arm and foot. *Just let there be a key in the SUV.*

There was.

I slammed the big car into reverse, shattering the garage door, before spinning the wheel and jamming the gear into Drive. The two Scottish Deerhounds raced up to the car. I reached back and opened the back door. The dogs jumped in.

After slamming the door shut, I floored the accelerator.

Gripping the wheel with a white-knuckled grip, I tore after Mary's Subaru. The gravel road gave little traction. At every curve, I fought to keep the SUV on the road. When we straightened for a moment, I snapped on my seat belt.

I finally caught a glimpse of red brake lights. I couldn't go faster without losing control.

Mary braked again as her car fishtailed on the loose surface. She lost control and spun, flying off the road, through a fence, and into a rocky field.

I followed, plowing after her.

She stopped, then jumped free of her car just as I slammed into it. My airbag deployed, temporarily blocking my vision. Both dogs ended up in the front seat. I unsnapped my belt and leaped out, followed by the dogs.

She was halfway up the small incline, holding up her cell phone and punching at the surface.

I'd never reach her in time.

She turned at my approach, grinning in the waning light.

"Get her!" I yelled.

Her grin disappeared as she spotted the dogs. Like two gray ghosts, they shot after their prey.

I didn't slow.

The dogs tackled her, knocking her to the ground.

I landed on top of her.

The cell flew from her hand.

She clawed at my face and screamed.

I smashed the palm heel of my hand upward into her nose.

She covered it, shrieking.

My next punch hit her throat.

I left her thrashing in the dirt and recovered her cell. She'd dialed, but hadn't any reception. I turned the phone off, then picked up a rock and smashed it.

Holding the rock, I pivoted back to Mary, still writhing on the ground.

I want to kill her, to crush her skull for the apocalyptic disaster she planned. And for making me forever lose my daughter. The thoughts welled up in my brain and left me shaken. I dropped the rock. *"As a man thinketh in his heart, so is he."* How far a journey was it between thinking of an idea and carrying it out?

I'd made it back to the SUV when the first patrol cars arrived. The gunshots, plus my dramatic exit from the garage, had drawn attention. Leaving Mary to one of the officers, I convinced the other to take me to Clan Firinn.

The studio was full of people, apparently staff and residents.

I pushed around them and rushed to the wounded men. Scotty was beyond help.

Dutch was conscious, with blood streaming from a deep wound on the side of his head. His fiberglass cast had shattered. It must have caused the bullet to ricochet upward. He waved me toward Dr. Brùn.

Dr. Brùn's skin was gray and blood lined his lips. He tried to talk.

"Don't move," I said. "Don't speak."

The ambulance seemed to take forever but finally arrived to transport Dutch and Dr. Brùn to the hospital. I followed in a patrol car with the same officer who had arrested me at Alderman Acres. He didn't speak for the first few miles, then asked, "What happened?"

I took a deep breath. "Long story."

EPILOGUE

CLAN FIRINN
SIX MONTHS LATER

Dr. Brùn was already seated and spreading preserves on his toast when Dutch entered. "How are you doing today?"

"I should be asking you the same thing." Dutch poured a cup of coffee into a mug and joined him at the table.

"Better. Grateful to be alive, thanks to you."

Dutch paused, coffee halfway to his lips. He knew the time would come when Dr. Brùn would talk about *that* night. He placed the mug back on the table.

"After the grain elevator fire," Dr. Brùn said, "you told me you threw away the third stone."

Dutch raised one eyebrow at the change of subject. "Yes."

Dr. Brùn took a bite of toast, chewed thoughtfully, then said, "You pulled Sam from the fire."

"Yes."

"You could say that both of us are alive today because of you."

"You know I didn't think about it that way. I just . . ." Dutch waved his hand.

"Yes. I know. You acted."

Dutch slowly nodded.

"Do you believe either Sam or I owe you something for saving our lives?"

"Owe me? I don't understand."

Dr. Brùn leaned forward. "You didn't pull Sam from the fire expecting she'd marry you, move in with you, have your children?"

Dutch's face grew hot. "No! Of course not! We're friends."

"Nor did you hope for fame, glory, money, or a reward when you took that bullet meant for me?"

"I did it because you're my mentor, my friend."

"That's right. The definition of a selfless act is one where you don't weigh the consequences, measure out the cost, add up how many crowns you'd receive in heaven." He looked at Dutch over his glasses. "Do you get what I'm saying?"

"Yes." Dutch stood and walked back to his room. He reached into the drawer of his desk, pulled out the small, dark cherry-wood box, and opened the lid.

The gold and red firefighter's challenge coin sat on top.

He reached in, removed the coin, and placed it in his pocket, then returned to the dining room. Dr. Brùn was still there.

Dutch placed the coin on the table.

Dr. Brùn smiled. "Now let's talk about your future."

I dropped my books on the kitchen table and headed for the flashing light on the answering machine.

"Samantha." Dr. Brùn's voice made me smile. "You really need to get a cell. I hate these machines. Believe it or not, the results finally came in on the DNA from the Suttonville case. A positive match, but then, we always knew that. Anyway, don't forget dinner tonight." *Click.*

How can I forget? I'd been looking forward to this for weeks. My new home, outside of Moscow, Idaho, was about an hour and a half from Clan Firinn. With the winter road conditions, I'd need to build in a lot of extra time. I planned on spending the night at Highland House to avoid traveling back late. I checked the time and headed to the shower.

With Dutch's encouragement, I'd started working on my PhD. I'd also taken short courses on forensic art. Life was full and complete. *Well, almost complete.*

As I headed to LaCrosse, the blustery winds of the Palouse sent the snow scurrying across the road and into deep drifts around the rolling hills. I drove slowly, concentrating on the icy roads and keeping my mind off the reason for the invitation. When Dr. Brùn first contacted me about the dinner, I assumed it was to celebrate his recovery. Between our frequent dates, Dutch's phone calls kept me current on his progress. But Mary's upcoming trial could also be the reason. It was due to start in another few weeks. Unless she got yet another continuance.

I was relieved to finally see the Clan Firinn gates, currently open. I drove through and parked next to several vehicles already at the main lodge. A woman opened the door to my knock, took my coat, and ushered me into a living room warmed by a crackling wood fire. A number of people were standing or sitting in small groups and talking quietly. I looked for, and quickly spotted, Dutch. As usual, I couldn't keep the heat from rushing up to my face.

He took my hand. "Glad you made it," he whispered.

"Me too."

Dr. Brùn slowly walked over to me. "Ah, Samantha, so good to see you again. I trust the roads weren't too terrible."

"Let's just say I appreciate the invitation to spend the night."

"Speaking of that, I hope you don't mind sharing Highland House with another guest. I think you've already met." He turned and waved someone over.

Janet, the woman who'd rescued me from hypothermia, crossed the room.

I couldn't speak. I just hugged her. I hadn't seen her since I returned her truck several months before.

When the lump finally subsided and I could talk again, I said, "I didn't know you'd met Dr. Brùn."

"Indeed we have." She turned to Dr. Brùn and patted him on the arm. "He called me several months ago to thank me for helping you. We went to dinner and have since become friends."

I looked back and forth between them. *If I didn't know better—*

"Yes." Dutch had sidled up to me and whispered in my ear. "The two of them have become an item."

I wanted to let out a whoop. Before I could cheer, a woman in a waitstaff uniform opened a pair of french doors and announced dinner. Dutch took my arm and led me to a seat on Dr. Brùn's left. Janet sat across from me. The meal was perfect and Dutch sitting next to me was heaven.

After the final course was served, Dr. Brùn stood. "Ladies and gentlemen, thank you all for coming out on such a stormy day. As many of you know, I've been planning on retiring for some time now. I wanted to make it official tonight. Clan Firinn will continue on. We still have important work to do in restoring the physical, mental, emotional, and spiritual lives of first responders and law enforcement suffering from PTSD. I'll be turning the work over to my friend and colleague, Dr. Van Seters."

I grinned at Dutch. "Congratulations."

He smiled back, sending my heart rate into the stratosphere.

After dinner, I tried to hide my yawn, but Dr. Brùn caught it. "My dear, you've had a long drive. Why don't you have Dutch walk you over to Highland House?"

The storm had strengthened, the wind driving the snowflakes almost sideways. Dutch kept a tight grip on my arm to keep me from slipping on the ice. When we finally reached Highland House and he opened the door, something huge, hairy, and black leaped on me.

"Fonzie!" I hugged the Black Russian Terrier.

After his enthusiastic greeting, he sat in front of me, mouth open in a doggie grin.

"I should have warned you Janet brought her dog." Dutch took my coat.

"The best kind of surprise. Fonzie saved my life." I snapped my fingers and Fonzie followed me into the living room. I sat on the sofa, hoping Dutch would join me.

He did. "You know, I'm hoping I can convince you to move closer to Clan Firinn."

"How close?"

"Well, since I'm going to be the new director, I'm hoping to hire an art teacher and therapist to the staff. We're looking at expanding to troubled children. We already have someone in mind to direct the youth program."

"Janet?"

He nodded. "So if you wouldn't mind working with both of us . . . ?"

I could only nod.

"Good. That's settled. Now just one more issue."

"Issue?"

Instead of answering, he took me in his arms and kissed me.

I wanted it to last forever.

He finally released me and looked at my face. "What are you thinking?" he finally asked. "You have the funniest look on your face."

"I'm thinking I'm so happy right now I wanted to cuddle up to you and whisper my favorite quotes in your ear," I blurted out, then clapped my hand over my mouth.

"That sounds wonderful," Dutch whispered. "I'll start.

Samantha McWilliams, in the timeless words of that famous philosopher, Christopher Robin, 'Always remember you are braver than you believe, stronger than you seem, and smarter than you think.' And twice as beautiful as you've ever imagined."

AUTHOR'S NOTE

I started the whole idea of Clan Firinn, Scottish Gaelic for "Family of Truth," several books ago. Because of my work as a forensic artist, and an instructor of forensic art, I am well aware of the evils that exist in this world. I attended the first FBI International Symposium on the Forensic Aspects of Mass Disasters and Crime Scenes in Washington, D.C., more than thirty years ago and was struck by the repeated comments of the presenters— that, at that time, no one really treated the first responders and law-enforcement personnel for the fallout from their horrible experiences.

When I started writing novels, I wondered what would happen if someone with a lot of money, and a personal burning desire to help, created a place for healing. Clan Firinn was born.

Where would I place such a retreat? I wanted to keep it in the Pacific Northwest, but no place that would be on anyone's radar. I essentially closed my eyes over a map and ended up with my finger near the tiny town of LaCrosse, Washington. Perfect. The Palouse region of Washington and Idaho were familiar to me. I'd attended Eastern Washington University, lived in Cheney, and my sister-in-law, Laurie, was from a dry-land wheat farm near Harrington.

LaCrosse also had something else I was looking for. It wasn't on the way to anywhere. You had to turn off the highway to reach the town.

When I shared this with my younger brother, Scott, he made a startling comment. "Our grandmother was born in LaCrosse."

How could that be? I had thought she was born in Walla Walla. Scott went on to say that we still had family living in the area. A bit of research showed that, indeed, Alvin Zaring had come to LaCrosse around 1862 in a covered wagon and homesteaded nearby. Alvin Zaring was my great-great-grandfather. Around 1908–1910, my great-grandfather moved his growing family, including my grandmother, Hazel Zaring, to the American Falls, Idaho, region. We became the "Idaho Zarings." I was able to connect with my previously unknown cousins still living in LaCrosse.

With the setting for my story chosen, I then looked for some historical threads to weave in—and I didn't have to look far to find the Hanford Nuclear Facility. Like everyone living in the Northwest, I was vaguely aware of its presence. But not its history. Hanford was a novel waiting to happen. Virtually all the information about Hanford in this book is accurate. Hanford built the bomb dropped on Nagasaki, released radioactive materials in 1949 called "Green Run," and has leaking and dangerous storage tanks. These tank farms contain fifty-six million gallons of radioactive waste.

Hanford *doesn't* have men in suits driving around in black SUVs waiting to pounce on unsuspecting citizens. Nor is there any such town as Suttonville.

For more information on the region, Hanford, and other tidbits, I'll post my resource materials and books on my web page: CarrieStuartParks.com.

Thank you for reading—and I'd love to hear from you. Carrie@stuartparks.com.

ACKNOWLEDGMENTS

Fallout is my ninth novel with Thomas Nelson, HarperCollins Christian Publishing. I thank the Lord for leading me to my publishing home. My thank-yous should start with my totally AWESOME editing team led by Erin Healy and Amanda Bostic. They take my (at times) blubbering wanderings and turn them into a novel. Thank you to Margaret Kercher, Nekasha Pratt, Savannah Summers, Taylor Ward, LaChelle Washington, Patrick Aprea, Jodi Hughes, and Kerri Potts (to name just a few of my wonderful team).

My agent, Karen Solem, is the best in the field and always provides me with guidance whenever I ask. Hugs all around. My writing buddies—Lynette Eason, Colleen Coble, Ronie Kendig, Robin Caroll, Voni Harris, and occasional others—stand by to help me with their inspiration. Frank Peretti, my mentor and friend, remains my writing hero. My husband, Rick, provided a sounding board for this book—between hockey games—and went on a day trip to see LaCrosse. He keeps hoping for a book set on a river cruise . . .

ACKNOWLEDGMENTS

The folks who gave me help and advice "in the field" include Angela Broeckel, the clerk/treasurer in the town of LaCrosse. A big thanks goes to Allyson Brooks, PhD, and Guy Tasa, PhD, and especially Annie Pillers, D-ABMDI, Whitman County Coroner. Thank you to Coleen Drinkard, the communication specialist, Department of Energy, Hanford.

For all things guns, bullets, and other advice, I need to thank my friend, Erin Hickson, Certified Forensic Artist, Forensic Scientist for the Phoenix PD. She also serves as Faculty Adviser, Comparative Forensics, ASU West.

For farming, grain silos, and regional inspiration, I have to thank my cousins, Roger and Peggy Zaring. My lovely sister-in-law, Laurie Stuart, proved to be wonderful help along with Greg Walker. A special thanks to Laurie's mom, Janet Scott, for serving as a template for Janet in the book.

Finally, most importantly, I thank my Lord and Savior, Jesus Christ, in whom all things are possible.

DISCUSSION QUESTIONS

1. Samantha's childhood was abruptly cut short by the murder of her family. She still clings to her children's books. Are there other ways she shows how her life has changed from this event?
2. On the farm, Samantha learned skills no longer taught to many young people today: canning, sewing, cooking, gardening. What skills do you have, and how did you learn them?
3. Were you shocked when you learned about Hanford, or did you know about this particular part of history?
4. The secret of what happened to Suttonville affected everyone differently. Talk about and contrast how Dr. Brùn, Beatrice, Mary's father, Sam's father, and Leroy's father dealt with that knowledge.
5. Have you ever blurted out a "Sneetch"?
6. Have you ever heard of the Hutterites before?

‌‌‌‌‌‌‌‌‌‌‌‌‍‌‌‌‌‌‌‌‌‌‌‌‌‌‌‌‍‌

7. What mother-daughter themes did you notice running through the story?

8. Are you aware the author has a web page just for book clubs? Take a look at carriestuartparks.com/for-book-clubs. Carrie loves to keep in touch with her readers.

From the Publisher

GREAT BOOKS

ARE EVEN BETTER WHEN THEY'RE SHARED!

Help other readers find this one:

- Post a review at your favorite online bookseller

- Post a picture on a social media account and share why you enjoyed it

- Send a note to a friend who would also love it—or better yet, give them a copy

Thanks for reading!

THE GWEN MARCEY NOVELS

"I love Carrie Stuart Parks's skill in writing characters with hysterical humor, unwitting courage, and page-turning mystery. I hope my readers won't abandon me completely when they learn about her!"

—Terri Blackstock, *USA TODAY* bestselling author of the If I Run series

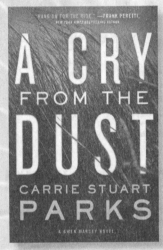
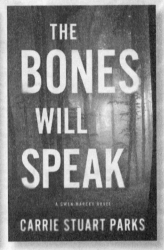

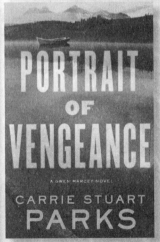

THOMAS NELSON
Since 1798

AVAILABLE IN PRINT, E-BOOK, AND AUDIO

9780785226130-A

"The action builds to a climactic, slam-bang fight with the killer as a hurricane sweeps the island. Those with a taste for modern Gothic family sagas will be amply rewarded."

—*PUBLISHERS WEEKLY*

"Danger and drama abide in this tale that takes a walk on the perilous side. With a flair for the macabre, the story will linger in your head long after the last page."
—**Steve Berry**, *New York Times* bestselling author

CARRIE STUART PARKS

A Novel

RELATIVE SILENCE

AVAILABLE IN PRINT, EBOOK, AND AUDIO!

THOMAS NELSON
Since 1798

ABOUT THE AUTHOR

Andrea Kramer, Kramer Photography

Carrie Stuart Parks is a Christy, multiple Carol, and INSPY Award–winning author. She was a 2019 finalist in the Daphne du Maurier Award for excellence in mainstream mystery/suspense and has won numerous awards for her fine art as well. An internationally known forensic artist, she travels with her husband, Rick, across the US and Canada teaching courses in forensic art to law-enforcement professionals. The author/illustrator of numerous books on drawing and painting, Carrie continues to create dramatic watercolors from her studio in the mountains of Idaho.

Visit her website at CarrieStuartParks.com
Facebook: @CarrieStuartParksAuthor

HER CAREFULLY CRAFTED LIFE IS ABOUT TO BE DEMOLISHED

After a difficult childhood, Samantha Williams craves simplicity: jigsaw puzzles, lectures at the library, and the students she adores in her role as an elementary school art teacher in the dusty farming community of LaCrosse, Washington.

But when an SUV crashes into the building where she teaches, her entire world is upended. Samantha manages to keep the children safe, but her car isn't so lucky. Oddly, her purse—with her driver's license, credit cards, and other identification—is missing from the wreckage.

After authorities discover that the driver in the accident was shot seconds before the crash, Samantha quickly becomes entangled in increasingly strange events that have her constantly looking over her shoulder.

Samantha has long tried to forget the tragedy of her past, but the twisting connections she discovers between the murdered driver, a deadly secret government project, and an abandoned town can't be ignored. Those involved are determined to keep the secrets buried, and they'll use any means necessary to stop Samantha's search for truth.

ALSO AVAILABLE:

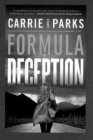

Visit us online:

TNZ Fiction

Cover design by Faceout Studio
Original package design
© 2022 Thomas Nelson
Cover imagery © Shutterstock

THOMAS NELSON
Since 1798

thomasnelson.com

FICTION
USD $16.99 / CAD $21.00
ISBN 978-0-7852-3985-7

51699

9 780785 239857

PRAISE FOR
CARRIE STUART PARKS

"Carrie Stuart Parks has penned a highly intriguing mystery full of secrets, lies, and murder. Fans of Parks will not want to miss this tale that manages to be both suspenseful and quirky at the same time."
—LISA HARRIS, BESTSELLING AUTHOR OF THE
NIKKI BOYD FILES, FOR *FALLOUT*

"Stunning! Carrie Stuart Parks has penned a masterful tale of intrigue with impossibly unpredictable twists and turns. Plagued by a mysterious past, Samantha Williams is a remarkable and quirky character that captivated me from the first page. I couldn't read *Fallout* fast enough."
—ELIZABETH GODDARD, *USA TODAY* BESTSELLING
AUTHOR OF THE ROCKY MOUNTAIN COURAGE SERIES

"This enjoyable thriller from Parks finds a sleuth investigating a string of accidents at a luxury resort . . ."
—PUBLISHERS *WEEKLY* FOR *WOMAN IN SHADOW*

"Unique, witty, and hilarious . . . The perfect mix of intrigue, mystery, and danger, *Woman in Shadow* is definitely a book for my keeper shelf."
—DANI PETTREY, BESTSELLING AUTHOR OF
THE COASTAL GUARDIANS SERIES

"Danger and drama abide in this tale that takes a walk on the perilous side. The story will linger in your head long after the last page."
—STEVE BERRY, *NEW YORK TIMES* AND #1 INTERNATIONALLY
BESTSELLING AUTHOR, FOR *RELATIVE SILENCE*

"*Relative Silence* is one of the most engrossing suspense novels I've read in a long time. Pitch-perfect pacing and characterization . . ."
—COLLEEN COBLE, *USA TODAY* BESTSELLING AUTHOR OF
ONE LITTLE LIE AND THE LAVENDER TIDES SERIES

"I love Carrie Stuart Parks's skill in writing characters with hysterical humor, unwitting courage, and page-turning mystery. I hope my readers won't abandon me completely when they learn about her!"

—TERRI BLACKSTOCK, *USA TODAY* BESTSELLING
AUTHOR OF THE IF I RUN SERIES

"Without fail, Parks delivers stories that reel me in and keep me turning the pages until I'm done and craving more. *Fragments of Fear* is sure to make you a Carrie Stuart Parks addict as well!"

—LYNETTE EASON, BESTSELLING, AWARD-WINNING AUTHOR

"The sinister tone of this fast-paced story line creates an almost unbearable tension that will keep readers glued to the page."

—*LIBRARY JOURNAL* FOR *FORMULA OF DECEPTION*

"Parks is a seasoned writer of inspirational 'edge-of-your-seat' suspense and mystery."

—*LIBRARY JOURNAL*, STARRED REVIEW, FOR
PORTRAIT OF VENGEANCE

"Parks has created an intriguing female sleuth with depth, courage, and grit."

—*PUBLISHERS WEEKLY*, STARRED REVIEW,
FOR *PORTRAIT OF VENGEANCE*

"The compelling crimes, inscrutable community, and resilient heroine propel Parks's latest thrill-packed installment."

—*PUBLISHERS WEEKLY* FOR *WHEN DEATH DRAWS NEAR*

"Parks's action-packed and compelling tale of suspense is haunting in its intensity."

—*LIBRARY JOURNAL*, STARRED REVIEW, FOR *A CRY FROM THE DUST*